Lost Pages

Also by Paul Di Filippo

Fractal Paisleys
Ribofunk
The Steampunk Trilogy

Lost Pages

by Paul Di Filippo

Four Walls Eight Windows
New York /London

© 1998 Paul Di Filippo
Published in the United States by
Four Walls Eight Windows
39 West 14th Street, room 503
New York, NY 10011
http://www.fourwallseightwindows.com

U.K. offices:
Four Walls Eight Windows/Turnaround
Unit 3 Olympia Trading Estate
Coburg Road, Wood Green
London N22 67Z

First printing August 1998.

Library of Congress Cataloguing-in-Publication Data:
Di Filippo, Paul, 1954–
Lost Pages / by Paul Di Filippo
p. cm.
ISBN 1-56858-099-1
I. Title.
PS3554.I3915L67 1998   98-8394
813'.54—dc21   CIP

The stories were originally published in the following publications:
"The Jackdaw's Last Case," *Science Fiction Age* (1997); "Anne," *Science Fiction Age*
(1992); "The Happy Valley at the End of the World,"*Interzone* (1997);
"Mairzy Doats," *The Magazine of Fantasy and Science Fiction* (1991);
"Campbell's World," *Amazing Stories* (1993); "Instability," *The Magazine of Fantasy and
Science Fiction* (1988); "World Wars III," *Interzone* (1992); "Linda and Phil," *Amazing
Stories* (1995); "Alice, Alfie, Ted, and the Aliens," *Interzone* (1997).

10 9 8 7 6 5 4 3 2 1
Printed in Canada
Book design by Acme Art, Inc.

Table of Contents

Introduction

Reprinted with permission from *The Journal of Popular Culture,*
Vol. XXXI No. 9, September 1998.

"What Killed Science Fiction?"

by Dr. Josiah Carberry, Professor of English,
Brown University at San Diego

ABSTRACT: The nearly extinct publishing and cinematic genre
once known as "science fiction" was born in 1926 and
reached its pinnacle in the year 1966, after which a series of
unforeseeable catastrophes, both literary and extraliterary, led
to its steep decline and virtual disappearance.

HARD AS IT IS TO BELIEVE TODAY, in our current media landscape
devoid of works of fantastic speculation, the worlds of literature and
cinema once bade fair to be dominated by a now-forgotten yet once
flourishing brand of entertainment called "science fiction." A few
surviving afficionados may very well fondly recall favorite works of
"SF," as it was familiarly called, while hoarding their disintegrating
first editions, flaking pulp magazines and deteriorating film prints,
but recent surveys reveal that—far from recognizing the peculiar
reading protocols and out-of-print landmarks of the genre—those
born since 1966 are mainly ignorant of the very notion of SF. This

severing of a generational link, in fact, represents one of the main hurdles to the resurrection of the genre.

Perhaps a very brief survey of SF's glory days is in order first, before examining the factors in its quick and infamous expungement.

When a Welsh immigrant entrepreneur named Hugh Gormsbeck launched his magazine *Amazing Stories* in April of 1926, he gathered a disparate body of stories and variety of writers under the rubric "scientifiction," a term later modified to "science fiction." Codifying the rules and playing field of the SF game, so to speak, Gormsbeck paved the way for sustained growth, popularity, and reader-writer camaraderie. For the next forty years, in various venues, the genre acquired an increasing complexity and sophistication, laying down benchmarks of excellence. Moving out of the magazines and into hardcover and paperback format (circa 1950-1960), SF began to produce genuine mature masterpieces, such as Theodore Sturgeon's *Other Than Human* (1953), Alfred Bester's *The Galaxy My Destination* (1957), and Henry Kuttner's *The Nova Mob* (1961).

Concurrently, SF began to infiltrate other media. Radio dramas like *The Shadow Lady* and *Dimension X Squared* thrilled millions. Daily newspaper strips such as *Flashman Gordon, Buckminster Rogers,* and *The Black Flame* vied with bound monthly comics such as *Captain Marvelous, Kimball Kinnison, Galactic Lensman,* and *Superiorman* for the attention of the average, slightly less literate reader. Hollywood weighed in with a variety of entries, ranging from the wonderful— *Things that Might Come* (1936) and *Destination Orbit* (1950)—to the execrable: *I Married a Martian* (1949) and the much anticipated but disappointing *Eye in the Sky* (1958).

The end half of the 1950s was a particularly exciting time for SF, as the Red Chinese launch of the first artificial satellite birthed a wider interest in the genre, reflected in dozens of new magazines, paperback publishers, and television dramas (e.g., Orson Welles's *The Twilight Zone*).

With the dawn of the 1960s, SF appeared primed to explode as a true mass pop phenomenon. Cult classics such as Robert Heinlein's *Drifter in a Strange Land* (1961), Thomas Pynchon's *Vril Revival* (1963), and Frank Herbert's *Dunebuggy* (1965) were wholeheartedly embraced by both older and younger readers, flirting with the lower ranks of best-seller lists. (The same happy fate was predicted by knowledgeable insiders for a triumvirate-in-progress of British fantasy novels—fantasy having been long allied with its more scientifically respectable cousin—tentatively called *The Lord of the Rings*. But the untimely death of author J. R. R. Tolkien in 1955, after the publication of only a single volume, precluded such a fulfillment.) Additionally, a vigorous new generation of writers employing sophisticated literary approaches (cf., H. Ellison, S. Delany, R. Zelazny, B. Malzberg, U. LeGuin) had begun to make themselves known.

All looked bright then for SF as the decade reached its midway point. But unbeknownst to all, doom for the field in all its manifestations was just around the corner.

And the name of SF's nemesis was *Star Trek*.

September 8, 1966, 8:30 PM EDT. Seldom before has it been possible to nail down so exactly a historical turning point. But in retrospect it was certainly this moment that marked the beginning of the end for SF.

A Hollywood stalwart best known for his aforementioned respectable *Destination Orbit*, George Pal had moved to the medium of television after the large-scale failure of his final theatrical release, the unintentionally hilarious *A Clockwork Orange* in 1965. Conceiving of the imaginary voyage of a twenty-third century interstellar cruiser named *The Ambition* as a clever device for using up a quantity of preexisting stage sets, Pal proceeded to exercise complete (un)creative control over every element of the new show.

Pal's first and biggest mistake was in the casting of his starship crew. Nick Adams played the histrionic Captain Tim Dirk as a third-rate James Dean. The alien officer named Strock was woodenly embodied by a narcotic-addled Bela Lugosi. Ship's doctor "Bones" LeRoi was laughably portrayed by Larry Storch. Engineer "Spotty" (so named for his freckles) found an aging Mickey Rooney far from his prime. And as for the female element—well, an emaciated young model named Twiggy (as Yeoman Sand) and a seedily voluptuous Jayne Mansfield (as Communications Lieutenant Impura) eye-poppingly contrasted each other like the ship's ludicrous "neutron-antineutron" drive. Lesser parts were filled with similar wince-provoking choices.

Pal's next major mistake was to insist on writing all the first season's scripts himself, as a money-saving measure. Ransacking every cliche of SF, as well as plenty from Westerns, WWII films, and a dozen other genres, Pal's scripts have to qualify in this critic's opinion as some of the worst writing ever to appear on television.

Given these two major strikes against it, the other factors mitigating against *Star Trek*'s success—primitive special effects, ridiculous villains, costumes more attuned to Oz than outer space, a theme song at once maddening and inexpellable from the mind—were mere icing on the cake of disaster.

Nearly every TV viewer of the requisite age can recall where he or she was when that infamous first episode of *Star Trek* (an ultra-confusing time-travel farrago entitled "When Did We Go from Then?") aired. Jumping the gun on the fall season, insuring that its only competition were reruns, the opening minutes of the deadly drama-bomb found millions tuned in. As jaws dropped across the nation and viewers phoned others, the attention wave surged. By the time the West Coast was treated to the debut of the new series, it had attained the highest ratings of any television show ever presented. This was not, however, a positive sign.

The next day found ridicule unanimous and at a high scathing pitch. Newspaper columnists and editorialists had a heyday with the spectacular failure, as did stage and TV comedians. (Johnny Carson, for instance, devoted his entire opening monologue of September 9 to the episode.) The following week, a special edition of *TV Guide* was given over to an abrasive assessment of *Star Trek* and televised SF in general.

Unwisely, NBC, wowed by Pal's lingering prestige, had already contracted for a full thirty-nine episodes of the new series. And rather than back out or seek help, Pal held the network to the letter of the agreement and bulled ahead in the face of ignominy.

Week after week, the viewing public was treated to one stinker of an episode after another. Numerous tag lines from the series ("He's—he's deceased, Tim!"; "I'm a twenty-third-century physician, dammit, not a Christian Scientist!"; "Bleep me up, Spotty."; "Highly non-axiomatic, Captain.") became the ironic stuff of everyday conversation. And then the inevitable happened.

Written SF became tarred with the same brush.

Latent prejudice against "all that Buckminster Rogers stuff," never far from the surface of public consciousness, resurged. To be seen reading an SF book in public became tantamount to wearing a "kick-me" sign on one's back. Whatever literary cachet SF had laboriously earned evaporated overnight.

As sales of book and magazine SF plummeted, fair-weather readers and writers began to desert SF in droves. Bankruptcies—both personal and corporate—proliferated. Movies in mid-production were written off. The field was caught in a downward spiral wherein failure begat further failure.

Finally, by 1968, long after *Star Trek*'s demise—brought on by a determined letter-writing campaign organized by true SF fans—yet while memory of its awfulness was still fresh, only a hard core of readers and authors remained, a shabby remnant of a once vital legacy.

There is little doubt that SF had the capacity, literarily, to recover from even a tragedy of this dimension. The field had always been prey to boom-and-bust cycles and had always bounced back before. It took a set of truly unique, large magnitude, extraliterary cataclysms to finally kill the whole genre, testament to its strength and its inherent appeal to human nature.

First and foremost came the Apollo 11 disaster in 1969. When the Lunar Excursion Module failed to depart the Moon's surface, the whole world was treated to a protracted tragedy that soured any technological optimism left intact by the Vietnam War and the growing awareness of mankind's pollution of the environment (cf., The Earth Day Riots, 1972-75). The perversion of computer technology for the maintenance of "Big Nurse" domestic counterintelligence databases by the FBI under the third Nixon administration, and the subsequent passage of laws limiting the manufacture of computers to low-capability machines, further diminished the allure of a future dependent on sophisticated machines. A final nail in the coffin of SF was the uncontrolled meltdown at Three Mile Island in 1979. Rightly or wrongly, SF had long been equated with nuclear power in the public's perception, and this seaboard-contaminating catastrophe made SF synonymous with mass carnage.

One final stroke of bad luck appeared in the shape of an underground sixteen-millimeter film that had the misfortune to gain notoriety shortly after TMI. Arising out of the San Francisco pornography scene, *Close Encounters of the Star Wars Kind* was an XXX-rated venture by the then-unknown directing duo of George Lucas and Steven Spielberg, starring equally unknown actors and actresses (Charlie Sheen, Rob Lowe, Hugh Grant, Louise Ciccone, Janet Jackson, Hilary Rodham, Sly Stallone, Arnie Schwarzenegger, et al). In this repugnant farce, representatives of a decadent interstellar empire made Earth their sex playground, only to meet with resistance from naked rebels who turned out to be more lickerish and reprehensible than the tyrants. After the Supreme Court finished with Lucas and Spielberg, no sane person would approach SF with a ten-light-year pole.

Nearly two decades after these various debacles, SF remains a form practiced only by a handful of eccentric amateurs, appearing in mimeographed samizdat publications limited to a circulation of a few hundred maximum (at least in the United States; the situation in the United Kingdom has a complex history of its own. See this author's previously published "The Media Empire of Moorcock and Ballard, Ltd.: Can Murdoch Offer Any Competition?"). That a once proud literary tradition should have ended up in this state seems inevitable, given the chain of circumstances herein adduced. Yet just for a moment, we might ponder—if it is not venturing too far into a heretical old SF trope known as "the alternate world"—how things might have been different.

The Jackdaw's Last Case

"Whatever advantage the future has in size, the past compensates for in weight. . . ."

—*The Diaries of F. K.*

PALE LIGHT THE COLOR OF OLD STRAW trodden by uneasy cattle pooled from a lone streetlamp onto the greasy wet cobbles of the empty street. Feelers of fog like the live questing creepers of a hyperactive Amazonian vine twined around standards and down storm drains. The aged, petulant buildings lining the dismal thoroughfare wore the blank brick countenances of industrial castles. Some distance away, the bell of a final trolley sounded. A minute later, as if in delayed querulous counterpoint, a tower clock tolled midnight. A rat dashed in mad claw-clicking flight across the street.

Shortly after the tolling of the clock, a rivet-studded steel door opened in one of the factories, and a trickle of weary workers flowed out in spurts and ebbs, the graveyard shift going home. Without many words, and those few consisting of stale ritual phrases, the laborers apathetically trudged down the hard urban trail toward their shabby homes.

The path of many of the workers took them past the mouth of a dark alley separating two of the factories like a wedge in a log. None of the tired men and women took notice of two ominous figures crouched deep back in the alley's shadows like beasts of prey in the mouth of their burrow.

When it seemed the last worker had definitely passed, one of the gloom-cloistered lurkers whispered to the other. "Are you sure she's still coming?"

"Yeah, yeah, don't sweat it. She's always late for some reason. Maybe tossing the boss a quickie or something."

"You'd better be right, or our goose is cooked. We promised Madame Wu we'd bag her one last dame. And the boat for Shanghai leaves on the dot of two. *And* we still gotta get the baggage down to the dock."

"Don't get ants in your pants, fer chrissakes! Jesus, you'd think you'd never kidnapped a broad before! Ain't the white slavery racket a lot better'n second-story work?"

"I guess so. But I just got this creepy feeling tonight—"

"Well, keep it to yourself! You got the chloroform ready?"

"Sure, sure, I'm not gonna screw up. But there's something—"

"Quiet! I hear footsteps!"

Closer the lonely click-clack of a woman walking in heels sounded. A bare white arm and a skirted leg swung into the frame of the alley-mouth. Then the assailants were upon the unsuspecting woman, pinioning her arms, slapping an ether-drenched cloth to her face.

"OK, she's out! You get her legs, I'll take her arms. Once we're in the jalopy, we're good as there—"

Suddenly the night was split by an odd cry, half avian, half human, a spine-tingling ululation ripe with sardonic, caustic derision.

The kidnappers dropped their unconscious burden to the pavement and began to tremble.

"Oh, shit, no! Not him!"

"Where the hell is he! Quick!"

"There! I see him! Up on the roof!"

Standing in silhouette on a high parapet loomed the enigmatic and fearsome bane of evildoers everywhere, a heart-stopping icon of justice and fair play.

The Jackdaw.

The figure was tall and cadaverous. On his head perched a wide-brimmed, split-crown felted hat. An ebony feathered cape, fastened around his neck, hung from his outstretched arms like wings. A cruel beaked raptor's mask hid the upper half of his face. From his uncovered mouth now burst again his piercing trademark cry, part caw, part madman's exultant defiance.

"Don't just stand there! Blast him!"

The frightened yeggs drew their pistols, took aim, and snapped off several shots.

But the Jackdaw was no longer there.

Facing outward, the forgotten woman behind their backs, and swiveling nervously about like malfunctioning automata on a Gothic town-square barometer, the kidnappers strained their ears for the slightest sound of movement. Only the drip, drip, drip of condensing fog broke the eerie stillness.

"We did it! We scared off the Jackdaw! He ain't such hot shit after all!"

"OK, quit bragging! We still gotta get this broad to the docks—"

"I think not, gentlemen."

The kidnappers swung violently around, teeth chattering. Bestriding the unconscious woman, the Jackdaw had twin pistols clutched in his yellow-gloved hands and trained on the quaking assailants. Before the thugs could react, the Jackdaw fired, his strange guns emitting not the flash and boom of gunpowder, but only a subtle *phut, phut.*

The kidnappers had time only to slap at the darts embedded in their necks before crumpling to the ground.

Within a trice, the Jackdaw had the men hogtied with stout cord unwrapped from around his waist. Picking up the girl and hoisting her in a fireman's carry over one shoulder, one gloved hand resting not unfamiliarly on her buttocks, the Jackdaw said, "A hospital bed will suit you better than a brothel's doss, *liebchen.* And I should still have time to meet that Shanghai-bound freighter. Altogether, this promises to be a most profitable night."

With this observation the Jackdaw plucked a signature feather from his cape and dropped it between the recumbent men. Then, with a repetition of his fierce cry, he was gone like the phantasm of a fevered brain.

When Mister Frank Kafka reached the office of his employer at 1926 Broadway on the morning of July 3, 1925, he found the entire staff transformed from their normally staid and placid selves into a milling, chattering mass resembling a covey of agitated rooks, or perhaps the inhabitants of an invaded, ax-split termite colony.

Hanging his dapper Homburg on the wooden coatrack that stood outside the door to his private office, Kafka winced at the loud voices before reluctantly approaching the noisy knot formed by his co-workers. The center of their interest and discussion appeared to be that morning's edition of the *Graphic*, a New York tabloid that was the newest addition to the stable of publications owned by the very individual for whom they too labored—that is, under normal conditions. All labor seemed suspended now.

The clot of humanity appeared an odd multilimbed organism composed of elements of male and female accoutrements: starched detachable collars, arm garters, ruffled blouses, high-buttoned shoes. Employing his above-average height to peer over the shoulders of the congregation, Kafka attempted to read the large headlines dominating the front page of the newspaper. Failing to discern their import, he turned to address an inquiry to a woman who resolved herself as an individual on the fringes of the group.

"Millie, good morning. What's this uproar about?"

Millie Jansen turned to fix her interlocutor with sparkling, mischievous eyes. A young woman in her early twenties with wavy dark hair parted down the middle, she exhibited a full face creased with deep laugh lines. Today she was clad in a black rayon blouse speckled with white dots and cuffed at the elbows, as well as a long black skirt belted with a wide leather cincture.

"Why, Frank, I swear you live in another world! Haven't you heard yet? The streets are just buzzing with the news! It's that mysterious vigilante, the Jackdaw—he struck again last night!"

Kafka yawned ostentatiously. "Oh, is that all? I'm afraid I can't be bothered keeping current with the doings of every Hans, Ernst, and Adolf who wants to take the law into his own hands. What did he accomplish this time? Perhaps he managed to foil the theft of an apple from a fruit-vendor's cart?"

"Oh, Frank!" Millie pouted prettily. "You're such a cynic! Why can't you show a little idealism now and then? If you really want to know, the Jackdaw broke up a white-slavery ring! Imagine—they were abducting helpless working girls just like me and shipping them to the Orient, where they would addict them to opium and force them into lewd, unnatural acts!"

Kafka smiled in a world-weary manner. "It all seems rather a short-sighted and unnecessary waste of time and effort on the part of these outlaw international entrepreneurs. Surely there are many women in town who would have volunteered for such a position. I counted a dozen on Broadway alone last night as I walked home."

Millie became serious. "You strike this pose all the time, Frank, but I know it's not the real you."

"Indeed, then, Millie, you know more about me than I do myself."

Kafka yawned again, and Millie studied him closely. "Didn't get much sleep last night, did you?"

"I fear not. I was working on my novel."

"*Bohemia,* isn't that the title? How's it going?"

"I draw the words as if out of the empty air. If I manage to capture one, then I have just this one alone and all the toil must begin anew for the next."

"Tough sledding, huh? Well, you can do it, Frank, I know it. Anybody who can write that lonely hearts column the way you do—well, you're just the bee's knees with words, if you get my drift." Millie laid a hand on the sleeve of Kafka's grey suitcoat. "Step aside, a minute, won't you, Frank? I—I've got a little something for you."

"As you wish. Although I can't imagine what it could be."

The pair walked across the large open room to Millie's desk. There, she opened a drawer and took out a small gaily wrapped package.

"Here, Frank. Happy birthday."

Kafka seemed truly touched, his self-composure disturbed for a moment. "Why, Millie, this is very generous. How did you know?"

"Oh, I happened to be rooting around in the personnel files the other day and a certain date and name just caught my eye. It's your forty-first, right?"

"Correct. Although I never imagined myself ever attaining this advanced age."

Millie smiled coyly. "You sure don't look that old, Frank."

"Even into my late twenties, I was still being mistaken for a teenager."

"Was that back in Prague?"

Kafka cocked his head alertly. "No. I left my native city in 1902, when I was only nineteen. That was the year my Uncle Lowy in Madrid took me under his wing and secured me a job with his employer, the Spanish railways."

"And that's what led to all those years of traveling the globe as a civil engineer, building railways?"

"Yes." Kafka fixed Millie with a piercing gaze. "Why this sudden inquisition, Miss Jansen? It seems purposeless and unwarranted."

"Oh, I don't know. I like you, I guess. I want to know more about you. Is that so strange? And you're so close-mouthed, it's a challenge. Even after two years of working almost side by side, I feel we hardly know each other. No, don't protest, it's true. Oh, I admit you contribute to the general office conversation, but never anything personal. Getting anything vital out of you is like pulling teeth."

Kafka seemed about to reply with some habitual rebuff, then hesitated as if summoning fresh words. "There is some veracity to your perceptions, Millie. But you must rest assured that the fault lies with me, and not yourself. Due to my early warped upbringing, I have been generally unfitted for regular societal intercourse. Oh, I put up a good facade, but most of the time I feel clad in steel, as if my arm muscles, say, were an infinite distance away from myself. It is only when—well, at certain times I feel truly human. Then, I have a feeling of true happiness inside me. It is really something effervescent that fills me completely with a light, pleasant quiver and that persuades me of the existence of abilities of whose nonexistence I can convince myself with complete certainty at any moment, even now."

Millie stood with jaw agape before saying, "Jiminy, Frank—that's deep! And see, it didn't hurt too much to share that with me, did it?"

Kafka sighed. "I suppose not, for whatever it accomplished. You must acknowledge that if I am not always agreeable, I strive at least to be bearable."

Millie threw her arms around Kafka, who stood rigid as a garden beanpole. "Don't worry, Frank! Everybody feels a little like a caged animal now and then!"

"Not as I do. Inside me is an alien being as distinctly and invisibly hidden as the face formed from elements of the landscape in a child's picture puzzle."

Releasing Kafka, Millie stepped back. "Gee, that is a weird way to feel, Frank. Well, anyhow, aren't you going to open your present?"

"Certainly."

Discarding the colored paper and bow, Kafka delicately opened the box revealed. From within a nest of excelsior, he withdrew a small carving.

"Very nice, Millie. A figurine for my desk, I presume."

"Do you recognize it?"

Kafka twirled the object, showing no emotion. "A bird of some sort, obviously. A crow?"

"A *jackdaw*, actually. How do you say that in Czech?"

"Why, something tells me you already know, Millie. Back home we say, 'kavka.'"

Smiling as if she had just been awarded a trophy, Millie repeated, "'*Kavka.*'" Then, rather alarmingly, she flapped her arms, crowed softly, and winked.

Closing his office door gently behind him so as not to make a loud report that would disturb his acutely sensitive hearing, Kafka bestowed a long appraisal on his desk, where a Corona Model T typing machine reigned in midblotter like a machine-age deity. Wearily, he shook his head. Nothing good could be done on such a desk. There was so much lying about, it formed a disorder without proportion and without that compatability of disordered things which otherwise made every disorder bearable.

Kafka set about cleaning up the mess. Soon he had a stack of unopened mail, one of interoffice memos, and another of miscellaneous documents. Finally he could truly work.

However, just as soon as he had positioned himself behind the writing machine, ivory-handled letter opener in one hand and faintly perfumed envelope in another, a male shadow cast itself on the frosted glass of his door, followed by a tentative knock.

Sighing, Kafka urged entrance in a mild voice.

Carl Ross, the office boy, was a freckled youth whose perpetually ink-smeared face bore a constant smile of impish goodwill. "Boss wants you, Mr. Frank."

"Very well. Did he say why?"

"Nope. He seemed a tad steamed though."

"Undoubtedly at me. Well, the fault is probably all mine. I shall not reproach myself, for shouted into this empty day it would have a disgusting echo. And after all, the office has a right to make the most definite and justified demands on me."

"Cripes, Mr. Frank, why do you want to go and beat up on yourself like that for, before you even get called on the carpet? Let the Boss do it if he's going to. Otherwise, you're just going to suffer twice!"

Kafka stood and advanced to lay a hand on Carl's tousled head. "Good advice, Carl. Perhaps we should trade jobs. Well, there's no point putting this off. Let's go."

At the end of a long, blank corridor was a door whose gilt lettering spelled out the name of Kafka's employer: *Bernarr Macfadden.* Kafka knocked and was admitted with a gruff "Come in!"

Bernarr Macfadden—that prolific author, self-promoter, notorious nudist and muscleman, publishing magnate, stager of beauty contests, inventor of Physical Culture and the Macfadden Dietary System—was upside down. His head was firmly ensconced on a thick scarlet pillow with gold-braid trim placed against one wall of his large office, against which vertical surface his inverted body was braced. In his expensive suit and polished shoes, his vibrant handsome mustachioed face suffused with blood, Macfadden reminded Kafka of some modern representation of the Hanged Man Tarot card, an evil omen one would not willingly encounter.

As if to reinforce Kafka's dire whimsy, Macfadden now bellowed, "Have a seat and hang in there, Frank! I'll be done in a couple of seconds!"

Kafka did as ordered. True to his words, in only a moment or two Macfadden broke his swami's pose, coiling forward in a deft somersault that brought him to his feet, breathing noisily.

"There! Now I can think clearly again! Sure wish I could get you to join in with me once in a while, Frank!"

"I appreciate your interest, sir. However, I have a nightly course of exercises of my own devising which keep me fit."

"Well, can't argue with success!" Macfadden snatched up a stoppered vacuum bottle from his desktop and gestured with it at Kafka. "Care for a glass of Cocomalt?"

"No, thank you, sir."

"No matter, I'll have one." Macfadden poured himself a glass of the chilled food-tonic. "Anyhow, I must confess you're looking mighty fit. You're following my diet rules though, aren't you?"

"Indeed."

"Good, good. You were on the road to goddamn ruin when you first applied for a job here. I can't believe you ever fell for Fletcherism! Chew every mouthful a dozen times! Hogwash! As long as you lay off the tobacco and booze, you'll be A-OK! Why, look at me!" Abruptly, Macfadden stripped off his coat, rolled back one sleeve, and flexed the bicep thus exposed. "I'm fifty-seven years young, and at the peak of health! A little grey at the temples, but that's just frost on the roof. The fire inside is still burning bright! You can expect the same, if you just stay the course!"

Kafka coughed in a diversionary manner. "As you say, sir. Uh, I believe you needed to speak to me about a work-related matter. . . ?"

Macfadden grew solemn. He propped one lean buttock on the corner of his expansive desk. "That's right, son. It's about your column."

"So then. I assume that 'Ask Josephine' is losing popularity with the readers of *True Story*. Or perhaps you've had a specific complaint. . . ?"

"No, no, no, nothing like that. Your copy's as popular as ever, and no one's complained. It's just that your advice to the readers is so—so eccentric! Always has been, but I just read the latest issue and, son—you're moving into some strange territory!"

"I'm afraid I don't see—"

"Don't see! Why, how do you justify this? 'Anxious in Akron' asks for your advice on whether she should have more than one child. Here's your reply in its entirety: 'The convulsive starting up of a lizard under our feet on a footpath in Italy delights us greatly, again and again we are moved to bow down, but if we see them at a dealer's by hundreds crawling over one another in confusion in the large bottles in which otherwise pickles are packed, then we don't know what to do.'"

"Very clear, I thought."

"Clear? It's positively lurid!"

Kafka smiled with his typical demure sardonicism . "A charge you yourself have frequently had leveled at your own writings, sir."

"Harumph! Well, yes, true. But hardly the same thing! What about this one? 'Pining in Pittsburgh' wants to know how she can get her reluctant beau to pop the question. Your counsel? 'The messenger is already on his way. A powerful, indefatigable man, now pushing with his right arm, now with his left, he cleaves a way for himself through the throng. If he encounters resistance he points to his breast, where the symbol of the sun glitters. The way is made easier for him than it would be for any other man. But the multitudes between him and you are so vast; their numbers have no end. If he could reach the open fields how fast he would fly, and soon doubtless you would hear the welcome hammering of his fists on your door. But he is still only making his way through the inner courts of a palace infinite in extent. If at last he should burst through the outermost gate—but never, never can that happen—the whole imperial capital would lie before him, the center of the world, crammed to bursting with its own sediment. Nobody could fight his way through there. But you sit at your window when evening falls and dream it to yourself.'"

For a space of time Kafka was silent. Then he said, "It's best, I think, not to raise false hopes. . . ."

Macfadden slammed down the magazine from which he had been reading. "False hopes! My god, boy, that's hardly the issue here! With such mumbo jumbo, who can even tell if you're talking about this planet or another one! I know the motto of our magazine is 'Truth is stranger than fiction,' but this kind of malarkey really beats the band!"

Kafka seemed stung. "The readers appear to take adequate solace from my parables."

"I'll grant you that if someone's heartsick enough they can find comfort in any old gibberish. But that's not what we're about at Macfadden enterprises. The plain truth plainly told! No flinching from hard facts, no mincing or obfuscation. If you can only keep that in mind, Frank!"

Rising to his feet, Kafka said, "I will do my best, sir. Although my nature is not that of other men."

Macfadden got up also, and put an arm around Kafka's shoulders. "That brings me to another point, son. You know I like to keep a fatherly eye on my employees and their home lives. And it has risen to my attention that you're becoming something of a reclusive loner, a regular hermit bachelor type. Now, take this advice of mine to heart, both as a stylistic example and on a personal level. You cannot work for yourself alone, and rest content. You need a satisfying love life, and the home and children with which it is sanctified. It is the stimulus of love that makes service divine. To work for yourself alone is cold, selfish, and meaningless. You need a loved one with whom you can double your joys and divide your sorrows."

During this speech Macfadden had been escorting his subordinate to the exit. Now, opening the door, he slapped Kafka with hearty bonhomie on the back, sending the slighter man staggering forward a step or two.

"Have a yeast pill, son, and get back in the harness!"

Silently, Kafka accepted the offered tablet and departed.

Back in his office, Kafka deposited the yeast pill in a drawer containing scores of others. Then he picked up the envelope the slitting of which had been interrupted by his boss's summons and extracted its contents.

"Dear Josephine," the letter began. "I hardly know where to start! My sick, elderly parents are about to be evicted from our farm because they had a number of bad years and can't pay their loans, and my own job—our last hope of survival—could be in danger itself. It's my boss, you see. He has made improper advances toward me, advances I've modestly refused. Still, I get the impression that he won't respect my virtuous stand much longer, and I'll have to either bend to his will or be fired! I've made myself sick with worry about this, can't sleep, can't eat, etc., until I almost don't care about anything anymore, just wish I could escape from it all somehow. Does this make me a bad daughter? Please help!"

Kafka rolled a sheet of paper into his typing machine. Attempting to keep Macfadden's advice in mind, he moved his fingers delicately over the keys.

"Don't despair, not even over the fact that you don't despair. Just when everything seems over with, new forces come marching up, and precisely that means that you are alive." Kafka paushed, then added a codicil. "And if they don't, then everything is over with here, once and for all."

Seated in the study of his Fifth Avenue apartment at a desk that was the tidy twin to its office mate, with the dusk of another evening mantling his shoulders like a moleskin cape, Kafka composed with pen in their native German his weekly letter to his youngest and favorite sister, Ottla, now resident with her husband Joseph David in Berlin.

> Dearest Ottla,
>
> I am gratified to hear that you are finally feeling at ease in your new home and environs. The claws of our "little mother" Prague are indeed difficult to disengage from one's skin. Sometimes I envision all of Prague's more sensitive citizens as being metaphorically suspended from the city's towers and steeples on lines and flesh-piercing hooks, like Red Indians engaged in ritual excruciations. Although I myself have been a wandering expatriate for some two decades now, I still recall my initial disorientation, when Uncle Alfred took me under his wing and forcibly launched me on my globe-circling career. I think that my strong memories of Bohemia and my intense feelings for our natal city were what prevented me from settling down until recently. Although, truth be told, I soon came to enjoy my peripatetic mode of existence. The lack of close and enduring ties with other

people was not unappealing, neither were the frequent stimulating changes of scenery.

Of course, all that changed after "The Encounter," which I have expatiated about to you in, I fear, far too copious and boring detail. That meeting in the rarefied reaches of the Himalayas with the Master—hidden like a pearl of great worth in his alpine hermitage— and my subsequent revelatory year's tutelage under him has finally resulted in my settling down to pursue a definitive course of action, one calculated to make the best use of my talents. My adopted country, I feel confident in saying, is now Amerika, practically the last country unvisited by me in an official engineering capacity, yet one of which I have often dreamed—right down to spurious details such as a sword-wielding Statue of Liberty! It is here, at the dynamic new center of the century, that I have finally planted sustainable roots.

As for your new role as wife and mother, you must accept my sincerest congratulations. You know that I esteem parenthood most highly—despite having many reasons well known to you for the likely development of exactly the opposite opinion. Once I actually dared dream of such a role for myself. But such a happy circumstance was not to be. For although there have been many women in my life, none seemed equal to my idiosyncratic needs. (Any regrets I may have once had regarding my eternal bachelorhood are long extinguished, of course.) Curiously enough, my employer, Herr Macfadden, saw fit to accost me on this very topic today. Perhaps I shall take his blunt advice to heart and resume courting the fair sex, if only for temporary amusement. Although the rigors of my curious manner of existence have grown, if anything, even more demanding than before. . . .

Fleshing out his letter with another page or two of trivial anecdotes and polite domestic and familial inquiries, Kafka paused at the closing endearment. After some thought, he finally inscribed it: "Give my regards to Mother—and Mother alone." Weighing the sealed letter with a small balance, he affixed the precisely requisite postage to it, then took the elevator down to the lobby of his building, where he left the missive with the concierge.

But then, instead of returning to his apartment or exiting onto the busy Manhattan street, Kafka moved to an innocuous door in a forlorn corner of the lobby. Looking about to ascertain whether anyone was observing him, he quickly insinuated himself through the portal.

A wanly lit flight of stairs led downward. Soon Kafka was in the basement. Crossing that nighted realm, Kafka reached another set of stairs. Within seconds, he was in a subcellar.

This underground kingdom seemed even darker than the level above, save for a distant flickering glow. Kafka moved toward this partially shielded light source.

Heat mounted. On the far side of a gap-slatted wooden partition, Kafka came face to face with an enormous, Moloch-like furnace. Its door was open, and from an enormous pile of coal a half-naked man shoveled scoop after scoop of black lumps.

For some time Kafka watched the brawny sweating man work. He knew neither the man's name nor his history. Kafka assumed he lived here, within reach of his fiery charge, for no matter when Kafka visited he found the stoker busy tending his demanding master.

The congruence with his own situation did not go unregarded by Kafka.

On the floor stood a pail of cinder-flecked water with a dipper in it. Kafka took up the dipper and raised it to the stoker's lips. Without stopping his shoveling, the laborer greedily drank the warm sooty liquid. After several repetitions of this beneficence, the man signaled by a grunt his satisfaction.

Feeling free now to tend to his own business, Kafka stepped around the bulk of the furnace. Behind this asbestos-clad monster was another door, seemingly placed without sense. Through this door Kafka stepped.

And into the Jackdaw's sanctum.

Strange machines and devices bulked in the shadows not entirely dispelled by several low-wattage bulbs. An exit leading who-knows-where could be vaguely discerned. Near the entrance door on a peg hung the famous feathered cape; on a table sat mask, hat and canary-colored gloves. In a glass case was a gun belt and sundry other portable gadgetry.

With lingering, almost fetishistic pleasure, Kafka donned his disguise. A transformative surge passed through him, rendering him somehow larger than life.

Emitting a mild *sotto voce* version of his shrill cry, the Jackdaw stepped to a ticker-tape device. Picking up the trailing paper, he began to scan its contents.

"Hmmm . . . The Mousehole Gang suspected in daring daylight bank robbery, but police on the case . . . Dogface Barton in prison break, but likely hideout believed known . . . The dirigible *Shenendoah* to make maiden flight . . . Ku Klux Klan to stage Washington rally . . . Yes, yes, but nothing here for me—Wait, what's this? 'The Federal Bureau of Investigation under its new director Mr. Hoover is pursuing reports of an extortion attempt upon oil and steel magnate John D. Rockefeller by a hitherto unknown Zionist agent provocateur using the pseudonym of "The Black Beetle. . . ."' Ah, this has the Jackdaw's name writ large upon it!"

The door to Kafka's office opened and Millie Jensen entered, carrying a sheaf of papers. She stood quietly for a moment, regarding the affecting sight before her, which evoked a tender sigh from her sympathetic nature.

Kafka's face rested insensibly on a surface definitely not intended for such a purpose: the uncomfortable keys and platen of his Corona typing machine. Gentle snores issued from the sleeping columnist.

Millie tried awakening him by tapping her foot. When this method produced no effect, she began to cough, at first femininely, then with increasing violence, until her ultimate efforts resembled the paroxysms of a tuberculosis victim.

Her ploy worked at last, for Kafka jolted awake with a start, almost like a caged dangerous beast, taking in his situation with a single wild-eyed glance before his usual mask of calm fell into place.

"Ah, Miss Jensen, please excuse my inattention. I was inspecting the mechanism. Its performance was unsatisfactory—"

"Oh, you don't need to make excuses with me, Frank," said Millie, not unkindly. "I know you're exerting yourself night and day to accomplish—certain things."

"Yes, quite correct. My, um, novel is presenting me with certain intractable difficulties. Important lines of the plot refuse to resolve themselves—"

"Yeah, gotcha, kiddo." Millie regarded Kafka slyly and with a humorous glint in her green eyes. "Say, did you ever think that by relaxing a little, you might find an answer to your problems unconsciously?"

Kafka smiled. "Why, Millie, you sound positively like a disciple of Herr Freud."

"Oh, a girl likes to keep abreast of the latest fads. But I'm serious. You like the movies, don't you?"

"I believe that the cinema represents a valid new sensory experience akin to the exteriorization of one's dreams."

"And their popcorn generally ain't so bad either. Well, it's a Friday, and the new Chaplin is playing downtown. *The Gold Rush.* Wanna catch it with me tonight?"

Kafka deliberated momentarily before brightening and giving a surprisingly hearty and colloquial assent. "Millie, I'm your man!"

Turning to leave—or so that she could regard Kafka coquettishly over one shoulder—Millie replied, "That remains to be seen!"

Streaming out from the doors of the Nature Theater of Oklahoma—a popular begemmed movie palace owned by the most famous and successful son of that prairie state, the comedian Will Rogers—the happy moviegoers soon dispersed into the evening bustle of Manhattan. Left behind were a single man and woman; the pair seemed hesitant or unsure of their next destination, like moths deprived of their phototropism.

After a protracted silence, Millie chirpily asked Kafka, "So, Frank, whadda'd you think? What a riot, huh?"

Millie's date seemed lost in thought, his dark features enrapt in a fugue of consternation. "That scene where Chaplin is starving and forced to eat his own shoe made me feel so strange. . . . It corresponded exactly to an enervating emotion I myself have had on numerous occasions."

"Really? Gosh, I feel plenty bad for you, Frank. Look at you—you're wound up so tight you're ready to burst to pieces! What you need is a feminine presence in your life, someone to take care of you and nurture you. Don't you think that would be nice?"

"If you speak of marriage, Miss Jensen, I fear that such a normal mortal luxury is forever denied me. A formal union with a woman would result not only in the dissolution of the nothingness that I am, but doom also my poor wife."

"Holy cats, Frank, you've been reading the fake sob stories in our rag too much! Or maybe you've even been dipping into *Weird Tales*! Life just isn't as complex or melodramatic as you or those three-hankie writers make it out to be!" Millie linked her arm through Kafka's and leaned her head on his shoulder. "A man and a woman together—what could be simpler?"

Kafka did not disengage, but instead, seeming to take some small encouragement from the simple human contact, managed to pull himself together with a visible effort.

"I'm sorry to be such a wet blanket, Millie, when all you sought was a gay night out. Truthfully, I have not felt so melancholy for nearly twenty years. This black humor was something I thought I had left behind in the dank and dismal streets of Prague. The cosmopolitan, globe-trotting engineer known as Frank Kafka was a mature, vibrant, self-assured fellow. But it appears now that he was only a paper cutout that quickly withers in the flames of frustration."

Since Kafka was at least communicating again, Millie's natural exuberance reasserted itself. "Oh, bosh and piffle, Frank! Everyone gets a dose of the blues now and then. It'll pass, you'll see! All we have to do is spend an hour or two doing something pleasant. What do you really, really like to do? How about grabbing a coffee and some pastry? The Hotel Occidental has a great coffee shop. I bet their jelly donuts will make you think of Vienna!"

"That sounds fine, Millie. But if you'd really like to know what I enjoy—"

"Yes, yes, Frank—tell me!"

"I like to contemplate the Brooklyn Bridge. Mr. Roebling's masterpiece reminds me of some of the humbler constructions I myself was once responsible for. Sometimes those noble buttresses alone seem endurable and without shame to me, amidst all the city's charade. But I don't suppose—"

"Frank, I'd love bridge-watching with you! Let's go!"

With Millie forcefully tugging on her coworker's arm, the mismatched couple began to move up Broadway. Soon, they were within sight of City Hall and not far from the majestic span across the East River.

As they crossed the small park in front of City Hall, the shrill scream of a hysterical woman brought them to an abrupt halt. This initial call of alarm was quickly followed by a swelling chorus of indignation, fear, confusion, and outrage.

Kafka raced toward the source of the noise, Millie trailing behind.

A growing, growling, agitated crowd lifted its gaze skyward. Atop the very roof of City Hall stood an ominous figure. Diminuitive yet powerful, with the warped back and hypertrophied cranium of a Quasimodo, he was clad in a form-fitting black union suit that merged into face-concealing, antennae-topped headgear. From his back sprouted small, wire-stiffened cellophane wings; from his torso, parallel rows of artificial abdominal feelers. The creature could be none other than—

"The Black Beetle!" shouted an onlooker.

"Where're the cops?" yelled someone else.

"Where's the Jackdaw?" yelled another.

Kafka stood quivering beside Millie like a dog on a leash faced with an impudent raccoon or squirrel.

The Black Beetle began to harangue his audience in a slightly accented English, showering them with incomprehensible slogans and demands.

"Down with all anti-Semites! Up with Zionism! Palestine for the Jews! The Mufti of Jerusalem must die! America must support the Zionist cause! If she does not do so willingly, with guns and money, we shall compel her to! Take this as a sign of our seriousness!"

There was nothing equivocal or esoteric about the round bomb which the Black Beetle now produced from somewhere on his person. The sight of its sizzling fuse raised a loud inchoate cry from the crowd, and people began to scatter in all directions.

"Long live the Stern Gang!" shouted the Black Beetle as he hurled his explosive device.

Kafka knocked Millie to the ground and covered her body with his lanky form.

The bomb went off, filling their world with noise and the reek of gunpowder, hurtling shrapnel, flying cement chips, and clumps of sod.

Immediately after the detonation, Kafka leaped to his feet and surveyed the situation. By a miracle of Providence, it appeared that no person had been caught in the blast, the destruction confined to turf, sidewalk, and park benches.

As for the Black Beetle—in the confusion, he had made good his escape.

Kafka slumped in despair, muttering, "Useless, useless, all ambition. And yet what joy, imagining again the pleasure of a knife twisted in my heart. . . ."

Millie had regained her feet and was brushing her clothes clean. "Frank—are you OK?"

Kafka straightened. "Millie, our night together is over. I trust you can find your own way home? I have—I must be going."

"Why, sure, Frank. See you in the office."

Kafka hurriedly departed. Millie hung back until he turned a corner. Then she slipped after him, always keeping a shield of pedestrians between them.

She followed her quarry as far as Times Square. There, in a squalid doorway apart from the more wholesome foot-traffic, as Millie watched from concealment behind a shuttered kiosk, Kafka approached two gaudy women of obvious ill repute, leaving, after a slight dickering, with both of the overpainted floozies, plainly headed toward the entrance of a nearby fleabag hotel.

"Oh, Frank! Why?" Millie exclaimed, and began to weep.

Dearest Ottla,

I write to you today hoping to clarify my own thoughts on one particular matter, that being our shared ancestry and heritage. A disturbing incident of late has unleashed a savage pack of old feelings and recriminations I thought long tamed. I have always admired at a

suitable distance your passionate embrace of an ultra-modern syn-
thesis of our old family religion—perhaps strictly for its certitude—
although I could never myself feel comfortable in its suffocating
clutches. Perhaps your perspective will aid me in seeing my own
status afresh.

We are Jews, of course. Jews by birth, an inescapable heritage of
the blood. You have affirmed this ancient taint wholeheartedly,
passionately enlisting in such causes as the rescue of the *Ostjuden* and
the formation of a Jewish homeland in the Palestine protectorate. I,
on the other hand, have violently abandoned any such affiliations
and attitudes, a decision enforced not solely by my rational intellect
and the study of comparative cultures enabled by my extensive
travels, but equally by my gut.

How you ever maintained any religious feeling, raised in our
household as you were, I cannot imagine. Dragged by *him,* we went
to synagogue a bare four times a year, and it was a farce, a joke. No,
not even a joke. I've never been so bored in my life, I believe, except
later on at dance lessons. I did enjoy the small distractions, such as
the opening of the Ark, which always reminded me of a shooting
gallery where, when you hit a bull's-eye, a door flips open the same
way, except that at the gallery something interesting popped out,
while here it was always the same old dolls without heads.

Later, I saw things in a slightly less harsh light and realized
what could lead you to believe. You had actually managed to salvage
some scraps of Judaism from that small, ghettolike congregation.
For me, it was not to be, and I firmly affixed a Solomonic seal to
the whole stinking corpse of my incipient, puerile Judaism and
buried it deep.

But now, this old specter has arisen again, lashed into an
unnatural afterlife by the chance meeting with a Zionist demagogue.

What I humbly request from you, dearest sister, are two things.
First, a well-marshalled explanation and defense of your own faith.
Second, and perhaps more vitally, some information regarding the
chief figures of the European Zionist scene, specifically any particu-
lars concerning a certain crook-backed firebrand . . .

The door to Kafka's office was thrust open so violently that it swung through a full half-circle of arc to bang against the wall in which it was hung, making the inset glass pane quiver like a shaken quilt.

Kafka clapped his hands to his ears and winced. "Millie, was that strictly necessary?"

Millie snorted, then stomped across the room. "That's 'Miss Jensen' to you, Mr. Kafka!" She flung an armful of papers down on Kafka's desk and pivoted to leave.

Kafka stood and moved to her side. "Millie—or if you insist, Miss Jensen. I realize that our date did not end in a particularly satisfying fashion, and that perhaps your nerves are still abuzz from our shared brush with death. And yet, I fancied that until that unforeseen, inaesthetic climax we were enjoying ourselves much like any other couple."

Millie's jade eyes flared with anger. "Oh, sure, right till we nearly got blown up things were hunky-dory. But what came *after* was the real shocker!"

"After? I don't understand—No, surely you couldn't have—"

"But I did, Mr. Barn Veeve-ant, Filly-der-joy Kafka! And let me just tell you this, buster! Any guy who'd pass up some heavy petting with me in favor of two clapped-out, gussied-up old trollops is not someone who's ever going to learn if I wear my stockings rolled!"

And with that obscure assertion, Millie departed as noisily as she had come.

Kafka sat down at his desk and cradled his head in his hands. There came a polite knock, followed by the entrance of officeboy Carl.

Kafka looked up. "The Boss?"

Carl simply nodded, his expression and demeanor conveying the utmost solemn sympathy.

Once more Kafka stood before the forbidding door to Bernarr Macfadden's office. Dispiritedly he knocked, wearily entered when bidden.

Macfadden was employing an apparatus of steel springs and Bakelite grips in exercises intended to strengthen his upper body. Seated behind his massive desk, he stretched and released the resistant springs like a demented candymaker fighting recalcitrant taffy. Sweat dripped from his agressive mustache as, grunting, he nodded Kafka to a seat.

Watching in horrified fascination, Kafka sought within him for some last untapped resource of strength. A phrase of the Master's came back to him unbidden: "The axe that cleaves the frozen sea within us . . . " Why could he no longer lay his grip upon that once familiar haft?

Finally Kafka's superior finished his exertions. Dropping the device, he wiped his brow and then poured himself some brown sludge from his flask. That Kafka was not offered any of the drink, the advice columnist considered a bad omen.

Macfadden began to lecture, on a topic of seemingly small relevance.

"I'm not one of your hypocritical, church-going, priest-worship-ping, narrow-minded Babbits, Frank. Far from it! Open-minded toleration and clear-sighted experimentation has always been my game plan. I'll endorse any mode of living that honors the body and the mind and the soul. But I draw the line at one thing. Do you know what that is?"

"No, sir. What?"

"Blasphemy!" thundered Macfadden. "Blasphemy of the sort contained in these galleys of yours, which I took the precaution of securing a look at before they reached print! And thank the Lord I did! I can't imagine the magnitude of the hue and cry that would have followed the publication of this corker!"

"Sir, to what are you referring. . . ?"

"This answer of yours to 'Doubting in Denver.' 'If we were possessed by only a single devil, one who had a calm, untroubled view of our whole nature, and freedom to dispose of us at any moment, then that devil would also have enough power to hold us for the length of a human life high above the spirit of God in us, and even swing us to and fro so that we should never get to see a glimmer of it and therefore should not be troubled from that quarter.'"

Weakly, Kafka replied, "You misconstrue my meaning—"

Macfadden crumpled the galleys savagely. "Misconstrue, hell! It's the most blatant decadent Satanism I've ever seen! That poor girl! I hate to imagine how her life could have been ruined by these abberant Nietzschean gutter-sweepings of yours! No, Frank, you've had your chance. You had a good job, but you threw it away. I want you to clean out your desk right now, collect your last wages, and be off."

Kafka said nothing in his own defense. He knew that all he could say would appear quite incomprehensible to Macfadden, and that whether a good or bad construction was to be put on his actions had all along depended solely on Macfadden's judgmental spirit. And besides, the summed weight of all the misunderstandings he was the center of now sat upon his shoulders like a sack of coal on a stevedore's back, robbing him of speech. A flickering, cool little flame had taken up residence in the left side of his head, and a tension over his left eye had settled down and made itself at home. Coming to his feet, Kafka turned to go.

Now that he had vented his spleen, Macfadden softened somewhat toward his ex-employee, to the point of offering advice. "Maybe you should try something that doesn't involve contact with the public so much, Frank. Go back to the railroads. Or you could always try the insurance industry. Lots of call for analysts and writers there."

Kafka left without a word.

On his way from the building, he was forced to thread an unwelcome, albeit generally friendly gauntlet of his ex-coworkers. Most of them uttered sympathetic farewells and useful advice, all of which pelted Kafka like hailstones.

The ultimate face in the series belonged to Millie. Seemingly genuine tears of sorrow had snailed her cheeks.

"Oh, Frank, I had no idea—"

Kafka came alert, straightening his back. "Millie, I regret anything I have done to cause you distress. For a time, I acted like a lost sheep in the night and in the mountains. Or rather, like a sheep which is running after this sheep. But now my course is clear."

"What's that, Frank?" sniffled Millie.

"To let my own devil fully possess me."

And with that, Kafka walked with what he hoped was a passably erect carriage through the door.

A wrinkled, disintegrating newspaper, half soaking in the wet gutter, half draped over the granite curb, bore large headlines just legible under the wan buttercup-colored glow of a streetlamp:

JACKDAW TERRORIZES UNDERWORLD!
POLICE HARD PUT TO JAIL ALL MALEFACTORS DELIVERED TO THEIR DOOR!
COURTS CLOGGED!
"WHAT IS HE AFTER?" ASKS PUBLIC
COMMISSIONER O'HALLORAN SPECULATES:
"IT SEEMS HE HAS A GRUDGE AGAINST THE BLACK BEETLE"

A booted foot ground down upon the discarded tabloid, pulping its substance. The foot moved on, followed by its mate, carrying their owner with determined stealth across the sidewalk and up to the very wall of a derelict building. There the boots halted.

The Jackdaw studied the structure before him. His keen eyes caught sight of a line of ornamental carvings above the second-story windows. Deftly the masked avenger uncoiled a grapple and cord from around his waist. In mere seconds he was standing on a ledge some dozen feet above the ground. From there he progressed rapidly up the side of the seemingly abandoned building until he crouched before the lighted panes of a sixth-floor window.

Inside, men clustered around a table on which bomb-making materials were scattered. Consulting a plan and arguing among themselves, they were oblivious to their watcher.

Chuckling softly to himself, the Jackdaw stood. Tugging the rope secured above him to test its stability, he next leaned backward into sheer space at an angle to the wall, supported by his yellow-gloved grip on the rope. With a kick, he propelled himself away from the wall. At the end of his short arc into darkness, he was aimed feet first for the glass and moving at some speed.

As he hit, glass and wood exploding inward, the Jackdaw emitted his nerve-shattering cry.

It was enough. The bombmakers fell cowering to the floor, failing even to reach for their weapons.

"We give up! Don't kill us! Please!"

The Jackdaw picked up one of the spineless hirelings of the Black Beetle with maniacal force. "Where is he! The Black Beetle! Talk!"

"Lower East Side! In the basement of Schnitzler's Market on Delancey Street! That's his headquarters! Honest!"

"Very well! Now, you gentlemen look as if you could use a little nap before your ride in the Black Maria—"

The pick in the lock of the rear door to Schnitzler's Market tickled the tumblers as delicately as a virgin toying with the strap of her camisole in some Weimar brothel. Within seconds, the Jackdaw had gained entrance. Tiptoeing across the shadowy storage room thus revealed the Jackdaw spied what was patently the basement door.

As he twisted its handle, there came a noise from above of rattling chains.

With a tremendous crash a large cage fell, trapping the Jackdaw!

Gas hissed out from hidden nozzles.

Consciousness departed from the Jackdaw like an offended customer offered inferior goods huffily exiting a carriage-trade establishment.

When he awoke, the Jackdaw found himself lying belly down on some kind of padded platform, secured at wrists, waist, and ankles, and stripped of his mask and cape. His chin was cupped in a kind of trough, and a leather strap went around his brow, forcing him to bend his neck at a strained angle. The sole sight before his eyes was a brick wall with flaking grey paint and blooming excrescences of niter.

Into the Jackdaw's view now walked a man.

The Black Beetle, bent of back, bulging of skull.

"So, we meet again after so long, Franz Kafka!"

Even in extremis, his careful deliberation of speech had not deserted Kafka. Far from blurting out a plea for mercy or a useless threat, Kafka now uttered a simple, "Again?"

An ooze of false sincerity and hollow bonhomie dripped from the Black Beetle's voice. "Ah, but of course! I am still masked. How discourteous! Allow me. . . ." The Black Beetle doffed his headgear, so that the attached piece of his suit with its antennae hung down his back like an improperly molted skin. Kafka saw the gnomish face of a stranger his own age, in no way familiar.

"I see you are still puzzled by my identity," continued the Black Beetle. "Naturally, there is no reason for you to remember such a nonentity as Max Brod!"

"Max Brod? Weren't you at the Altstadter Gymnasium with me as a youth? But that was over two decades ago, and we hardly ever spoke a single word to each other even then!"

"Of course we never spoke! Who would bother to seek out conversation with a crippled, graceless overachiever such as I was then? Not the haughty, handsome Franz Kafka, by any means! Oh, no, he never had time to see the pitiful, adoring youngster who idolized him, who hung on the fringes of his precious little circle— Pollack, Pribam, Baum, that whole bunch!—desperately hoping for some little crumb of attention! And then, when you left me behind in Prague, the agonies of severed affection I suffered! The sleepless nights in a sweat-soaked bed, writhing under the lash of your image! The long hikes and swims intended to burn away your memory, but which only succeeded in somewhat alleviating my childhood bodily afflictions. Even your absence became a kind of presence, for the glorious figure of Engineer Kafka and his faraway glorious deeds were forever thrust before my eyes by all and sundry in the small world of Jewish Prague society."

The strain on Kafka's neck was beginning to nauseate him. "And—and have you tracked me down then only to sate your unnatural obsessions and take revenge?"

Brod laughed sourly. "Even now you cast all events with yourself at the center! Far from it, Mr. Vaunted Jackdaw! This victory is merely a sweet lagniappe. You see, the only way I was able to forget about you and recover my wits and energies was to plunge myself into a cause larger than myself. Zionism was the flame that reignited me!

"At first, I allied myself with one of your old buddies, Weltsch, and his journal *Selbstwehr*. But he proved too meek and mild for my tastes, and I soon found more radical companions. Willingly, to spite all those who see the Jew as the cockroach of civilization, I adopted this disguise. Now I and my comrades wage a worldwide campaign of terror and coercion with the aim of establishing a Jewish state in Palestine. You in your foolish crimefighting role stood in the way of my goals here in America, so I simply chose to stomp on you. The wonderful irony of our early connection was merely a token that Yahweh continues to smile on me."

"And now what will you do with me?"

From somewhere on his person, Brod produced a crisp crimson apple. After polishing it on his sleeve, he began to crunch it, chewing avidly, as if to mock his captive. "I shall enlist you in a scientific experiment. You are secured, you see, to the bed of a unique apparatus intended to convince the enemies of Zionism of their folly. Above you is an adjustable clockwork mechanism which can be set to reproduce certain movements in what we call 'the Harrow,' to which it is connected by various subtle motors.

"The Harrow features two kinds of needles arranged in multiple patterns. Each long needle has a short one beside it. The long needle does a kind of inkless tattoo writing directly into your flesh, and the shorter needle sprays a jet of water to wash away the blood and keep the inscription clear. Blood and water are then conducted here through small runnels into this main runnel and down a waste pipe."

"I see. And what text have you chosen to inscribe on my flesh?"

"A portion of the Talmud dealing with traitors to the Jewish race!"

Discarding the core of his apple, Brod moved out of Kafka's view. In the next second, Kafka felt his garments being slit open to expose his back.

"I am sorry you will not survive your reeducation, my dear Franz. But the process, to be effective, must be repeated hundreds of times over many hours!"

Kafka waited tensely for the start of the physical torture. But what came next was the last thing he expected.

"By the way," said Brod with fiendish glee, "your beloved *father* sends his usual sentiments!"

Kafka swooned straight away.

When he regained consciousness, the reeducation machine was already in action.

What felt like a bed of nails now touched Kafka's back, and he was instantly reminded of enduring a similar sensation under the Master's tutelage. Yet even those lessons in self-mastery were bound to disintegrate under repetitive assaults of the Harrow, especially when his psyche was weakened by the Black Beetle's psychological thrust.

Kafka strained against his bonds, to no avail.

"Perhaps you'd care to vent that ridiculous cry of yours once more? No, I thought not. Very well, prepare yourself—"

Suddenly a loud crash sounded from above them, followed by the clamor of urgent gruff voices.

"Damnation! Well, I see I must leave my fun. But not before witnessing the first prick!"

Dozens of dancing needles pierced Kafka as if he were Saint Sebastian, and he swore his skin could interpret the agonizing shapes of the Hebrew letters. It took all his Oriental training not to scream.

Footsteps galloped down a flight of wooden stairs. The needles continued their cruel and arcane tarantella. Shots rang out. Kafka lost his senses.

He swam up out of blackness apparently only moments later, and felt that his bleeding form was freed from the Harrow and cradled in a soft embrace. The tearful face of Millie Jensen regarded him from above.

"Oh, Frank! Tell me you're going to make it!"

Kafka groaned. "The palimpsest of my hide still has room for a few more passages . . ."

Millie bent to kiss him. "Thank God! I was sure we'd be too late! I've been haunting the police since the day you were fired, trying to convince them I knew who the Jackdaw was, trying to stop you for your own good! When those bombmakers finally came around and the police beat some information out of them, I tagged along! Everything's fine now, Frank!"

A certain lifelong tension inherent in his very sinews and musculature seemed to have been drained from Kafka along with his blood. Momentarily, he thought to ask whether the Black Beetle had escaped, then realized he didn't care. Max Brod's fanaticism would lead to his own undoing sooner or later, much as Kafka's had nearly led to his.

"Millie?"

"Yes, Frank?"

"Have you ever considered what marriage to me might entail?"

Millie kissed him again. "Well, you're nothing to crow about—"

Kafka winced. "Millie, please, my writer's sensibilities have not been extinguished—"

"But you'd be a feather in any girl's cap!"

Anne

THE NIGHT TRAIN FROM FRANKFURT WAS LATE.

Nothing went nowadays as it should.

The simple businessman awaiting the arrival of the German coaches at Amsterdam's Central Station began to grow nervous. The telegram in his pocket said that his two brothers-in-law had managed to board the express. But suppose something had happened to them. . . . The worst of the pogroms in their native city had ended, and they had emerged unscathed. But the turbid current of anti-Semitism still ran strong, throughout all Europe. What if there had been a last-minute inspection, a questioning of documents or motives at the border? The man could picture his in-laws all too plainly in the hands of the Gestapo.

A chill December wind blew in off the Het Ij, the Amsterdam Harbor. To the man standing on the exposed platform, it smelled like the breath of a wolf.

Nothing could be counted on in this bad year of 1938.

The man's anxiety increased. His chest felt filled with sand. This simple delay—undoubtedly innocent—was somehow driving home to him with more force than many a greater outrage the tremendous uncertainty of the times, the danger under which they all lived.

What a responsibility, to care for a family, a wife and two daughters, under such conditions!

He had thought they were safe in Holland. For five years they had lived here in relative security. He had been able to convince himself that the madness in Germany would not touch them in their adopted country. But now he knew differently. Not one inch of the continent would be spared the insanity of Hitler and his followers.

Suddenly he was possessed by a flash of prescience, a moment of revelation of Old Testament proportions.

If they stayed here, they would all die. Sooner or later, despite all possible delaying tactics, all the tricks and dodges of the pursued, the Germans would get them. They were foredoomed.

Under the impact of the vision, the man began to weep. The arrival of the Frankfurt train brought him back to himself. He dried his tears on his coatsleeve and searched the faces of the disembarking passengers for his wife's brothers.

There they were!

"Hans, Dietrich, how good to see you again!"

"And you, Otto."

They embraced, then stepped apart.

Otto said, "It's a walk of a mile or two home. Do you mind? It would save trolley fare. . . ."

"Not at all," said Hans. "It will feel good to stretch our legs after the long journey."

"And it will give us time to talk," added Dietrich. "Man to man, without troubling Edith or the girls."

"I understand."

They departed the station and soon picked up the Oz Voorburgwal south.

"We live in the River Quarter, South Amsterdam," explained Otto. "Many Jewish families have gathered there."

For some minutes the brothers brought Otto up to date on the affairs of those relatives and friends who remained in Frankfurt. The news was welcome, but at the same time disturbing. Things were worse than he had guessed.

At last, within sight of the town hall, Hans broached the real meat of their discussion.

"We are not settling here, Otto, despite your kind offer. We are determined to move on. In fact, we have already purchased passage to America."

Otto was stunned. "America . . . Why so far? We'll never see you again. And what will you do there?"

Dietrich answered, "To my mind, it's just far enough. Let us not fool ourselves, Otto. The Nazis will not stop until they've conquered all of Europe. It's as plain as the yellow star they force all Jews to wear!

Even England is not safe. As to how we shall manage—well, we are
skilled German optical craftsmen. Surely such talents are in demand
everywhere."

They crossed the Amstel River. Ice floes resembling partially
surfaced U-boats passed beneath the many bridges. Otto did not speak.
He could not bring himself to contradict what the brothers had said,
not after his revelation.

As they crossed Prinsengracht Dietrich said, "Will you and Edith
and the children join us, Otto? There are some steerage berths left on
our ship. It's not too late. . . ." Despite his recent vision of doom, Otto
could not bring himself to instantly agree. His nature was more timid
than the two bachelors'.

"I don't know. . . . It means starting from scratch. Life would be
hard at first. I'm not sure that Edith would like America. . . . And I
have an obligation to my current firm—" Hans suddenly stopped and
grabbed Otto by the upper arms. "*Mein Gott!* Otto, wake up! This is
your last chance!"

Otto's voice quavered. "I just don't know what's necessary. It's all
too confusing—"

Deitrich intervened. "Hans, please. Otto will make up his own
mind. All we can do is offer our advice." He looked keenly at Otto.
"And let me reiterate, we strongly recommend flight. If not all of you,
at least the children."

This possiblity had never occured to Otto. "Split up the family? I
couldn't—"

"Think on it. We could present it to the girls as a little vacation
with their two rediscovered uncles. Not upsetting in the least. Come,
man! If you and Edith won't save yourselves, you must at least save
the children."

They were silent the rest of the way home.

Number Forty-Six Merwedeplein was brightly lit. When the door
was opened a gust of warm air, scented with heavenly odors of
cooking, washed over the three men. Edith stepped forth from the
kitchen, drying her hands on her apron. Upon sighting her brothers,
she began to cry. They hastened to hug and comfort her, while Otto
stood uselessly by.

Attracted by the noises, an adolescent girl wearing glasses emerged from the parlor. She was followed closely by her sister, some three years younger.

Otto reintroduced the girls to the uncles they had not seen in many years.

"This is Margot," he said, indicating the elder. "Margot, give your uncles a kiss."

Margot did so.

"And this is Anneliese Marie."

The younger girl had dark hair and grey green eyes with green flecks. Dimples were prominent in her cheeks and chin. She had a slight overbite.

Now her interesting eyes flashed. "Pim," she said forthrightly and with great dignity, using her father's nickname, "you know I prefer to be called Anne."

Her uncles laughed at her seriousness. "Very well," said Hans. "Little Miss Anne Frank it shall be."

Thursday, June 14, 1939
On Tuesday, June 12th, I woke up at six o'clock, and no wonder; it was my first screen test.

Oh, yes, it was my tenth birthday also. At the breakfast table, I was treated to a rousing chorus of "Happy Birthday" from Uncle Hans, Uncle Dietrich, and Margot. Silly old Hans had stuck a candle in my Cream of Wheat, and I had to blow it out. Then I received my presents. From the uncles, a subscription to *Screen Romances*, along with some new publicity stills for my collection; and from Margot, this diary I am now writing in. It has a marvelous picture of Rin-Tin-Tin on the cover. A trifle babyish, perhaps, for a young lady of my years, but I like it nonetheless.

But the celebration could not take my mind off the upcoming test. I confess I was a little nervous and kept fussing with my hair at the mirror for so long that Uncle Dietrich had to call out, "Hurry up, *liebchen*, or we'll be late!"

Riding to the studio in our big Packard, I sat between the uncles up front, a rare treat. Normally Margot and I are consigned to the back.

Uncle Hans, driving, said, "Are you sure you want to go through with this, Anne? After all, you're still quite young to be thinking of a career."

"Only a year younger than Shirley Temple," I replied. "And she has been making films for ages. And after all, it's been my only dream for years and years now."

"Very well," he said. "But don't set your hopes too high. There are dozens of pretty young girls for every role. I see them arrive at the studio every day, and most go away heartbroken."

"Not me, Uncle. I am grateful just for this chance to audition. If I fail, I will go back happily to my studies. Why, there're lots of other careers I could have. Perhaps I could be a journalist, for instance."

"I am glad to find you so sensible, Anne. I had to call in many favors to get you this opportunity, but it is still far from a sure thing."

Soon we were through the studio gates. The lot was bustling with glamorous people, and I thought to myself, Little Anne, you have certainly come a long way from that Montessori schoolyard halfway around the world!

Almost before I knew it, we were on the soundstage. The lights, the microphones, the cameras, and the spectators, although just as I had always imagined them, were enough to make my head spin. With cameras whirring, I was asked to recite one of Temple's speeches from *Captain January,* which I managed to do without flubbing it. A voice from beyond the lights next asked me to "sing something." I obliged with Captain Spalding's big number from *Animal Crackers,* And then it was over, almost before it had begun.

Uncle Dietrich had gone to work already, but Uncle Hans was waiting for me.

"Do you know who that was who asked you to sing?"

"No. Who?"

Uncle's voice assumed a reverent tone. "That was Louis Mayer himself!"

Accompanying Uncle to the workshop, where I would spend the day (what bliss!), I actually saw in the flesh the beautiful Lane Sisters, Lola, Rosemary, and Priscilla, the stars of *Four Daughters.*

Lola and Rosemary were busy chatting gaily with some men, but Priscilla—my favorite—was kind enough to bestow a warm smile on me.

To think that once, back in Amsterdam, I had a fantasy of Priscilla Lane becoming my special friend—And now it might actually come true!

Saturday, June 16, 1939
I haven't written for a few days, because I wanted first of all to think about my diary. I don't want to set down a series of bald facts in a diary like most people do, but I want this diary itself to be my friend, and I shall call my friend Priscilla (after whom, we all know!).

I shall start by sketching out my life since Margot and I arrived in America, under the guardianship of our uncles.

We landed, of course, in New York. Soon, we were living with Jewish friends on the Lower East Side. Unfortunately, work was hard to find, even for such talented craftsmen as Hans and Dietrich. One day a month or so after our arrival, Margot and I were told that we were moving.

"Before our savings are eaten away, we intend to try our hand at life in California, girls. They say Hollywood needs lots of camera technicians and repairmen."

"Hollywood!" I shouted. "Hurray! Oh, thank you, thank you, dear uncles!"

"Oh, Anne," said Margot, somewhat snippily, "please spare us. Don't make it sound as if our uncles are catering to your foolish obsession. It's strictly a practical move." I knew this was true, but I could still maintain my fantasy, couldn't I?

You see, diary, ever since I was in kindergarten, I had been enthralled by the cinema. The walls of my room back in Amsterdam were positively covered with photos of my favorite stars. I could recite the plots of all the films I had ever seen, as well as the names of many of the actors and crew involved. In short, I was a regular little starstruck fan.

Well, we packed our meager belongings and set out on the westward train journey, rather like the hardy souls in John Ford's *Stagecoach*. I was much taken with the vastness of my new home, its immense and varied terrain. I found the farms most impressive; one could never go hungry in this land!

Upon arrival, just as we had hoped, Hans and Dietrich quickly found jobs. And not just with one of the "Poverty Row" studios either, but with the biggest: Metro-Goldwyn-Mayer.

MGM has twenty directors, seventy-five writers and two-hundred-fifty actors and actresses on permanent payroll! Last year, its profits were over five million dollars. It's just tops!

And, diary—your friend, Anne, was just singing to its head, Louis B. Mayer!

Monday, June 18, 1939
Dear Priscilla,
I hardly know where to begin.

Honestly, living in America ages one entirely beyond one's years! (And although most people would not credit it, pleasant experiences can sometimes be as trying as unpleasant ones. . . .)

I know I've always been a precocious child. (Haven't Pim and Mums forever delighted in scolding me for it?) But since coming to Hollywood, I feel as if I've gone from childhood to young womanhood overnight. Even though I have just turned ten, I feel at least a good five years older. (Although my figure surely lags behind!)

But I am circling around the important issue I have to relate. It seems that I am afraid to set it down on paper, lest it prove the merest soap bubble of my overactive imagination.

Today, Mr. Mayer offered me a role!

And not just any old role, but the starring role in a new family film. (Mr. Mayer always says he will never put his name on a picture he's ashamed to let his family see.)

It happened like this.

At eight this morning, the phone rang. When Uncle Hans hung up, he wore a stunned expression.

"That was Mayer's secretary, Anne. He wants to see you in his office at ten."

I walked around the house in a daze. The drive to the studio passed unnoticed by me. The next thing I knew, I was sitting in Mr. Mayer's office in front of his huge desk, Uncle Hans by my side.

"So, Miss Frank—your uncle tells me you'd like to become an actress."

"Yes, sir. I've been told I have a talent for mimicry. I could always imitate my friends back home. Strangers too."

"Your test shows promise, real promise. Normally, we'd start you out small, a bit part here and there. But it just so happens that something's come up where your inexperience might actually be valuable. Have you ever read *The Wizard of Oz*?"

"Mr. Frank Baum's book? Of course."

"Well, we're filming it. Or at least, we're trying to. I don't know what's the matter with this project, but at times it seems cursed. I wanted to begin it last year, but couldn't free up Vic—Vic Fleming—from *Gone with the Wind*. My son-in-law, Selznick, had a lock on him. Then as soon as he was ready, just a month ago, we lost Judy." An expression of genuine grief passed over Mr. Mayer's face. I knew that Judy Garland had been one of his personal favorites.

"It was a horrible accident," I said, though I fear my words were little consolation. "I cried when I read about in *Photoplay*."

Mr. Mayer looked approvingly at me. "I appreciate that, Anne. Not only was it wrenching for me, but also for the studio. Judy's death in that car crash threw a monkey-wrench into the filming. We had already shot several key scenes with her too. Then, on top of that, just last week Buddy Ebsen developed an allergy to his Tin Man makeup. It was almost enough to make me abandon the whole project. But then you showed up, as if by a miracle."

Mr. Mayer got up and came around to sit on the edge of his desk. "Anne, I think you'd be perfect for the part of Dorothy. The more I thought about it, the more I realized Judy was a bit too old at seventeen for the character. Baum had a younger, more innocent kid in mind, someone kinda naive, and I think it's you. Are you interested?"

I could hardly breathe. Yet somehow I managed to reply.

"Interested? Mr. Mayer, I'd die for such a part!"

Mr. Mayer slapped his hands on his knees. "Great! It's settled then. Now, all I've got to do is line up someone to replace Ebsen."

Uncle Hans and I got up to go, but a word from Mr. Mayer stopped us.

"Oh, one more thing, kid. That last name. It's got to go. Too Jewish. German too. Your accent's almost unnoticeable, and lessons'll clean up the rest, but the name's a dead giveaway. Now don't get me wrong, I'm a Yid myself, there's no prejudice involved, it's just that the public likes its stars nondenominational, if you get my drift."

I admit I was taken somewhat aback, never having thought of my heritage as anything to be ashamed of. But I recovered quickly.

"Perhaps I could use my uncle's name?"

"Hollander? Kinda long. Say, what if we shorten it? How does 'Anne Holland' grab you?"

I considered it for only a moment before agreeing. "Sounds swell."

Mr. Mayer smiled, and came to shake my hand. "Kid, I can see we're going to get along fine."

Tuesday, June 26, 1939
Dear Priscilla,

My first day of filming was a huge success, but more wearying than I ever could have imagined. I got off on a good footing with my costars, disarming what I suspected was some initial jealousy that a newcomer like myself should suddenly leap into such a prominent role. By the end of the day we were all clowning together between takes like old chums.

I have been assigned a chaperone and tutor to accompany me on the set. (How I wish Mums could have taken this role; perhaps it would have brought us closer together. . . .) Her name is Toby Wing, and I'm afraid that, try as I will, I can only consider her a rather harsh and vulgar person. She had a few small parts several years ago, mostly for Paramount, but hasn't really worked since 1934's *Search for Beauty*. Somehow—I hate to imagine the circumstances—she ended up on the MGM payroll. She's quite glamorous, in a showgirlish way, with platinum hair and long legs (which she doesn't hesitate to show off at the slightest provocation!), but she snaps her chewing gum and has horrible diction.

When I contrast her with you, Priscilla, my dream friend, how coarse she appears!

Fancy this: attempting to give me a math lesson during lunch, she said, "Your figure comes first, honey, but it don't hurt to know figures too. Else how you gonna count your diamonds?"

Diamonds! As if that's why I'm doing this!

Oh, well, best to keep all this between you and me, Priscilla, as I do with everything.

Sunday, September 2, 1939
Dear Priscilla,
Please forgive me. Filming has kept me so busy that I haven't written to you in all these days. But yesterday's events compel me to. Hitler has invaded Poland. No more need be said. The war that everyone dreaded for so long is underway.

Oh, what will become of my dear Pim and Mumsie, not to mention all my other friends? Peter, Miep, Elli, Lies, Jopie, Sanne— For now, they are safe. But I have an awful intuition that they will soon be in harm's way.

All Margot and I can do here in America is pray. I cannot imagine what life must be like in Europe now. My days in Amsterdam seem so far away. I guess I am truly an American now.

Thursday, April 30, 1940
Dear Priscilla,
Ten months of filming. Who could ever have predicted it would take so long? I feel as if I've passed through a kind of fire that has burned away all I was before. Out of the ashes I emerge a new person, stronger and more mature, one who has earned to right to utter those magic words:

"It's a wrap."

My first film is in the can. It turned out to be the studio's most expensive project to date. In fact, months of postproduction work still await, some of which involves me. But for most of my time, I'll be working on a new film. Mr. Mayer already has another project lined up for me. He wants me to play the daughter in an adaptation of the classic *Swiss Family Robinson.* I've just read the book, and it's a thrilling tale. Hard to credit though, a family isolated and trapped like that, living off their wits, surrounded by wild beasts, struggling just to get enough to eat. But Mr. Mayer thinks it will go over big with the public, and I trust his judgment.

I guess it's as Toby said, "Sweetie, you're on your way to the top now!"

Friday, May 10, 1940
Dear Priscilla,
Holland, dear Holland, my namesake, has been invaded! The uncles, Margot and I were glued to the radio all day. (Luckily, there was no shooting scheduled.) I can't begin to picture what the innocent country is undergoing. Our hearts go out to the poor helpless citizens there. If only America would get involved in the war— Perhaps there is something I could do as an actress to help.

I shall ask Mr. Mayer for his advice.

Wednesday, June 12, 1940
Dear Priscilla,
What should I receive for my birthday from Mr. Mayer but the most fabulous present imaginable!

Fox studios has had a project on hold for some time, while they gauged public sentiment toward the war, and Mr. Mayer has bought it for me. I'll dive into it as soon as the Swiss pic is finished.

I am to play the daughter of the female lead in *I Married a Nazi*. I've read the script, and it's a corker! In the end, I get to denounce my "father" as a spy, and save Hoover Dam from blowing up. Now I don't feel quite so useless and powerless.

Friday, September 15, 1940
Dear Priscilla,
Tonight was the best night of my life.

I attended the premiere of *The Wizard of Oz* at Grauman's Chinese Theater.

Stepping from the limousine, adjusting my mink (a beautiful stole by Adrian) around my shoulders as the flashbulbs popped, I could hardly believe that I was soon to see my name, Anne Holland, on the silver screen. I moved as if in a dream. Throughout the whole screening, I felt transported. I was proud of my work, glad that my name was associated with such a fine picture, one that will, I am sure, last for generations and serve as an inspiration of how courage, brains, and heart may triumph over adversity. (Is it too much to see in the Wicked Witch a symbol of Nazi tyranny?)

And, dear Pris, just to show you that I am still, under my new exterior, the same little fan I once was, I must exclaim that the premiere was simply studded with stars! (Although much to my disappointment *you* were not there, since you were busy filming *Four Mothers*, the sequel to *Four Daughters*, and *Four Wives*.) It was keen to meet so many of the people I've admired all these years. I even got to shake hands with Charlie McCarthy and his "partner," Edgar Bergen.

As the musicians say, "They're a gas!"

Sunday, December 2, 1940
Dear Priscilla,
The queerest thing happened to me yesterday, and I feel I must tell you about it.

Having developed a headache on the set, I called a halt to filming and asked for a few minutes to recover myself by lying down. Opening my dressing room door, I was shocked to encounter my chaperone, Toby, in an amorous embrace with one of the stagehands. Her dress was hiked halfway to the sky, and her lipstick was all smeared. She looked a fright. Instead of expressing repentence, she just laughed and said, "Oh, honey, you don't mind, do you? A girl's gotta amuse herself somehow. I wasn't cut out to be no teacher."

I made no reply and was soon alone in the room, a cold compress on my forehead.

I couldn't get the image of Toby, pressed down by the grip, out of my mind. A mix of repulsion and attraction filled my bosom.

I have had these kinds of feelings subconsciously before I came here, as well as more recently. I remember that once when I slept with a girlfriend (Bonita Granville) I had a strong desire to kiss her, and I did so. And in fact, I go into ecstasies every time I see the near naked figure of a woman, such as Jean Harlow, for example. It strikes me as so wonderful and exquisite that I have difficulty in stopping the tears rolling down my cheeks.

Am I too young for such feelings? Sometimes I feel as if my whole life that was to be has been accelerated beyond all comprehension by forces beyond my control.

If only *I* had a boyfriend too!

Thursday, June 12, 1941
Dear Priscilla,
Yet another marvelous present from Uncle Louis! (This is becoming a regular tradition. . . .)

He plans to revive the *Andy Hardy* series of films, which has been in abeyance since Judy Garland's death. And I am to play in them, opposite Mickey Rooney! Uncle Louis says that, at twelve, I am now mature enough to serve as a "love interest" for Mickey, who is seven years my senior, but looks much younger. (Just a couple of years ago, in *Boy's Town*, for instance, he was still playing a child's part.)

I can't tell you how excited I am to be working with Mickey. He's so cute!

Don't be jealous of me, Pris!

Monday, July 1, 1941
Dear Priscilla,
At the oddest moments, the plight of my poor parents will recur to me, shattering my mood of the moment and making me forget my lines. Sometimes I feel incredibly guilty that I should have left them behind, to suffer in my stead. At other times, I imagine that my safety and that of Margot must serve as an inspiration to them in their unimaginable difficulties, for I know that they truly do love us both, despite whatever unavoidable fallings-out we might have had.

Would I have accomplished as much with my life had I stayed in Amsterdam? That is a question I will never have the answer to, although sometimes, just before dropping off to sleep, I sometimes catch a ghostly glimpse of what might have been, and that unreal alternate life both scares and thrills me.

Monday, July 8, 1941
Dear Priscilla,
I've read the script for *Love Finds Andy Hardy* and must say that several times I blushed. Not that there's anything indecent in it—far from it! It's just that it will be a supreme test of my professionalism to keep my true emotions separate from the role.

You see, I've fallen in love with Mickey!

It's true, Pris. One meeting was all it took. That's what an adorable little charmer he is! (Not that he flirted with me at all. He's the perfect gentleman and probably feels nothing for me. . . .) But that night, all I did was dream of him.

I was completely upset by the dreams. When Uncle Hans kissed me this morning, I could have cried out, "Oh, if only you were Mickey!" I think of him now all the time, and I keep repeating to myself the whole day, "Oh, Mickey, darling, darling Mickey. . . !"

Who can help me now? I must live on and pray to God that when Mickey someday reads the love in my eyes he will say, "Oh, Anne, if I had only known, I would have come to you long before!"

Sunday, December 7, 1941
Dear Priscilla,
Well, we are in the war now for sure. The destruction at Pearl Harbor has finally awakened the slumbering giant, America. Already Hollywood is shifting gears to do its bit. Who knows? Perhaps one day soon, I will be reunited with Pim and Mumsie. I will buy them a big house in the hills, with lots and lots of rooms, even a secret annex where we can hide together from my public!

Thursday, February 14, 1942
Dear Priscilla,
A valentine from Mickey! Is he just being considerate, or can it be that—?

Toby advises, "Don't throw yourself at him like you're desperate, kid. Keep him guessing and hanging on a little longer."

It seems like a cruel and sneaky tactic, but perhaps I should heed Toby's greater experience.

Monday, March 3, 1941
Dear Priscilla,
Whether it was Toby's advice or my own pure heart, I don't care to know. Suffice it to say that Mickey has kissed me!

It happened like this.

We had just finished a very emotional scene and were refreshing ourselves with sodas from the studio commissary, standing outside in a secluded corner of a Western set. I was still trembling from the stress of concealing my emotions, and Mickey, the angel, seemed to sense how vulnerable I was and how delicately I needed to be treated. He came towards me, I impulsively flung my arms around his neck (he's not much taller than me) and gave him a kiss on his left cheek and was about to kiss the other cheek, when my lips met his and we pressed them together. In a whirl we were clasped in each other's arms, again and again, never to leave off.

Is it right that I should have yielded so soon, that I am so ardent?

I simply don't care. My happiness is complete.

Sunday, June 14, 1942
Dear Priscilla,
At age thirteen, my life is over.

Mickey has just been drafted. No strings that Uncle Louis can pull have been able to get him a deferment.

The love which has so recently bloomed between us must now undergo the immense strain of separation and anxiety which so many other couples are experiencing in this war torn world.

What, oh, what is the use of war? Why can't people live peacefully together? Why do they make still more gigantic planes, still heavier bombs? Why should millions be spent daily on the war and yet there's not a penny available for medical services, artists, or poor people? Why do some people starve, while there are surpluses rotting in other parts of the world? Why are people so crazy?

I have no answers. All I know is that I shall wait forever for Mickey to return.

Thursday, October 16, 1944
Dear Priscilla,
We have just had a letter from Pim and Mumsie!

After receiving a call-up notice from the SS, they resolved to flee Holland. By many torturous strategems, they made their way to Switzerland, where they can now sit out the war in safety.

I am so relieved. I doubt they would ever have made it, if they had been burdened with Margot and me. Finally the wisdom of our uncles' advice reaches its triumphant pinnacle!

Now, if only I had fresh news of Mickey. He survived D-Day, but the war is hardly over yet. . . .

Saturday, November 12, 1944
Dear Priscilla,
Mickey is coming home.

He has lost a leg.

Tuesday, January 3, 1945
Dear Priscilla,
The war has changed Mickey so much. Gone is the carefree boy I fell in love with. The horrible sights he witnessed, the events he participated in, have all scarred his soul.

Even I, safe at home, have been deeply shaken by the news out of liberated Germany of the so-called concentration camps. . . . All the friends of my youth seem to have vanished into them, consumed like so many moths around a klieg light.

I still love Mickey, of course, and forever shall. But I know that the brief childlike interlude we enjoyed will never return. After we are married, we shall enter our adulthood with no chance of stepping back. (Odd, I never could quite picture myself as an adult.)

I resolve now to devote the rest of my life to taking care of Mickey.

And of course, to my art.

Friday, December 19, 1949
Dear Priscilla,
Why do I write now, after all these years of silence, during which I was

so busy with so many things that I neglected my oldest, my dearest friend? Only to mention that Margot has emigrated to Israel, to be with Mumsie and Pim. So much for my dream of us all living in one big house. (Though how anyone besides your long-suffering Anne could stand to live with poor Mickey is beyond me. . . .)

How I wish I could believe in something, anything, as fervently as Margot does. But I fear my faith in anything outside the glorious artifice of the soundstage has completely disappeared.

I never really acknowledged to Margot how much her presence meant to me. We fought, as sisters will, but beneath it all was a deep understanding and affection. As a final instance of her sisterly devotion just before her departure, she managed to extract from Mickey a promise to stop drinking.

Saturday, June 12, 1951
Dear Priscilla,
The divorce is final.

The proceedings were extremely messy—vile, in fact. In accordance with California state law, I was forced to prove mental cruelty charges against Mickey. Not a hard task, given his abusive nature when drunk, but nevertheless an unpleasant one. When I think back to the days of our innocent courtship, even to those few months after the marriage, when Mickey was making an honest effort to restart his career, I find myself in tears at what was lost in the war's cruel embrace. Could anything possibly have been worse? I ask in self-pity.

But then I take a couple of Miltowns, straighten my seams, and go on like the trouper I've long become. Anyway, Mickey's lawyer in retaliation brought up that old scandal with Vincent Minnelli. Luckily, there was never any proof of my pregnancy—I made sure to avoid all photo-ops in those last few months—and no one's ever traced little Liza to that Minnesota orphanage. So, as I hoped, the judge's decision went completely in my favor.

Still, the whole affair was incredibly complex, wasteful of both my time and money. I still sometimes can't believe what my life has become these days.

Oh, Priscilla, if only I had stayed with Pim and Mumsie in Amsterdam! Surely, we could have escaped together to Switzerland! Surely after the war I could have gone back to the lovely little house at Number Forty-Six Merwedeplein, taken up with one of my old boyfriends, and gone on to become an average Dutch *hausfrau*! What a sweet life it would have been! No agents, no fractious costars, no face-lifts looming just down the road.

But the horrors I've just described are my only life now. There is no other path.

Yet—you know what?

Despite everything, way down deep, beneath the pancake makeup, I still believe in the goodness of man.

The Happy Valley
at the End of the World

IN THE CUT-ADRIFT BRITISH COLONY OF KENYA, East Africa, Year of our Lord 1939, beneath the shadows of the Aberdare Mountains, by the shores of treacherous, man-swallowing Lake Naivasha, where the cool and fertile highlands with their vertigo-inducing skies began to stretch their limbs, there stood the creamy stone mansion familiarly called Djinn Palace, home to Joss and Molly Erroll, frayed nerve center of the castaway European settlers in Happy Valley.

At a small remove from the large pillared and porticoed house and its many outbuildings and guest cottages, several lovingly tended emerald polo fields maintained their European breeding in the face of the patient African foliage—jacaranda, flame trees, eucalyptus, thorn, and cedar—held at bay only by the constant efforts of an extensive staff of Masai, Kikuyu, Kavirondo, Wakamba, and Somalian servants. Upon one of the fields a game was now in progress. There sounded the sod-softened thunder of hooves, the whack of mallet upon ball, and the jubilant braying English voices of men and women, players and spectators.

"Jolly nice play!" "Bloody hell!" "I say, you cad!" "Well done!" "Queen's knickers!" "Bit of all right there!"

In the midst of this frenetic, sweaty game a low droning noise as of an aggrieved hornet, swelling in intensity, eventually made itself obtrusive. One by one the players reined up their mounts, forming a small spontaneous cluster of riders, all angled toward the direction of the noise. The unattended ivory ball rolled to a stop amidst the blades of grass, revealing a strange asymmetry.

Shading his eyes, Joss Erroll, an overpoweringly handsome man in his thirties, straight pale gold hair brushed up into wings on either side of his head, spoke. "I see it now. By God, it is a plane. First one in, what, ten months? There, above that peak—"

His wife Molly, petite, auburn-haired, said, "Who *can* it be? I thought all the locals were grounded, by order of dear old Gwladys. . . ."

A tall, cruel-eyed fellow, John Carberry, master of the ranch at semi-distant Nyeri called Seremai ("Place of Death" in Masai), said with languid gruffness, "Not a shabby European, I venture. That lot has had it. Dead as the dodo, or near enough so as not to matter, the whole filthy, weak-limbed passel of them. No, if anyone survives, it'll be the Americans."

Used to Carberry's self-slighting invective, his compatriots ignored him.

Alice de Trafford, a slight, elfishly beautiful woman, possessor of high cheekbones and violet eyes, said, "Lizzie, you've got the best sight amongst us. Can you see what kind of plane it is?"

Julian "Lizzie" Lezard, one of the audience, a bumble-footed, untidy, unshaven, yet somehow attractive youth with the air of a perpetual schoolboy cutup, replied, "I never rely on my own talents alone if I can help it, Comtesse. As it happens, thanks to my intense cultural swotting up recently, I've got just the thing we need right here." Lizzie held aloft a pair of opera glasses and received a round of delighted applause. Focusing the glasses, he announced, "I do believe, based on observing some trials a year or two ago in Paris, that it's a Frenchie vehicle. A Simoun, perhaps. Let's see if I can make out the registration—yes, it's Eff dash Ay En Ex Are—"

As the buzzing plane rapidly approached, even the unaided eye could soon discern that its mode of progression was alarmingly erratic. Its wings dipped first left, then right; its nose drooped, then jerked up.

"Five pounds says it crashes!" called out Carberry.

"You're on!" answered Joss.

Now soaring above the ring of trees surrounding the polo fields, the plane was so low its landing gear clipped the leafy crowns. The unseen pilot appeared unaware of or oblivious to his plight, failing to gain height or even throttle back. And so as it crossed the perimeter of the lawn, the Simoun was aimed like a runaway missile straight at the groundlings.

"Scatter!" called out Joss, spurring his own horse.

At approximately one hundred miles per hour, the plane plowed into the soft lawn, drawing a long loamy gouge. So violent was the impact that the plane's engine was expelled from its frame like a spit-out seed, traveling a further distance beyond the plane's final grave.

Silence reigned for a moment. Then Carberry spoke.

"Pay up, old man."

"Of course," replied Joss sanguinely. "Back at the house. Meanwhile, I suppose we should have a look at our visitor."

"Oh, he's dead," Carberry maintained in a hopeful manner. "No one could survive that."

As if on cue, the mangled cockpit door of the crumpled steaming wreck emitted a hideous grating squeal as it was pushed open from within, falling thence, hingeless, to the turf.

From inside, a bulky figure in blood-stained coveralls unfolded itself. Clutching something, levering himself one-handedly and painfully through the door frame, the oversized pilot followed his door to the grass, landing face first.

The players and spectators rushed over to him. Hands turned the aviator over onto his back. In his grip was a hatbox which, opened, proved to be full of scribbled papers and one printed book.

Kiki Preston, an American, black sheep of the Whitney clan, said in her ineffably gay manner, "Why, it's that fabulous flyboy-writer-whatchamacall-him, Saint Soupy! His face was all over New York last year." Kiki saddened. "New York. To think it's no more—"

Joss dismounted, took off his neckerchief, wet it on his tongue—several women sighed melodramatically—and dabbed gently at the aviator's unconscious bloody face. Removing the pilot's shattered glare glasses, he said, "I believe our Miss Kiki is correct. I too recognize the famous Antoine Saint-Exupéry."

Standing, Joss snapped his fingers and was instantly surrounded by richly uniformed servants.

"Yes, Bwana?"

"Fix up a stretcher and carry our guest to the East bedroom. Send a car to Nairobi for Doctor Vint."

"Yes, Bwana."

"Listen!" cried Kiki with delight. "He's trying to say something!"

Saint-Exupéry's feebly murmured words sounded like nonsense. "Tayara boum-boum, tayara boum-boum . . ."

"He's attempting to sing!" claimed Lizzie. "Ta-ra-ra-boom-de-ay!"

Joss shook his head with wry disdain. "I think not, Lizzie. But we'll find out for certain if he survives."

After Saint-Exupéry had been carried off, Joss remounted.

"Well, considering all the wagers placed, I propose we continue our game on the adjoining field, as this one is now decidedly unsuitable. Will someone get the ball, please?"

Lady Idina, Joss's ex-wife, galloped over and, bending down from the saddle without stopping, scooped up the ball. Returning, she held it aloft: a polished human skull, *sans* jawbone, bearing the fracture marks of many solid mallet whacks.

"It looks as if old Playfair is about ready for retirement," Lady Idina said blithely. "I know he asked us to keep him part of the game as long as we could, but we can't play with inferior equipment now, can we?"

Joss smiled at his former wife. "I daresay there'll be other candidates soon enough."

Antoine de Saint-Exupéry—Tonio Saint-Ex to his extensive net of friends and family—awoke to a variety of sights, sounds, and smells.

Gauzy curtains fluttered at a tall open window, whence poured in sunshine reminscent of the glorious light that once drenched his mother's home at Saint-Maurice. Also from outside came exotic birdsong and the scents of many blooms: jasmine, frangipani, bougainvillaea. From within the house breakfast smells wafted up, accompanied by the clatter of dishes and the muted hum of voices.

Saint-Ex levered himself up instinctively, then collapsed back upon the crisp clean sheets with a loud groan. His entire body was a mass of aches and pains. What had happened, how had he gotten here, wherever "here" was—?

It all washed over him in an instant. Fueling the Simoun himself at deserted Le Bourget field (pushing aside the blood-drenched corpse of a mechanic, a friend, who had collapsed across the pump). Taking off down the body-strewn runway without benefit of weather forecast or copilot for what would, if he prospered, be at least a three-day flight. Crossing the vast cemetary that was France, its cities now necropoli. His mind left free to confront the enormity of the world's tragedy, once the pathless waters of the Mediterranean were below him, hours in which there was no assurance, as he had once written, of possession of anything in the world. Sighting the familiar beloved coast of his North Africa, picking up the old Aeropostale route at Algiers, following it for a while east before veering south, his path dictated by *pifometre,* sheer flier's instinct. The night coming on, the darkness he had once loved—when only the glow of the instruments seductively beckoned—now a mockery. His eyes growing gritty with fatigue, his mouth tasting of too many cigarettes and brandy swigged from a Thermos. The first dawn, and a refueling stop at Malakal on the Nile, where all the natives had been astonished to see a white man still alive. Then back in the air for an eternity of landscape unpeeling as if off a enormous roll hidden below the horizon. Popping two Benzedrines at dusk, another dawn, refueling at Juba (for one hallucinatory moment he thought he was not at *Juba* but at *Juby,* that first halcyon posting now lost in a nostalgic haze). The third dawn coming up after a lost, Benzedrine-hazed twenty-four hours to reveal the Great Rift Valley below him, its herds of wildlife exuding what he could swear was a renewed exuberance in the face of mankind's great defeat.

And then, sighting the green field he prayed was at least some-where near his destination. Fighting for control of the plane with flickering consciousness, but losing it, raking that final cruel furrow across Mother Earth's fair bosom—

Saint-Ex dragged one big hand with its oil-stained cuticles across his rugged, not unalluring countenance, and monkish tonsure, the latter a product not of choice, but of familial baldness. How had he gotten from the wreck to this bed? He lifted up the soothing sheets (thoughts of Marguerite Chapeys, the ancient housekeeper at Saint-Maurice and her endless mending of linens surfaced, then melted away). His sturdy frame (Saint-Ex's somatotype was dubbed *style armoire à glace,* or "hulking brute") was sporting green silk pajamas with a crest on the bosom. Incredible! Once again his luck had held.

How many forced landings and crashes had he survived? The minor ones were innumerable and forgettable, just part of the job, but the larger ones he would always recall. The Libyan desert, the Indochinese swamp, the bay at Saint-Raphael, the takeoff in Guatemala—That last and most inglorious incident—an overloaded plane he should have double-checked, without relying on Prevost—had left him with nagging disabilities that would only be exacerbated by another hard landing so soon. Yet he would not mourn nor indulge in self-pity! He was alive, was he not, when so many others, so many millions, were dead? His mother, his sisters, Consuelo, Louise, all his *mignonettes*, the beautiful women he had adored, if only for a moment or a night. God, what a waste! The extinction of so many unique worlds within the skull . . .

There came a polite knock on the bedroom door, interrupting Saint-Ex's sad reverie. He tried to call out a welcome, but disused speech apparatus produced only a croak.

Taken as assent, his croak caused the door to swing open. In stepped a handsome blonde white man wearing a plaid skirt, followed by a string of servants bearing trays of food, shaving equipment, hot towels, and hampers of fresh clothing.

"Joss Erroll," said the white man. "Servants heard your exclamation and summoned me. How are you feeling?"

The smell of the food brought a freshet of saliva to his parched throat, and Saint-Ex found speech reluctantly returning. "I beg your pardon, M'sieu' Erroll, I speak only French."

Instantly switching languages, Joss continued in a somewhat fractured patois. "Of course. Saint-Exupery's love and mastery of his native tongue is well known. I'm afraid my own French, drilled into me at Eton—before I was sacked, that is—is somewhat rusty."

Joss came to sit on the bed beside Saint-Ex. The close presence of the epicenely good-looking stranger made the aviator uneasy, and he struggled to move away a bit and sit up. Seeing this, Joss hastened to aid Saint-Ex, lifting him with easy strength and adjusting pillows around him.

Settled, Saint-Ex asked, "Where am I? What happened?"

Joss recounted Saint-Ex's abrupt and near fatal arrival into Happy Valley, concluding, "You've been unconscious for several days, but Doctor Vint and a team of volunteer nurses—most of the ladies in the Palace, in fact, all quite eager to, um, lend a hand—have been giving you the very best care. The Doctor couldn't believe you escaped with only a few fractures and a minor concussion. But when I told him who you were, he understood completely."

This appeal to Saint-Ex's legendary reputation had its predictable effect, lifting his spirits considerably. "I have a guardian angel, M'sieu' Erroll. She keeps me safe from storms, cheating publishers, and jealous husbands."

Joss smiled. "You won't find many of the latter hereabouts, I wager." His host laid a soft hand on Saint-Ex's forehead, startling him. "Your fever seems gone. Think you could eat anything?"

"I could do justice to at least six breakfasts!"

Joss stood. "Very good, since that's just what we've brought." The skirted master of Djinn Palace snapped his fingers, and servants soon turned Saint-Ex's bed into a shining plain of silver platters.

"We've paw-paws, bacon *na mayai*, partridge, fried bananas, eggs. Coffee, of course, from Thika—Well, you can see for yourself. Be sure to try the *piri-piri* juice and the tommie meat. Nothing like them back home."

Mention of Europe brought a cloud to Saint-Ex's countenance. "The plague, the dying world—that's why I've come! I have a scheme, a plan for recovery! We must begin now to restore civilization—"

Saint-Ex made as if to get up, but was restrained by Joss.

"Can't restore civilization on an empty stomach now, can we, Tonio? May I call you Tonio? Of course I may! I'm the lord of the manor here, after all. Though you wouldn't know it to ask my wife! Now, why don't you tuck in first, enrich your blood a bit, then we can all bash together and pitch right in to picking this old sot of a world up and brushing its pants off."

Simultaneously mollified and a trifle irked by his host's levity, Saint-Ex decided his advice was nonetheless sound. Lifting up a fork, he was struck with another thought.

"My papers, that book—!"

"All safe and sound, man! Don't fret, they're right on your nightstand. I'm going to leave you now. The boys here will groom and dress you when you're done, if you feel up to coming down."

Joss moved to exit, then stopped and turned with an inquisitive look. "May I ask you a question? Right after you climbed from the plane, you were mumbling something. It sounded like 'tara-boom-boom?'"

Saint-Ex pondered a moment. "Oh, I must have hallucinated I was back in Libya, after another crash. It was then I told the Bedouins who found Prevost and me dying of thirst, 'Tayara boum-boum!' Airplane fall!"

"Splendid! I believe I shall go collect on a small bet now. Enjoy your meal."

Alone, Saint-Ex swooped down on his food like a famished bird of prey. When he had stuffed himself to the limit, he eagerly assembled his papers and the lone volume on his lap, motioning off the servants for a moment longer. Picking up the book, he bestowed a kiss on it, ran his finger down the spine and its title: *Things to Come: A Film.*

"Ah, *M'sieur* Wells—together, you and I will set things right!"

When Saint-Ex awoke for the second time in his new bed, it was to syrupy darkness mitigated by a single lit candle and to the unmistakable coughing calls of lions. For a moment, he once again had no idea of where he was. When memory returned, he knew chagrin.

He was lying atop the coverlets, dressed in a white tuxedo. After breakfast, after the silent yet efficient servants had bathed and shaved and kitted him out—in formal wear, despite his protestations—Saint-Ex had lain down, weary, for just a minute's shut-eye. That had to have been at least twelve hours ago.

Saint-Ex got to his feet. Inventorying his powers, he was surprised to find himself feeling rather well. All the accounting of old pains was there, with new ones added to the tally, but the sum was not more than he could pay.

Picking up the candle and his copy of *Things to Come*, Saint-Ex ventured from his bedroom.

Following music and voices, he found stairs and descended.

A parlor, lit by oil lamps, contained a dozen or more people of mixed sexes, seated on elegant European furniture and hide-strewn tiled floor. Saint-Ex spotted his host (champagne flute in hand, still mysteriously beskirted), but naturally recognized no other face.

Upon Saint-Ex's entrance, shouts of jubilation and assorted good-natured catcalls were raised.

"A new warm body for the game!" "Bring that chap a drink!" "Pink gin for the brave flier!" "Gin Palace forever!" "Pinkies all around!"

Making little sense of the English phrases, Saint-Ex came into the lighted circle, bowed and waited for his host to observe the proprieties.

Joss spoke up. "Our new guest would be grateful to hear conversation in his native tongue. Perhaps if you could all introduce yourselves—"

All the Englishmen and -women seemed fairly well conversant in French, judging by their opening remarks, and Saint-Ex breathed a sigh of relief. There was nothing worse than being marooned among a group of non-Francophones. The names of the women stayed easily with him, and he knew those of the men would come eventually.

A servant approached with a glass. Saint-Ex, no foe of a friendly drink himself, his large frame able to surround liters of wine with no apparent diminution of sobriety, took it willingly and sipped moderately to wet his pipes. Now, since there was no time to lose, he would immediately broach his mission.

"Friends, citizens of this sad new world we now inhabit, I have made the perilous trip to your hospitable land because I heard rumors that your brave colony was less devastated than other realms by this hideous doom that has swept the globe. How happy I am to see that this one time Dame Rumor did not lie! Now, having found each other, all the components of civilization's resurrection have come together. In me, you see a humble man with a certain vision—a vision borrowed from one of your own countryman's prophetic volumes! I come as the bearer of a plan that will impose order on the chaos now churning around us. In you, I see a cadre of men and women at the peak of their powers, the fruit of Western enlightenment and education, heirs to the grand tradition of two millennia, holders of vast territories, commanders of large forces of loyal natives. Together, between us, we have the power and the will to raise the world up Lazarus-like from its grave!

"Let me start to detail what we must do. First—"

"Show us a card trick!"

Saint-Ex peered into the circle of faces. Several people were stifling yawns. The woman called Kiki had actually nodded off.

"Who said that?"

The puppyish youth who had named himself Lizzie thrust his hand up like an eager schoolchild and said, "I confess! That was me! It's simply that I heard Saint-Ex was famous for his card tricks."

"It is true, I am capable of extraordinary feats of legerdemain with an ordinary deck of playing cards—"

"Bring them out!" "Let's see some *new* tricks!" "I'll be his assistant!" "Hussy! You will not!" "Ladies, ladies, please—remember the last time!"

The uproar had awakened Kiki. "I have to visit the little girl's room," she said langorously. "Who else wants to come?" She and Alice de Trafford left, arm in arm.

A servant was standing by Saint-Ex, proferring a sealed deck on a silver salver. Automatically, Saint-Ex took it up.

"Very well. But only a few . . ."

Two hours later, his brain spinning from the diabolical pinkies, Saint-Ex found himself reclining at his full length of six-feet-two inches, with his head resting on *Things to Come*, which in turn rested in the lap of Kiki Preston, who had returned after a fifteen-minute absence considerably enlivened and wide-eyed, chafing the inside of one elbow.

"Time to play Blow the Feather!" called out Lady Idina during a momentary lull in the roistering.

Kiki leapt up, letting Saint-Ex's head thump to the zebra-hide rug. Unperturbed, he rolled over on his side to observe.

A bed sheet was brought out and unfolded. Kneeling in a rough circle, the partygoers took up the sheet by its edges, holding it at chest-level. A feather was deposited in the middle of the snowy expanse. Immediately, everyone began to purse their lips and puff. The feather fluttered erratically across the terrain while the players shrieked and laughed. Eventually the feather wafted up to settle on one woman's shoulder.

A hush fell. Lady Idina put a finger to her lips as if in deep contemplation. "Patricia Bowles," she plummily pronounced. "Now, who haven't you been paired with lately? Let me see. . . . Ah, I have it! June Carberry!"

The players applauded as June and Patricia stood, clasped hands and kissed.

"Take the Ostrich Bedroom, dears. Now, let's resume—"

Saint-Ex had been slow to perceive the reality of the game, befuddled as he was with drink. But when understanding dawned, he was outraged. Leaping to his feet, he transfixed the crowd with an outstretched finger.

"What decadence! Have you no shame? The world is bleeding into the gutter, and you amuse yourself thus? I—I cannot—"

Dizziness suddenly overtook him, fatigue, wounds, and drink conspiring. His collar and shirtfront seemed to tighten, and he felt himself beginning to fall backwards, consciousness departing down a whirlpool colored, of all shades, pink.

Once more Saint-Ex awoke, this time with a throbbing skull. He kept his eyes closed against the bright sunlight he vaguely sensed beyond his lids.

"Here, old chap. Try some of this. It'll help in a jif."

Saint-Ex risked a look. He found himself outstretched on a sofa in a room littered with discarded clothing, empty glasses, half-eaten food and a pool of vomit. Seated near his ankles was Joss Erroll, looking dapper and unruffled despite the previous evening and his currently bare legs, puffing on a cigarette and offering a drink.

Whatever the liquid was, it could only improve his condition. Saint-Ex took and quaffed the beverage. True to Joss's promise, the aviator felt quickly enlivened. The scent of his host's cigarette even reawakened that old craving in Saint-Ex, and he asked, "Have you a smoke to share?"

"Indeed. Genuine Craven A's. Enjoy it, for soon we shan't see their like again in our lifetimes."

Saint-Ex swung his legs down so as to sit upright. His white tuxedo was blotched with various stains. *"M'sieu'* Erroll, you seem like the most sensible and civic-minded person in this madhouse—"

Joss waved a negligent hand, scrawling a line of smoke in the air. "Tut-tut, it's all appearances. It only comes from breeding and hereditary responsibility. I *am* the lord high constable of Scotland after all. Although since practically every other royal is dead, I just might qualify as king of England too, for all I know."

"Scotland. That would explain—"

Joss lifted the hem of his kilt, revealing a traditional absence of undergarments. "Do you like the clan colors? I find them fetching."

"M'sieu' Erroll, please! Can we discourse not like children, but like grown men? One cannot remain a little boy forever, after all, as charming as such a destiny might seem. And after all, I have not journeyed thousands of miles simply to reenact the court life of Louis the Sixteenth! I have a plan to rebuild civilization, and I am counting on you as local leader to assist me."

Joss smiled ruefully. "I'm afraid I'm not much of a leader here, Tonio. Not that my fellow settlers consent much to be led anyway. Lord Delamere and his wife, Gwladys—she's mayor of Nairobi, by the by— are more in that line."

Saint-Ex shot to his feet. "It's they I must see then! We must begin at once to assemble Wings over the World!"

"I'm not quite sure what you intend, Tonio. But if it has anything to do with flying, you can rule it right out."

"Rule it out? But why?"

"Gwladys has issued an edict banning flying, in order to conserve fuel for our land vehicles. No one's making any more of it, after all. Or if they are, they're not delivering it to us. Why, there hasn't been a plane aloft in months. That's why we were so surprised to see yours."

Saint-Ex spluttered. "But, but—this is idiotic! Aviation is the key to restoring civilization. Without it, we shall revert to savagery!" His eye fell on *Things to Come*, its cover warping from having absorbed a spilled drink. Saint-Ex picked up his cherished volume, now fragrant with alcohol. "Look, the whole answer is in here! Your own H. G. Wells outlined this entire scenario four years ago, before any of it began. I met the man once myself, and I tell you he was a genius! True, there was no war, as he predicted, but that was only because the plague came first. Hitler was obviously ready toward the end to invade his neighbors. It was only the mass dying that disrupted his plans."

Joss grew reflective. "Ah, yes. Having one's soldiers and civilians and politicians, as well as those of one's enemy's, turn into leaky sacks of blood and melted organs is a rather effective deterrent to bellicosity. Shame no one ever thought of trying it before. Say—would you care to hear my theory as to why we Africanized Kenyan whites were as relatively immune as the natives?"

Saint-Ex was brought up short. "Why, yes, I would."

"Basically, we were already immunized, just as the savages were. This country boasts blackwater fever, malaria, dysentery, cholera, typhoid, bubonic plague, and sleeping sickness, just to name a few. Having already survived those, we had a measure of protection against the nameless hemorrhagic flux."

Saint-Ex recalled his own bouts with many diseases, both African, Asian, and South American. "It makes as much sense as any other theory I have encountered. But do you not see," said the flier with increasing vehemence, "that such a stroke of good fortune demands even more of you? The rescue of the world sits squarely on your shoulders!"

"Tonio, this lot here—and I fully include myself—has spent twenty years living out their most morbid and self-indulgent fantasies like pashas in the lap of luxury. They had no interest in contributing to the empire when it actually existed. Why should they exert themselves to revive it? Like flogging a dead horse, isn't it?"

"I refuse to believe that everyone shares this attitude! I will scour this land until I find people capable of great deeds and selfless action!"

Joss yawned. "Now you begin to sound like old Beryl—"

"Beryl? Not Beryl Markham? But I thought she was still in America—"

"Well, if she is, there's a damned good imposter living on her ranch at Njoro."

"*M'sieu'* Erroll, you must lend me a car immediately."

"Haw! I think not, Tonio. You've already cost me a week's petrol just to fetch Doctor Vint. But you *are* welcome to a horse. Not one of the better ones, you understand. We reserve those for polo. But it'll be quite serviceable."

"But I have never ridden before!"

"Better get used to it, then. It's the wave of the future."

"Never! I reject such pessimism utterly!"

A woman's voice cried, "Bravo! Bravo!"

A barefoot, tousle-haired, pajama-clad Kiki Preston stood in the doorway. "What spunk! What pep! Take me with you, Tony! Fly me to the moon, you gorilla, you!"

"What is she saying?" Saint-Ex asked his host.

Joss smiled. "I believe she is offering to be your copilot, or to fill some allied position."

"Can she fly?"

"No. But she owns a plane."

"Very good! Tell her she will soon have a chance to play her part."

"Not necessary. She always does anyway."

The lands surrounding Njoro were at seven-thousand feet of elevation, on the Mau Escarpment: a mix of open, tall-grassed pastures and dense forests of junipers, acacia, and mahogo. The air was cool and invigorating, the views equally so. To Saint-Ex's right, looking north, the land fell away to the ceaseless emerald swatch of the Rongai Valley, with the cobalt-colored Molo Hills and the peak of the extinct volcano Menengai looming in the distance. It was like riding on the rim of a dish garden of the gods.

None of this spectacular scenary, however, helped to alleviate Saint-Ex's aching buttocks and thighs. To the contrary, all the mocking beauty had put him in a foul mood. Irrepressibly loquacious, without any companions, he was reduced after nearly three days of traveling to complaining aloud.

"To think that I could have flown over this same distance in under an hour! I, who once thought nothing of soaring the length of the

Andes! How are the mighty fallen! Not just I, of course, but the whole grand, scientific dream of the twentieth century. Alas, what use in wishing things were different? Still, even the damned train would have been tolerable in comparison. But without spare parts, they fear to run it overmuch, debating every journey, quibbling and qualifying. Such indecision and cowardice! And to think that they are mankind's last best hope! If only the colonies of France had offered a better foundation, I would have headed there. Was I seduced by Wells's vision into unconsciously favoring the British? A nation of shopkeepers! Listen to me! What am I saying? Nations are dead, and only the brotherhood of the air now exists. In any case, my hand is now drawn, and I must play it. . . ."

Noontime saw Saint-Ex crossing the border of cultivated lands planted in flax and ground maize. An hour later he came upon a well-established homestead, presumably Lord Delamere's estate. Gratitude overswept him, especially as his horse had begun to falter, favoring one leg.

"Curse all beasts of burden! Give me a sturdy, reliable machine anytime!"

No white person was in sight, only natives moving with slow deliberation on errands and chores. Trying his French on them, Saint-Ex was met with total incomprehension. Reduced to simply asking for "Beryl Markham, Beryl Markham!" over and over, he eventually received pantomime directions that indicated he must ride some small distance further to find "Memsahib Beru."

Cursing, he urged his limping horse—an otherwise tractable mare ironically (and, he believed, precisely so chosen) named Winged Victory—onward.

After another ninety minutes (Delamere's holdings, Equator Ranch, constituted one-hundred-sixty-thousand acres, and Saint-Ex was cutting across a small corner of them), during which time he passed several Masai encampments, their beloved cattle lowing plaintively, Saint-Ex reached a second ranch, this time boasting both a sawmill and a flour mill. Further pantomime directed him toward the stables.

Rounding the corner of an outbuilding, Saint-Ex saw Beryl Markham—grey flannel pants, white blouse, brown denim jacket—standing with a western-dressed native outside the stalls.

Pangs of sexual longing in his loins began to compete with the pains of riding.

Beryl Markham was two years younger than Saint-Ex, born in 1902 to his 1900, and nearly as tall, grazing six feet. With her wavy blond hair, flashing blue eyes, painted nails, slim figure, patrician features, and immense self-composure, she had often been compared to Garbo. Twice married, now separated from her second husband, scandalous ex-lover of Britain's Prince Henry, promiscuous as any man (as, say, Saint-Ex), she was fully as much a living legend as Saint-Ex himself.

The only white child on the ranch of Charles "Clutt" Clutterbuck, Beryl Clutterbuck had been raised by a busy farming father more known for his extravagant affection than his daily attention. Left to her own devices, she had been practically adopted by the respectful natives, growing up like a wild creature, roaming the forests and plains, spear in hand, *panga* blade at her waist, pack of dogs by her side. Upon reaching adulthood, she had cast about rather aimlessly for a career before falling in love with flying, inducted and trained by another superb pilot, Tom Black. Achieving her unrestricted license in record time, she was soon overflying the bush, spotting elephants for white hunters such as Bror Blixen and Denys Finch Hatton (both ex-lovers). On a whim one day she set out solo for England, in a plane whose most advanced instrumentation was a compass. It took her seven exhausting days to get there, and when she arrived she borrowed some evening clothes and went dancing at the Savoy.

Then, in 1936, in an aircraft borrowed from the very John Carberry Saint-Ex had just met at Naivasha, its cockpit nearly filled with jury-rigged fuel tanks, she had set a world record, the first woman to fly alone and non stop from England to North America. (Her goal had been to land in New York, but she had crashed in a Newfoundland bog. To the two fishermen who had found the bloodied aviator, she had calmly introduced herself. "I'm Mrs. Markham, and I've just flown from England.")

All this and much more Saint-Ex knew about Beryl, thanks to a continuing interest manifested in a long correspondence, much like that he had carried on with Anne Lindbergh. Saint-Ex had met Beryl only once in person, in 1932 at the King's Cup air races in England.

But that one meeting had impressed her image and essence on his heart. Beryl was his dream woman, both physically and in her character, unattached and available. Yet, married to Consuelo only a year, Saint-Ex had felt it unchivalrous to start an affair so soon, although Beryl had given signs of not being averse. (And what irony, Saint-Ex thought, since his new bride—wild, capricious, hot-blooded Latin that she was—had begun to cuckold *him* not much later.) For years, although his paths had not crossed hers again, Saint-Ex kept abreast of his female counterpart's exploits, both through news reports and her own well-written letters.

And now, here they met at last once more in the miraculously spared flesh, amidst the ruins of the globe!

Saint-Ex raised a hand in a friendly wave, catching the eye of the native. The man tugged at Beryl's sleeve, she turned to take in the sight of the approaching visitor. Then from nowhere there sprouted a pistol in her hand, and she called forcefully, "Get off that poor horse, you fool, or I'll drill your black heart!"

Saint-Ex understood a bit more English than he let on (pretend ignorance was a useful ruse at times). But such a situation was rather easily interpreted in any event. He reined his horse to a dead stop, then wearily dropped to the ground.

Beryl advanced with that peculiar, sexy, ball-of-the-foot lope of hers that she had learned from the Nandi hunters. "You damned idiot, riding a horse in that condition! Do you want to cripple it for life! I swear, I—"

The angry woman, now only feet from Saint-Ex, froze, gun dropping to the turf, her face transforming from wrath to joy. "Tonio! Can it really be you! I thought you were dead!"

"Only a moment more and I might have been," said Saint-Ex dryly.

Beryl hurled herself into his arms. "Oh, Tonio, you *know* I would have only bestowed a flesh wound for such relatively minor mistreatment of a horse." Mention of the mare caused Beryl to turn her attention to the animal. Rapidly and intuitively assessing its condition, she issued a stream of instructions in the native's language to her assistant, who bowed and led the horse away.

"Arap Ratu, my brother, will see that the mare fully recovers."

"Your brother?"

"We were raised together, Ratu and I. There's more of a bond between us than I share with most of my blood relatives."

"And what of them?" asked Saint-Ex delicately.

Beryl seemed unperturbed by the question and delivered her answer plainly, without emotion. "Mother and Richard were in England, of course, where they'd been for ages. They were never here long enough to develop immunity to the flux, I believe. They can only be dead. Gervase and his father, the same. Clutt, thank goodness, is safe in South Africa. One of the last steamers brought a letter from him."

"Your situation is identical to mine." Saint-Ex grew solemn for a moment, considering all the dead, his own and those millions unknown to him. Beryl used the silent interval to size up the bearish Frenchman with flashing eyes, before he spoke again. "Do you still have your plane, Beryl my sweet?"

"Of course! And a field to launch it from! Not that it does me much good, with this fuel embargo old Gwladys has imposed. Would you care to see it?"

"By all means!"

Beryl conducted her guest to a long grassy landing strip where sat her pride and joy: a streamlined Vega Gull identical to the one she had piloted across the Atlantic.

"Isn't she a beauty! Stingy old Carberry had to buy a new one when I ruined the first. You should have heard him swear! But he's given up flying since the collapse, and he signed her over to me. I've christened her the *Messenger II*. She's got a two-hundred-horsepower De Havilland Gipsy Six engine, and variable-pitch props. Cruises at over one-hundred-and-sixty!"

Saint-Ex ran his hand admiringly over the fuselage. "A beauty. Like her glamorous owner, she is a combination of—"

Startled by the sudden appearance of a boy's white face in the cockpit window, Saint-Ex pulled back. "Who is that?"

Beryl laughed. "Oh, that's just Jimmy. His own parents died of the flux. They had just been transferred here by the husband's company from Shanghai and evidently hadn't benefited yet from our salubrious climate. Nice couple, the Ballards, but that didn't save them. Somehow, Jimmy ended up with me. He must be a natural immune, or a mooncalf favored by the gods. He's nearly the same age my Gervase would have been, and I suppose I was feeling maternal. Lord knows, it's a rare enough emotion with me. Here, you should meet him."

Beryl opened the cockpit door. "Jimmy, come out please." She turned to Saint-Ex. "I should warn you, he's rather a strange child, especially since his parents' deaths. Doesn't speak much. All he cares to do really is sit behind the controls of the plane and pretend to fly."

A gawky, long-limbed youngster in shorts and striped shirt cautiously emerged. He had the look of a hunted animal or visitor from another world. Saint-Ex squatted before the boy and proceeded magically to pluck coins, pencils, and other unlikely objects from behind his ears. Smiling with grave dignity, Jimmy submitted to the game, but it was clear his mind was elsewhere.

After Jimmy had returned to his fantasy flight, Beryl and Saint-Ex headed back to the main house.

"I can offer you plenty to eat, as long as you don't mind tommie meat—"

"No, I have tried it once already and find gazelle quite palatable, if accompanied by a decent wine."

Beryl laughed. "Good, good! We've a fine cellar. And there'll be a hot bath waiting for you, as well as fresh clothes." For the first time, a slight note of constrained hysteria crept into Beryl's strong voice. "Nothing like a plague to insure plenty of hand-me-downs for the survivors, after all." She visibly pulled back from some private abyss, regaining her easy tone. "Then, when you're washed and fed, we shall drink and talk ourselves silly, reminiscing about old times! It's been so long, Tonio, so long. . . ."

Saint-Ex took her hand. "I agree, my flower, with one condition. That we shall also speak of the future."

"Oh, Tonio, you scare me, but it feels good!"

"How so?"

"It's been so long since I could imagine any of us had such a thing as a future!"

After the meal with its wine accompaniment and brandy chasers, Beryl and Saint-Ex switched to pinkies, delivered to them in the candle lit, trophy hung parlor by a somber Arap Ruta. With a crackling fire pushing back the evening cold of the Highlands, cigarette smoke curling into the rafters, the two aviators soon found themselves deep in easy and animated conversation, dissecting personalities and events of olden days.

Beryl tossed one arm backward in a dramatic gesture. "So then Bunny says to Petal, if it's good enough for Cockie and Sonny, then who the hell is Hemingway to bitch!"

Saint-Ex laughed heartily. Beryl was a vivid storyteller.

"Did you ever consider putting your adventures down in print, Beryl dear?"

She swirled her drink. "Like you? Oh, I suppose I've briefly contemplated it now and then. Karen Blixen was going to help me at one point, but then there was that awful scandal and she left for Denmark for good. I still miss her. I often speculate that she's still alive. After all, she was resident here from 1914 on, so she should have picked up our miraculous resistance. Perhaps we'll meet again some-day, just as you and I have. . . . Anyway, I had even come up with a title, *West with the Night*. Evocative, don't you think? But I was never as serious about writing as you seem to be. I thought of it mostly when I was desperate for funds!"

"My own main spur for composition! But it is not too late, you know. In fact, I am working on a new manuscript myself." Saint-Ex indicated one of his satchels. "Something very different, a child's fable."

"Now you are carrying optimism too far, Tonio! Who's going to print this book or read it? Such civilized amenities are extinct."

"Come now, Beryl! You exaggerate tremendously! Humanity has been in much worse fixes than this. Take the Middle Ages, for instance."

"*You* take them. I myself prefer Paris around 1925."

"Who does not! But my point is that life will go on. And it will unroll much smoother with our help."

Saint-Ex stood and fetched his satchel, from which he withdrew *Things to Come*. "Here, you must read this. Immediately, without delay."

"Oh, Tonio, I'm too smashed—"

"Read it, Beryl. Or I am gone."

Huffing prettily, Beryl took the book and drew a candle closer. With melodramatic motions, she opened the book and turned the pages. Soon, however, she was reading with real interest and plainly captivated.

Just as he had so often done while waiting for friends to finish reading his first drafts, Saint-Ex paced the room dramatically, smoking and drinking.

Two hours later, Beryl set the book down. Tears welled from her blue eyes. "I don't know what to say. It's all so true and tragic, yet fanciful and hopeful at the same time. To think he saw it all coming. What a genius! That speech of Mary's—'This nightmare of a world we live in— that is the dream, that is what will pass away.' If only it could be true. . . ."

Saint-Ex fell to his knees before Beryl, taking both her hands in his. "But it *can* be, Beryl! Together, you and I and the other pilots in Kenya can become Wings over the World! A new breed of sane men and women! We only need to *will* it for it to be so!"

They were kissing then, frantically, tongues and mouths on each other like thirst-stricken desert travelers face first in an oasis spring. Beryl ripped the shirt from Saint-Ex's back, and he whipped her cloth belt out of its loops, gripped the hem of her trousers and pulled them off, upending her onto the couch, much as he was wont to whisk tablecloths from under dishes, but with less grace. Beryl leaped up and tackled Saint-Ex, bringing him crashing to the floor. She was atop him, pinning him down one-handed while wriggling out of her step-ins, then popping the buttons off her own shirt.

"Mother of God, girl! You are a savage!"

"You're not the first to tell me that! And you won't be the last! Now, get those flannels off!"

Saint-Ex felt it wisest to comply.

Then talk ceased.

They finished coupled like spoons. Saint-Ex felt every minute of the extra two years and additional crashes he held over Beryl. When his breathing had slowed and he opened his eyes, he was confronted with a set of old faded scars on Beryl's back he had been too busy to notice earlier. Tracing them, he asked, "What are these from, pretty one?"

Sleepily, Beryl replied, "Paddy, the Elkington's pet lion. When I was ten, he attacked me."

"What a horror! And were you scared?"

"Of course not, silly. Clutt was nearby. And besides, I had already killed one myself by then."

Nairobi, at lower elevations, was much warmer than the White Highlands. Standing outside the Muthaiga Country Club in the hot sunlight, sweat speckling his face, chocolate-colored dust kicked up by the horse-drawn vehicles that rumbled by tickling his nose, Saint-Ex felt stifled in his formal wear.

"Beryl—is it strictly necessary that I wear this monkey suit? You know my preference for informal attire."

"Do you think I'm any happier in this getup in the middle of the day? But if we want to get Lord Delamere on our side, we can't afford to look like a couple of mechanics! Now, straighten your bow tie and we'll go in."

Saint-Ex did as he was told. This seemed to be the new pattern of his behavior around Beryl, since their intimate reunion nine days ago. Used to giving orders to friends and subordinates alike, comfortable mostly when leading and directing both recreations and missions, Saint-Ex found that a certain amount of tongue-biting was necessary in their relationship. He kept telling himself that he was not on familiar ground, and that Beryl knew best. But at times he wanted to bull ahead, tossing aside her subtle machinations. (Beryl's second, nonsavage self was fully at home in the intricately mannered colonial milieu, very much a wily player.)

This meeting with Lord and Lady Delamere seemed one such move. As Beryl had explained back at Njoro, before their long wearisome horse ride into the city, "Nothing gets done in Kenya without Uncle Hughie's approval. And Uncle Hughie does nothing without consulting Gwladys. She's a nettlesome one, though! Much younger than Uncle Hughie—his second wife in fact. And she's not a patch on Aunt Florence, God rest her soul."

"Are you truly related to the Delameres?"

"Not by blood. But I've known Uncle Hughie since I was three. He and Aunt Florence were awfully good to Clutt and me, and I've trained Uncle's racehorses for a decade now. I can wrap him around my little finger. Gwladys, however is another story. But since she has a penchant for virile, adventurous men, she'll be your assignment."

"You flatter me, Beryl."

"Oh, don't try to kid me, Mr. Saint-Ex! I know your notorious ways with the ladies perfectly well. And don't think I won't have my eye on your every move from here on in!"

"And a more charming eye one could not imagine."

"Now who is flattering whom, hey?"

The Muthaiga Country Club, a sprawling, multiwinged, partly colonnaded structure, was comprised of huge stone blocks covered with pink pebbledash and surrounded by a golf course, squash courts, and croquet lawns. It was the buzzing social center of Nairobi social life, a hive where one could easily be stung to death.

Standing now on its doorstep, Saint-Ex braced himself for his assault on the Queen Bee.

Beryl was greeting an employee in English. "Hullo, Philip. This is my guest, Mr. Saint-Exupéry."

"Not a Jew by any chance, is he?"

Saint-Ex understood the question. "A Jew? With the fabric of the world rotting around us, he wonders if I am a Jew! This is insane! And what if I were? Were the flying abilities of my good friend Jean Israel any less because he had his dick clipped! I cannot believe this!"

Philip smiled approvingly. "Your friend seems the exciteable type. He'll fit right in. Have a nice meal, Mrs. Markham."

Beryl took Saint-Ex's arm and shepherded him through the busy, cool interior of the club, with its cream and green walls and parquet floors. Saint-Ex noted a few familiar faces from the Djinn Palace, dotted among the many strange ones: the Carberrys, the Errolls, Kiki Preston. The latter, catching sight of Saint-Ex, semaphored extravagantly to him, causing Beryl to cast a cold glance Kiki's way. Saint-Ex smiled, Beryl harumphed, and they turned their backs toward her.

All the guests were impeccably attired, Saint-Ex noted, just as if nothing in the world had changed, and he felt a sudden sense of unreality, unable to reconcile this willfully ignorant finery with the carnage he had witnessed in his escape from the charnel grounds of the Continent. The feeling passed, leaving him sour-souled.

"Tonio, you were much too vehement with Philip. It's true he's just a servant, but you must rein yourself in. Remember our mission."

"Very well, very well! But when Air Command is running things, we shall insist on and enforce liberty, fraternity, and equality!"

"Let us crawl before we try to run, though."

In the dining room, Beryl steered straight for a certain table with two diners seated. Once there, she introduced Saint-Ex.

"Lord Delamere, may I present the famous French aviator, Antoine, Count de Saint-Exupéry."

Saint-Ex was embarrassed by the use of his title, but tried not to show it. He stuck out his hand for Lord Delamere. The man stood, a small, once-muscular fellow, with homely, wizened face and bald pate, and addressed Beryl first.

"Beryl, you scamp! How dare you take any time off from training my nags! How will I sweep Race Week if you continue so slothful? Well, I'm glad to see you anyway. You look damn fine! You're poured into that dress like oats into a feedbag!"

Lord Delamere turned his attention on Saint-Ex. "Glad you could escape that mess back on the Continent, lad. Kenya needs all the good white men it can get, if we're to keep on top of things."

Beryl translated. Saint-Ex replied, "I am glad to hear you speak so, Lord Delamere, as this is my very purpose in coming to Africa."

"And this is Gwladys, Lady Delamere, Mayor of Nairobi."

Saint-Ex turned to confront a woman in her early forties. Pale-skinned, dark-haired, petulant, and puffy-faced, half again as massive as her elderly husband, she was a once attractive woman gone to mental and physical seed.

Taking her offered hand, Saint-Ex planted a kiss on it. "Such a combination of managerial skill and beauty does not seem strictly fair to the rest of Eve's daughters."

Lady Delamere tittered, and Saint-Ex could tell she had already been drinking for some time. "What a charmer! I hope you will not keep yourself secluded at Njoro entirely, Count."

Saint-Ex fought a grimace. "Certainly not now, that I have seen the attractions of Nairobi."

Lady Delamere tittered again, and Saint-Ex visualized, improbably, a drunken frog.

The newcomers sat, and the meal commenced with Lord Delamere bellowing out to the Somali staff, "Boy! More champagne!"

During the fish course, Saint-Ex could contain himself no longer and began to discuss business. He outlined his dream of Wings over the World, stressing its British origin.

"And Kenya is ideally fitted to provide the nucleus of such a force. I believe that this country boasts more planes and living pilots than any other in the world."

Lord Delamere banged a withered fist on the table. "Yes, but what of the petrol situation, damn it! We've barely enough for rudimentary ground transport, let alone gallivanting through the clouds! Where are you going to get your bloody fuel!"

Saint-Ex tried to speak as convincingly as he could, dividing his gaze between husband and wife. "There are depots here and there which we could commandeer. I stopped at one such at Malakal on the way here. But the ultimate answer is the one Wells foresaw. He placed the headquarters of his Air Command at Basra, amidst the refineries and oil deposits. We must do the same."

"What are you getting at exactly?" Lady Delamere asked.

Saint-Ex leaned forward. "I am asking you for enough petrol to get to Basra and back. This first flight shall be a simple reconaissance mission. I suspect that the facilities lie unattended, ours for the plucking. If there are Arabs present, possible survivors of the plague, they will surely welcome the reimposition of European rule. I know the Arabs, have lived among them, and speak their language. We will need them, in fact, to run the refineries and wells. We will mount a larger mission upon my return, establishing full control, a secure beachhead from which to ressurect the world. Soon, you will have all the petrol you need. Kenya, the new global capitol, will flourish as never before!"

Lady Delamere seemed dubious. "I don't know, it all seems so chancey. What if you meet some kind of opposition. . . ?"

Saint-Ex took the mayor's hands in his. "Gwladys, I promise you, it will be a piece of cake! I stake my name on it! What do you have to lose?"

"Well, I suppose it's a small enough gamble. We can spare a few hundred gallons of fuel. We'll just have to cut back on the safaris a bit, I suppose. Don't you agree, Hugh?"

Under the influence of the bubbly, Lord Delamere had been growing visibly sleepy. Beryl gripped the drowsy man's elbow and shook him gently. "Uncle Hughie—"

The results of this intervention were dramatic. Lord Delamere rocketed to his feet. From a holster beneath his jacket he produced a Colt .32 pistol.

"Intruders? Where are they? Loose the hounds!"

Fixating on his own movements in the mirror behind the long bar across the room, Lord Delamere raised his gun. With a *sang-froid* that bespoke similar occurences in the past, the bartenders dropped below the thick mahogany counter. Just in time, for Lord Delamere began to fire. He took out the mirror, several liquor bottles, and a rack of cocktail glasses before Beryl could gently and efficently subdue him. The inebriated estate holder and founding father sank sleepily down again into his overstuffed chair.

Saint-Ex was amazed at the unconcern exhibited by the other patrons of the Muthaiga. What kind of lunatics had he cast his lot with?

Lady Delamere took a long sip of champagne, then said, "I think you've roused Lord Delamere's sense of adventure, Count. At least it wasn't as bad as the time he doused the club's piano with paraffin and set it afire. Still, he'll be rather a handful for the next few days. Despite that, I shall send a tanker truck out to Njoro with the fuel tomorrow."

Dressed in comfortable, rumpled dirty coveralls, head under a raised cowling on Beryl's Vega Gull, his arms smeared with grease to the elbows, Saint-Ex felt as relaxed as he ever did while still standing on the ground. And what made his joy as complete as it could be was that beside him, similarly busy and likewise accoutered, stood Beryl herself, his long-sought life's mate, the woman whom only a strange, world-wrenching twist of fate had made his.

Beryl pulled out from beneath the raised hinged metal engine cover, her face streaked with shiny black. "Done! What about you?"

"*Moi aussi, ma chérie.*"

"Let's eat, then. I'm famished!"

Sitting beneath the wing-shade cast by the fully fueled plane, they ate their fruit and sandwiches quietly for a time, then enjoyed a reflective smoke, before Beryl spoke.

"You know, I always believed that the important, the exciting changes in one's life took place at some crossroad of the world where people met and built high buildings and traded the things they made and laughed and labored and clung to their whirling civilization like beads on the skirt of a dervish. Everybody was breathless in the world I imagined. Everybody moved to hurried music that I never expected to hear. I never yearned for it much. It had a literary and unattainable quality, like my childhood rememberance of Scheherazade's Baghdad. And now that world is gone, dead as Scheherazade herself. And you and I find ourselves on this elevated scrap of earth, where one would expect only commonplace things to emerge. And instead, we very well might be the Adam and Eve of a new world."

Saint-Ex took Beryl's hand tenderly. "Ah, my sweet, how glad I am to share this common and disinterested ideal with one such as you. Truly, you have learned life's lesson, that love does not consist in gazing solely at each other, but in looking outward together in the same direction."

"Well, I do think this great work we are attempting is wonderful and exciting. Of course, it's also our obvious responsibility, especially since we aviators were the cause of all this misery—"

At first Saint-Ex could literally not parse this last thought. It seemed like the sheerest gibberish. When its meaning penetrated, he still could not fathom what Beryl meant.

Spying his confusion, Beryl said, "Surely you have heard the theory before, Tonio. I think it quite the most likely. The hemorraghic flux obviously originated here in Africa. This is evident from the patterns of immunity. The disease must have existed in equilibrium with its environment for thousands of years before Europeans arrived. In the early days of settlement, it couldn't travel far. Its victims just died too soon to spread it. It was only when air travel became routine that the virus was enabled to hopscotch around the globe. *We* spread it, Tonio! All of us in the bright brotherhood of aviators, ferrying infected passengers. *We* killed all those millions, Tonio, as surely as if we had mowed them down personally with machine guns."

Saint-Ex felt something shatter within him. Without willing it, he was on his feet. Beryl rose too and hugged him to her.

"There, there, Tonio, it hit me hard also the first time. But you can't let the knowledge paralyze you. No one living has hands unbloodied. We're just unprecedentedly bloodier than most. The only way we can atone, even partially, is to keep on doing what we're doing."

Finding his tongue, which felt like a wheel chock, Saint-Ex said, "All—all my life I have despised war and killing. And now I learn I am one of the biggest murderers ever to live. This—this will take some growing into, Beryl."

"Precisely, dear. So let's get growing."

Beryl's clear voice rang out from inside the plane at dawn. "Switches on! Contact!"

An experienced Arap Ruta spun the prop and jumped back. There came a splutter, a strangled cough like the premature stirring of a sleep-slugged laborer. Then the full roar of the mighty engine as Beryl throttled up.

The *Messenger II* began to taxi down the short Njoro airstrip. The green marge of brush rushed at them with astonishing speed, until, with only inches to spare, the four-seater was aloft.

Inside the cockpit, Saint-Ex turned to Beryl—looking exceedingly attractive in her signature gear of fur-trimmed leather jacket, white silk shirt, cravat, and flowing white trousers—and said, "Very nice takeoff, my sweet. A true example of flying *à l'oeil et à la fesse.*"

"I don't recognize the idiom, Tonio."

"Ah, let me see—'by the cloth of one's trousers'?"

"Seat of the pants?"

"*Oui, c'est vrai!*"

Behind the couple were stacked various supplies for their trip, mostly boxes of food, water, medicines, and ammunition, all covered with a tarp. Their voyage was to be broken in half: twelve hundred miles to Aden, where hopefully refueling would be possible; then a second leg of equal length to Basra. Total estimated travel time, one-way: fifteen to twenty hours. Eminently doable by one toughened pilot of the old school, decidedly easy for two.

Although Saint-Ex detested the copilot's chair—he experienced headaches aloft if he were not in supreme control—he had deferred out of chivalry and love and sheer rights of ownership to Beryl when it came to takeoff. Now, his hands itching to grasp the controls, he tried to concentrate instead on the landscape below as they climbed to their cruising height of three thousand feet.

Yesterday's revelation, that in all probability the global plague had been spread by the activities of dedicated, technophilic, fatally ignorant men like himself, still smoldered within him like the remnants of a funeral pyre. What would Wells have thought? Saint-Ex knew it would take many days and many deeds before he would ever possibly assuage the sense of guilt.

And yet, up in the air once again, Saint-Ex found it hard to be too morose. With such a stalwart companion beside him, one possessed of *débrouillardise* (the ineffable "right stuff" of a true pilot), with a clear mission, a fine craft, the elements placid, the vistas broad—how could any man feel blue?

Casting his eye around the cramped compartment (when Beryl had flown in this plane's duplicate across the Atlantic, jury-rigged fuel tanks had filled all space except for a tiny pilot's niche), Saint-Ex spotted the butt of a pistol sticking from a door pocket.

"Beryl, I don't recall packing this. Our rifles, yes, but not this weapon . . ."

"Oh, no, that's just part of the *Messenger's* standard equipment. It's for the ants."

"The ants?"

"Do you know the *sansevieria?* A waste of weeds that jut up like an endless crop of sabers near the coast? A crash landing there skewers your plane, and if you're very lucky you die too. Otherwise, you face the *siafu.* Innocent little red ants, half the length of a matchstick. Within a few hours, a horde of them will have a healthy horse slaughtered and half-consumed."

"But I don't see how the gun—"

Beryl fixed him with her steely gaze, and Saint-Ex said, "Oh, of course. Quite proper."

For many miles afterward they were silent, rapt in the dream of flight. Slipped from the trammels of the world, surrounded by a bubble of noise and cloven slippery air, mundane reality fallen away, they were as eagles. Only a few hours from home, they were already as distant from it as if they were in India, or on an asteroid whirling amongst the stars. Below them, vast herds grazed or raced, as if exulting in mankind's premature demise.

Soon, Saint-Ex's stomach—which he was never loath to pamper, when duty permitted—commenced to rumble. "Beryl, dear, with your permission I believe I shall break into our provisions—"

Lifting high a corner of the tarp, Saint-Ex was astounded to confront the squint-eyed face of a young boy.

"The sun," said Jimmy Ballard with a scowl. "It's too bright—"

"Jimmy!" exclaimed Beryl, momentarily nonplussed. "What *could* you have been thinking!"

Jimmy smiled in his abstracted way. "I wanted to see where the dreams come from."

"This is untenable," Saint-Ex pronounced. "Not only does it throw off our fuel calculations, but the danger—"

Beryl seemed less disagreeable to their stowaway. "Oh, Tonio, come off it. You know you would have done the same thing at his age if you had had the chance. As for the fuel, we have a margin of tolerance. And the danger—well, where *isn't* there danger these days?"

Saint-Ex fumed for a while, but eventually managed to reconcile himself to the new situation.

Now the flight assumed a monotony of forward motion that gave the illusion of a fixed vehicle above a spinning ball of a world. Trading off duties, Beryl and Saint-Ex stayed fresh right up until the midpoint of their destination, the aerodrome at Aden. Intimately familiar with the landing facilities there from his Aeropostale days, Saint-Ex assumed the controls for touchdown. With nose high to insure that the tail wheel touched ground first, they made a perfect descent. Taxiing up to the refueling station, Saint-Ex breathed a sigh of relief at the seemingly uninhabited conditions at the once-bustling aerodrome. (Although the many scattered dessicated and half-eaten corpses were not exactly pleasant.)

At the pumps the three fliers disembarked, the adults armed, Beryl with rifle and Saint-Ex with ant-gun tucked into his waistband. A vast inhuman silence broken only by the exhalations and twitterings of nature reigned. It left Saint-Ex feeling mournful. After stretching their limbs, Beryl stood guard, Jimmy poked around, and Saint-Ex manually pumped their tanks full.

"Jimmy! Stay away from those dead men!"

"But Aunt Beryl, I just wanted to see the smiles beneath their faces. . . ."

As soon as their tanks were topped off, they were in the air again, with Saint-Ex at the controls. Now that they had left Beryl's stomping ground of Africa behind and were in Saint-Ex's domain of the Levant, he insisted on doing the actual piloting. Heading north across the ancient Mediterranean lands, the Frenchman felt as if he were Moses leading some ragtag remnants of his people towards a promised haven.

They passed the tedious hours in various ways. Snacks were taken, catnaps snatched, and Saint-Ex introduced Beryl to the addictive "game of the six-letter words." Conversation turned both speculative and practical. Saint-Ex tried to interest Beryl in some of his most recent, pre-Collapse reading, the work of physicists Planck and de Broglie, their speculations on entropy and the quantum nature of spacetime, branching futures and all, but she found it too dry. In turn, she attempted to convey to him the excitement of horse training, its scents and sensations, half a ton of flesh in motion, but discovered him likewise unexcited.

"Thank God we both like to fuck," she said drily.

"Beryl, please, the innocent child—"

Jimmy, however, was unheedful of their talk. Seated in Beryl's lap, hands on the decoupled dual controls, eyes riveted on cloud sculptures, he was plainly flying them to a destination more exotic than Basra.

It was coming on dusk when they reached the head of the Persian Gulf, leaving water for land. Dropping below a thousand feet to gauge local conditions, Saint-Ex was pleased to see an absence of humanity. It appeared that Basra would be theirs for the taking.

Such sanguine forecasts, however, were soon revealed to be premature.

Below them, campfires came into view. Tethered horses clustered around Bedouin tents. The sound of the Vega Gull brought the occupants of the tents out into the open. Shading their eyes with free hands, ancient carbines in the others, the groundlings soon spotted the plane.

"Ah, my old comrades, the tribes of the sands. Well do I recall their language and ways. Certainly their range has expanded since the days when I would host them in my room at Port Juby. Yet I venture to say they are as friendly now as then—"

Shots began to ring out. A bullet pinged off a strut.

"Yes, just as friendly."

Saint-Ex pulled back on the stick and the *Messenger* reared up like a stallion. Continuing north, they left the Arabs behind.

"I think they were saddling up," said Beryl.

"Ah, the follies of mankind. The one undeviating standard in a changing universe."

Saint-Ex insisted on completing their mission by overflying the refineries, despite the potential threat offered by the Arabs left behind. Miraculously, the installations appeared pristine, mankind's demise having been too rapid for social chaos, yet not so rapid as to preclude shutting down the plants in an orderly fashion.

"Here is the rock whereon I shall build my church," Saint-Ex declaimed grandiosely.

"Here is the rock on which you'll *crash*, unless we forget the speeches and fuel up soon, *mon vieux*."

Saint-Ex canted the plane around and headed for the Basra aerodrome, soon setting them down neatly.

"I am not so familiar with this layout. . . ."

Unlike the forgotten refineries, the airport had been the scene of much insane activity, as people sought madly and uselessly to flee. Here was much damage from the end times. It took them nearly an hour to find a workable pump and full reservoir. As Saint-Ex heaved away, Beryl kept a cocked ear.

"I hear hooves—"

Out of the twilight poured the *raffia* of ululating riders. Stepping out boldly into the open on the passenger's side of the plane, Beryl brought her rifle up to her shoulder with assurance and took out the lead rider with a single shot. The others wheeled about and retreated a few hundred yards. The dead man lay on the tarmac like a sack of wheat, while his mount galloped on by their plane.

"Keep pumping," ordered Beryl sternly.

"I was not planning to stop!"

By the shouted arguments, it was clear that the confused Bedouins were plainly working out some leadership problems. But they would not desist forever.

"Don't bother to fill the tanks, Tonio. Let's just get out of here!"

Saint-Ex hurriedly uncoupled hose from tank. He rushed to the pilot's side of the plane.

At that moment the Arabs charged, carbines blasting.

"Get in," urged Beryl. "I'll hold them off."

"No, I insist, after you, Alphonse!"

Beryl laughed, then turned to fire at the attackers. Golden hair streaming in the dusk breeze (Saint-Ex was automatically calculating takeoff vectors), she reminded the Frenchman of a Valkyrie. Drawing his pistol, Saint-Ex rushed to her side.

A bullet took Beryl in the shoulder and she yelped, spinning and falling.

Saint-Ex gave a wordless howl, raised his ant-gun and squeezed the trigger.

A magnificent roar like the resurgence of the Red Sea after its parting filled his ears, and a cloud of bitter smoke engulfed him.

When his senses returned, Saint-Ex saw before him an astonishing sight. Two horses and their riders had been turned into partially ground hamburger, and the rest of the Arabs were groveling on the macadam as if in the presence of their sacred Rock.

Saint-Ex stared incredulously at his pistol. Then he looked behind him.

Protruding from the plane's cabin were the enormous twin steaming barrels of a full-bore elephant gun, hefted by young Jimmy.

"They wanted to see heaven, and I let them," said the boy.

Without further hesitation, Saint-Ex hoisted Beryl quickly into the plane, then ran to its front.

"Jimmy! Help me!"

The boy slid willingly behind the controls. Saint-Ex spun the prop, the engine caught, and he scrambled in. Heedless of the living or the dead, he zipped down the runway and was quickly aloft.

Jimmy was cradling the unconscious woman's head in his lap. On her shoulder bloomed a greedy red rose.

"Will Aunt Beryl ever play with us again, Uncle Tonio?"

"We hope," said Saint-Ex in English. "We hope a lot."

The big balding man sat on a piano stool in the candle illuminated parlor of the Djinn Palace. Barefoot, clad in Kenyan formal dinner pajamas, he clutched in each massive hand an orange. Seated on his shoulders was a voluptuous woman wearing only her undergarments and high heels. She hefted a half-filled champagne bottle and a glass. Now pouring herself some, she sloppily dribbled some of the bubbly on the man's head. It ran down the side of his face and he darted out his tongue to catch the rill.

"*Très bon!* Now, *attendez-vous!* Debussy!"

Using one orange for the black keys and one for the white, the man produced a surprisingly melodic mishmosh that indeed resembled minor Debussy.

The listening crowd applauded wildly. The man stood abruptly, as if to take a bow, nearly upsetting his rider, who shrieked, dropped her burdens and clutched the giant around his brow.

"I am blind! Who turned out the lights? Are we now to play 'Pin the tail *sur un âne*'? Very well!"

The big man began to career around the room, arms extended, taking full advantage of his plight to grope all the women, none of whom made any serious move to avoid him.

Finally even his great strength faltered under the woman's weight, and he set her down on a tabletop. Spotting an empty couch, he hurled himself onto it with a noisy grunt.

"More wine! And bring me more shrimp! Shelled, *s'il vous plaît!*"

A pair of bare hairy legs materialized at the man's eyelevel. He looked up to a familiar, world-weary face.

"I'm glad to see you finally enjoying yourself, Saint-Ex," said his host, Joss Erroll. "All work and no play makes Jacques a dull boy."

"Ah, work," exclaimed Saint-Ex melodramatically. "Work does not exist anymore. We are now in a final age of self-indulgence which even my childhood hero Baudelaire could never have imagined."

"And your dreams?" inquired Joss gently in a tone not entirely cynical.

"Gone with the snows of yesteryear. And good riddance."

"But," said Joss enigmatically, "atop a mountain peak all the snows of yesteryear still remain." And he walked off.

"Pah!" said Saint-Ex. Resting an arm across his eyes and temporarily blinding himself again, he let his mind wander while he awaited the servants with his wine and food.

The flight back had been as arduous and nerve-wracking as any in his experience, even including the three days from Paris to Africa. Once stable at a safe altitude, Saint-Ex had warily let Jimmy handle the controls for a moment while he attended to Beryl. Stripping her of jacket and shirt, he found the Arab bullet still lodged in the wound. Fearing to provoke renewed bleeding, he merely cleansed and dressed her torn flesh, then tried to make her comfortable with a blanket. Resuming the pilot's seat, he popped several tablets of Benzedrine, then settled in for the long haul.

By Aden, after a day and a half in the air without more than a hour's scattered sleep, he felt his mind crumbling. He dared not rest, for fear of Beryl's condition worsening. Somehow he refueled and climbed into the skies once more.

By the end of the trip, it was only Jimmy's wordless crooning over Beryl's restless, fevered form that kept him awake.

He landed once more by the shores of Lake Naivasha, this time keeping plane and body intact. On this occasion he interrupted a round of croquet (played, he was grateful to see, with wooden balls). Upon seeing his human cargo, Joss had greeted him with, "Not another call to Doctor Vint, Saint-Ex! I swear, I waste more petrol on you than on ten mistresses!"

But Joss's tender handling of Beryl belied his mock indignation.

Saint-Ex slept around the clock and awoke with immense *deja vu* in the same bed and room that had sheltered him—could it be only two weeks ago? After looking in on a sleeping Beryl and learning that Doctor Vint had successfully removed the bullet and predicted a full recovery, Saint-Ex prevailed upon his host to drive him to Nairobi.

"You shall soon have all the petrol you wish, man! You can fill your swimming pool with it! Let us not quibble about a few gallons!"

In the city Saint-Ex tracked down Gwladys, Lady Delamere, mayor of Nairobi, in the cool rooms of the Muthaiga Club. Dropping unbidden into a seat at her table, Saint-Ex launched into a recitation of his exploits, not stinting on the heroism of both himself and Beryl and even little Jimmy. Throughout, Lady Delamere said nothing, listening with imperial mien.

"My good Count," she finally ventured as Saint-Ex sat expectantly, "we appreciate all your efforts to establish a toehold for Kenya in the Middle East. Once, we thought it was a feasible idea. But I am afraid that your news of armed opposition at Basra, combined with new developments here, render such a foray most unlikely."

"Unlikely! But, madame, the future of civilization rests on such a campaign!"

Lady Delamere fanned herself nonchalantly. "Oh, I think not, Count. Kenya has plenty of natural resources other than oil on which to build a very comfortable little life for we few surviving whites. The brute labor of the natives alone should suffice. And with careful rationing, our fuel stocks will last for many years yet."

Saint-Ex thumped the table. "And what then! What of all the children, born and yet to come! The future Mozarts and Lindberghs?"

Lady Delamere sniffed haughtily. "As you might have observed, Count, we are not a proletarian clan that tends to reproduce overmuch."

Striving to repress his natural indignation, Saint-Ex asked, "What are these new developments locally, if I may inquire?"

Lady Delamere had sufficent tatters of conscience left to look slightly abashed. "It's the fishing at Lake Victoria. Suddenly, Lord Delamere's frightfully keen on it. And then there's a clinic there with fabulous mud treatments for us ladies." Gwladys giggled coquettishly, producing an effect akin to story boards from the Disney studios of tutu-clad hippos which Saint-Ex had seen when he had visited Hollywood in 1933 for the filming of his *Night Flight.*

Saint-Ex was stupefied. "Lady Delamere, you are throwing away your heritage. Future generations shall curse your name!"

And then he stormed out.

All the way back to Djinn Palace, Saint-Ex had raved to Joss, who listened attentively. When the Frenchman finally subsided, the Scottish lord had said, "Do you want to know your first mistake?"

Saint-Ex growled.

"It was framing your appeal to all our so-called better instincts. Same mistake old Herbert George Wells made with all those dreadful utopias of his. We haven't any! Not a shred! No more than the general run of mankind does, anyhow. You should have preached to our self-interest."

"I thought I was."

"No, not at all."

"Bah! You are all hyenas!"

"Maybe so. But we're *your* pack of hyenas now."

At the mansion, Saint-Ex raced to Beryl's bedside, finding her awake and taking some broth as her first nourishment.

"*Ma chérie*, you look almost your old formidable self!"

Beryl did not smile or greet him, but continued sipping her broth.

"What troubles you?" Saint-Ex asked, dropping onto the bed beside her.

Beryl pinned him with her steely look as if he were insect specimen. "You left me alone, Tonio. I woke up and you weren't here. I don't care for that kind of treatment. Not one bit."

Saint-Ex slapped his forehead. "*Mon dieu!* I was pursuing our common goal, Beryl! Talking to that witch in the city—"

"Evidently your schemes are more important than my well-being."

"Yes, of course! They are more important than my own life also!"

"Well, I'm no longer sure about how I feel. When I was in my fever, I dreamed of all those beasts we saw in our flight. To see ten thousand animals untamed and not branded with the symbols of human commerce is like scaling an unconquered mountain for the first time, or like finding a forest without roads or footpaths, or the blemish of an axe. You know then what you had always been told—that the world once lived and grew without adding machines and newsprint and brick-walled streets and the tyranny of the clock."

"Surely my ears betray me! This is purest defeatism! There can be no turning back on the road of progress. What are the two hundred years of the history of the machine compared with the two hundred thousand years of the history of man? Only a step! We are in truth still emigrants who have not yet founded our homeland. Would you give up now?"

Beryl set down her cup and turned away from him. "Tonio, you trouble me. Go away now. Please."

And so he had gone from her room. And Beryl had returned several days later to Njoro without saying farewell.

Then had Saint-Ex plunged fully into the heedless life at Djinn Palace.

"Your shrimp, sir."

Saint-Ex unblinded himself, saw the waiting Somalian servant. The guest patted his stomach to indicate the tray's proper resting place. After the servant had deposited it, Saint-Ex dug in while still reclining, trying to sate himself like an ancient Roman. Meanwhile, around him the nightly debauched activities of the white colonists, unfazed by Armageddon, soared and spiraled in their ever-changing intricate patterns, producing shrieks, giggles, crashes, and yelps.

A snippet of talk winged into Saint-Ex's ear. "Why, she loves jewelry so much, do you know what she says when she crosses herself? 'Tiara, brooch, clip, clip!' "

When Saint-Ex was finished he got to his feet, sending the tray sliding to the floor with a clatter. Woozily, he began to wander the maze of the Djinn Palace, looking for distractions from the ache tamped down within him.

In one dark corner, he spotted two feminine shadows seated on a loveseat. Moving closer, he was able to discern the bouncy American Kiki Preston and her inseparable British friend Alice de Trafford. Neither appeared to be their usual giddy selves. They clutched each other and shivered. Kiki appeared to be sobbing.

"Beautiful ladies, what frightens you?" Saint-Ex inquired in a gallant manner spoiled only by a terminal belch. "Point out any monsters that need slaying, and I will sally forth."

Alice seemed the more composed of the two. "You can't slay this monkey, Count. He feeds only on magic powder, and the less he has, the stronger he grows."

Saint-Ex was puzzled. "I don't comprehend—"

Suddenly Kiki hurled herself at the Frenchman like a wildcat. "Soupy, Soupy, Soupy, you've got to fly me to Port Said! I've got a plane, haven't I? Port Said's where the junk comes from! I need my junk!" She began to wail like a banshee. "Where's Frankie! Oh, where's Frankie! He always had all the horse I needed!"

Saint-Ex disentangled the girl's clammy limbs from his own, and she collapsed back across Alice's lap.

Petting the other woman's hair, Alice said, "Frankie Greswolde Williams. The colony's connection for heroin. He didn't make it back from his final run, and now almost all the smack in Kenya is gone. Except of course for Lady Delamere's stash." Alice's voice assumed a manic quality that frightened Saint-Ex. "How I hate that woman! A greedy, puffy *pig*! Look what she's done to poor Kiki. Oh, I hurt too, of course. But Kiki's got the jones worse than I. Kiki, Kiki, love, hang in there. I'll help you somehow, I swear. . . ."

Shaken, appalled, confused, Saint-Ex staggered off, feeling as if he were ambling through Dante.

The first door he came to, he grabbed the knob, twisted it, and entered.

There was a young teenage girl, entirely naked, doubled over the back of a chair, her rump high. Over her towered the lean clothed figure of John Carberry, a riding crop in his hand.

With a swish and thwack, Carberry brought the whip down on her scarred buttocks.

"I'll teach you a thing or two, young miss!"

In the next second, Saint-Ex had spun the master of Seremai around and planted a solid roundhouse punch on his jaw. Carberry went flying across the room. Saint-Ex rushed to the girl.

"*Mam'selle,* are you hurt?"

Without changing position, the girl turned a teary face to Saint-Ex and said, "He can't hurt me, really. Not your own bastard Daddy. I only take it so he doesn't do it to Mummy."

Saint-Ex sprang back in shock. What a nest of vipers!

From behind Saint-Ex came Carberry's voice. "I said you were dead when your plane arrived. Unfortunately, I was wrong. Now I shall correct the situation."

The death-faced man held a gun calmly pointed at Saint-Ex. Without further oratory, he began to squeeze the trigger.

Saint-Ex lunged.

A roaring filled his ears, bitter smoke his nostrils, darkness his sight.

For the third time after recent great travail, Saint-Ex awoke in the same sun-flooded bedroom at the lunatic asylum by the shores of Lake

Naivasha. He felt bound on some wheel of continuous, duplicative suffering. Would he ever escape this place?

The voice of Joss Errroll interrupted his musings. "Bloody lot of shooting last night. Can't say I approve. Deucedly hard to clean up all that blood."

His unflappable host came across the room from where he had been sitting and put a hand to the side of Saint-Ex's head.

"Ouch! What a pain!"

"Oh, you overgrown child, it's just a flesh wound. Even I could recognize that. Damn swell of you to save me the trouble of fetching Doctor Vint this time, though. It's just as well he got what sleep he could before they summoned him for the Delameres. Not that he could do much for them."

Saint-Ex shot bolt upright. "The Delameres! What happened?"

"They were found by two milk boys at first daylight. Sitting in their Buick at the intersection of the Karen and Ngong roads. Shot in the head, both of them, right behind the ear, as if the killer had been in the backseat. No signs of struggle, so they plainly knew the assassin." Joss shivered. "I've always felt superstitious about that spot. Gloomy place, just right for an ambush by one's enemies. That's why I try not to make any."

"But, but—this changes everything! Who has authority now here?"

"Rather precipitous, old chap, to talk politics before the bodies of the old king and queen are even cold, don't you think? No mourning for the dead? No, I suppose not, not after what this tattered old world has seen. Well, to answer your question: *c'est moi*. As long as I have the support of the others, that is, who can't be bothered to govern."

"And would you—that is, can I convince you—?"

Joss held up a hand. "Didn't I just say I try to please everyone, Tonio?" He dropped his hand to Saint-Ex's knee. "If only everyone could try to please me . . ."

Saint-Ex was aghast, but hid his feelings. After no response, Joss lifted up his hand and sighed melodramatically. "Well, I had to try. You rest now, Tonio, for your grand assault on the future."

At the bedroom door, Joss stopped. "Did I ever tell you what dear little Alice once did? Shot her cheating husband right in the middle of a Paris train station. 'Fastest gun in the Gare du Nord' was what we called her for a while. Damned determined little chit. Especially when her friends are in trouble."

Wilson Airways had been the *de facto* Kenyan flagship line. Cofounded by the same Tom Black who taught Beryl to fly, Wilson possessed the best facilities from which to mount the assault on Basra.

This bright morning, some two weeks after the murders of the Delameres, the runways were once again, as of old, full of planes, their burnished parts gleaming in the sunlight.

Here was the nucleus of Wings over the World, summoned from across Kenya and nearby localities.

Mostly British and French models, hardly any two were alike. There were several different Gipsy Moths and a Puss Moth, as well as a few other De Havilland types, along with an old open-cockpit Breguet-14. An Avro Avian IV stood between a Hanriot-14 and a Caudron-59. Several different Latecoere models flanked a Potez-25. There were even a Piper Cub, a Lockheed, and a Messerschmitt to render the fleet truly international.

And of course, there was Beryl Markham's Vega Gull, the *Messenger II*.

Only the pilots outshone the planes in Saint-Ex's eyes.

In a loose cluster they stood now, at mission's start, leather-jacketed, insouciant, brash, goggles pushed up on their brows. They were his to command, proud vassals, just as he was their sworn leader, selfless in service to the greater whole. In near-symbiotic unison, they would be invincible.

Tom Wilson was present, chatting with his good friends, the husband and wife team of Jim and Amy Mollison. Sydney St. Barbe, former instructor for the London Aeroplane Club, seemed to be trying to seduce the beautiful "Silver Jane" Wynne-Eaton. June Carberry, wife to the man who had tried to kill Saint-Ex, was in conversation with Tom "Woody" Woods. To Saint-Ex's surprise, she had broken away from her husband's cruel rule enough to join in the enterprise.

(Carberry himself had retreated to Seremai to sulk and lick his wounds, and Saint-Ex had breathed a sigh of relief.)

All the pilots had Saint-Ex's approbation. But there were two (well, three, although one female still wasn't speaking to him) who had a claim on his heart. There they stood, living miracles: Henri Guillaumet and Jean Mermoz, his bosom companions from the Aeropostale days.

The two had appeared in Nairobi several days ago, and their reunion with Saint-Ex had been a tearful carnival. When Saint-Ex had been able to ask them how they had gotten here, Guillaumet cavilierly replied, "Why, we mostly walked, after our hunch as to your whereabouts! Is that not so, Jean? Just as I walked out of the Andes that time, Jean and I set out to visit our old friend on foot. The boat from Suez to Mombassa was incidental. And why? We were hungry for his card tricks, of course. That is all."

Saint-Ex had immediately appointed them his second and third in command.

Internationalism was all well and good, but there was—would ever be—only one France!

Now Saint-Ex climbed atop an upended crate and lifted his arms for silence. The massed aviators of Happy Valley turned to face him. In the rear of the crowd, Beryl removed a cigarette and blew smoke rings in his general direction, a sly smile on her lips.

"*Mes amis*," began Saint-Ex, then switched to English. "Today, we make some history, no? Here are some words to think on, from *M'sieu'* Wells."

Lifting his battered copy of *Things to Come*, Saint-Ex recited.

"The first man in this drama says, 'My God! Is there never to be an age of happiness? Is there never to be rest?' His comrade answers, 'Rest enough for the individual man. Too much of it and too soon, and we call it death. But for Man, no rest and no ending. He must go on—conquest beyond conquest. This little planet and its winds and ways, and all the laws of mind and matter that restrain him. Then the planets about him, and at last out across the immensity to the stars. And when he has conquered all the deeps of space and all the mysteries of time—still he will be beginning.'"

Saint-Ex closed the book with a sharp slap. Someone sniffled in the crowd. Then came the bumptious voice of Julian "Lizzie" Lezard.

"I say! Do any of you blokes know which end of this bloody dynamite one lights?"

Each plane was to carry a nonflier supercargo whose job would be to bomb the recalcitrant Arabs into submission. As much as Saint-Ex wished for Wells' nonviolent pacification gas, this was his only option. Even more hapless men must die, before the world could be reborn.

When the laughter died down, Saint-Ex called out, "*Allons!* We fly!"

Jumping down, Saint-Ex headed toward Kiki Preston's plane. The scatterbrained heiress was already onboard, her *joi de vivre* fully restored with access to Lady Delamere's drugs and the prospect of a renewed pipeline.

"Yoo hoo, Soupy! Don't forget the brandy!"

Saint-Ex patted his hip pocket significantly.

"If I find so much as a single hair on your collar when this is over, I'll scratch the eyes out of that little baggage. What I'll do to you will be unspeakable."

Beryl strode beside him, leonine hair catching glints of solar radiance. Saint-Ex pretended not to have heard her.

From her Vega Gull, Jimmy Ballard poked his head out and called, "Aunt Beryl, hurry! We musn't keep our new friends waiting!"

Now Saint-Ex feigned to see Beryl for the first time. "Oh, *Mam'selle* Markham. I am so grateful you could spare us time from your beloved horses. Is it that you wish some final advice on your flying? Do not continue to handle the stick like child with its lollipop—"

"Child with a lollipop! Why, I'll show you!

Grabbing him by the chinstrap of his leather helmet, Beryl tugged Saint-Ex's head down the inch or two necessary to reach her level. Her breath washed across his face with odors of tobacco and coffee. Saint-Ex felt hypnotized, as if facing a carnivore of the veldt. Without warning, she locked her burning lips to his for a full minute, during which their arms enwrapped each other.

When they unclinched, the whole company broke into applause.

"Beryl, my princess."

She poked his ponderous stomach. "Princess! And you're—what? Oh, I have it! My little prince!"

Mairzy Doats

TAPED TO THE WALL above the big atomic-powered Underwood typewriter was a page torn from an issue of *Life* magazine. Held in place by curling masking tape at the corners, the spread was an advertisement for Rheingold beer. Miss Rheingold of 1948—a sexy redhead named Anita Mann—lay on a striped towel on some beach. Sand, surf, umbrellas, gaily colored inflatables, and the like. Surrounded by male admirers, she and her beaus were naked as snakes. So was everyone else frolicking on the sand and amidst the waves. A block of big text floating in the blue sky proclaimed: "My beer is Rheingold—the dry beer!" Pictured in a border at the bottom, along with further text on the virtues of Rheingold, was a squat bottle and thick-lipped can of the product, arranged in a still life with a package of rubbers. Small type read: Brewed by Liebmann Breweries, est. 1837. Miss Rheingold's hair styled by Slipstick Studios. Prophylactics donated by B. F. Goodrich. Remember: Surgeon General Kinsey says, "Only you can help eliminate VD!" There was a sandwich consisting of carbon paper between some bond and onionskin rolled into the loudly humming typewriter. On it was typed author's name, address, and the title of a story:

Henry Gallagher
1212 Flatbush Avenue
Brooklyn, New York

Sex Slave of the Spaceways
by Carter Burrows

The typewriter carriage quivered, as if eagerly waiting for the first word of the story to appear. In fact, the whole typewriter seemed to throb with the power of its small nucleonic motor.

A radio was on, delivering the play-by-play for a Dodgers game. "And now, a word from owner Branch Rickey—" The Dodgers were away from home, on the West Coast, and the broadcast—live by satellite—was poor quality.

A loud belch erupted over the static, followed by the sound of a can—presumably of beer; presumably Rheingold—being crushed.

A man stumbled over to the Philco radio and leaned on the huge cabinet for support. The wood of the cabinet was warm from the Sylvania vacuum tubes that glowed within.

The man wore a white sleeveless undershirt and baggy GI-surplus khakis belted tightly around his slim waist. His feet were bare. His black hair was uncombed, his face stubbled, his dove-grey eyes bleary. He whacked the radio with the flat of his palm, soft at first, then harder. When the reception did not improve, he began to fiddle with the tuner. Stations flowed in and out of audibility, news segueing into commercials into soap operas and comedies. *Allen's Alley*, Spike Jones, *Ozzie and Harriet*, Eddie Cantor and the Mad Russian. A familiar strain of music popped up, and the man stopped playing with the dial.

"I love this fuckin' song," he said drunkenly and turned up the volume. "The Merry Macs, there's a fuckin' band!" He began to jitterbug clumsily around the room, knocking into the shabby furniture, while the singer sang: "Mairzy doats and dozey doats, And little lambsie divey. A kiddley divey too, Wouldn't you?" There was a knock at the door.

"C'mon in!" yelled the man.

The door was opened by a young woman. She wore a light pink angora sweater, madras skirt, pink ankle sox, and saddle shoes. Her moderate length blonde hair was done up like Joan Blondell's.

The man grabbed the woman around the waist and began to whirl her about.

"Little Lambsie Divey, Little Lambsie Divey!" he called out, as if that were her name.

The woman seemed exasperated, but allowed the man to spin her around. Eventually she started to participate willingly. The man swung her legs off the floor and high into the air. Her skirt fell down around her torso, revealing thick white cotton underwear that extended from her navel to well down below her buttocks. He set her upright on her feet and quickly shot her backward between his outspread legs. He spun around to face her, and she jumped up to wrap her legs around his waist. Off-balance, the man staggered backwards under her weight and they fell sideways onto the unmade bed as the song ended.

"Let's screw, Little Lambsie Divey," said the man.

Pushing him away, Little Lambsie Divey said, "Oh, Hank, forget it. You're drunk again, and you know how I feel about that."

"Am not," Hank said petulantly.

Little Lambsie Divey waved at the eight crushed beer cans on the floor. "Who drank these?"

"Little green men."

"Little green men can kiss my ass."

"I bet they'd just love to." Hank lunged at Little Lambsie Divey, but she rolled away off the bed and to her feet, leaving Hank clutching the pillow instead.

Little Lambsie Divey brushed the folds of her skirt into place. Hank lay still with his face in the pillow.

"Oh, Elsie, my head hurts. . . ."

Elsie looked down at Hank unsympathetically. "It's your own fault. I'm going to make some instant Maxwell House for us. Maybe it'll pep you up."

Elsie walked toward the kitchen. On her way past the table that bore the typewriter, she stopped to read the page in the machine. Shaking her head, she toggled off the nucleonic motor—the machine made a diminishing whine, like a dynamo running down—then disappeared into the kitchen.

There was the sound of running water and the soft ignition of a gas flame on the Crosley range, followed by the opening of the door of the Kelvinator refrigerator. In a short time, Elsie returned with two steaming mugs of milk-tinctured coffee.

"Sit up and take this."

Hank slowly assumed as much of a vertical position as he could, until he sat with forearms on his thighs, hands dangling between his knees, spine and head bent forward.

Elsie wrapped his fingers around the mug. "Drink," she ordered. Hank complied. Elsie sat down beside him.

Together they sipped at their coffee in silence for a minute or so.

"Hank. What's the matter?"

"You know darn well."

"The writing?"

"What the hell else?"

"Well, why do you keep on churning out that awful stuff? 'Sex Slaves of the Spaceways.' You know as well as I do that it's all junk."

"There's a market for it, and it pays the rent. Sixty dollars a month, don't forget."

"But it's killing you. Face facts. You hate it."

"Everyone hates their job."

"I don't mind mine so much.

"You were destined for it. Goddamn parents named you after that fuckin' cartoon Borden's cow."

"Advertising is honest work."

"So's sellin' dope."

"Listen, let's forget my job. Why don't you start on that novel you keep talking about?"

Hank looked up with wild eyes. "Novel! Swell . . . Who'd buy it? Not the magazines, not if I do it right. If I get down on paper half of what I've got in my skull, they wouldn't touch it. The editors and readers may not know shit from Shinola, but they know heresy when they read it. And that's what I intend to write. A story of the real future, not one of these wish-fulfillment escapist fantasies set ten thousand years from now. No, my book wouldn't be one of those. For one thing, it'd be told from the perspective of the street. No rich Harvard boys or millionaire's dilettante sons with jutting jaws. The hero'd be a real lowlife, living right here in New York." Hank laughed bitterly. "My God, I know enough about that particular slice of life to get it right. And for another thing, I'd extrapolate from all the real science people are doing right now, stuff that no one's picking up on. There's this guy named Claude Shannon at Bell Labs, just invented something he calls information theory. I hardly understand it myself, but I've got a hunch it's gonna be big. And then there's Linus Pauling's work with the alpha helix—Do you realize that we could be on the verge of understanding the mechanics of inheritance? I know nucleonics is important, but this other stuff— Jesus!"

Hank was staring up at the ceiling now, as if seeing the text of his novel engraved in fiery letters on the flaking plaster. Elsie reached over to hold his hands. She stared at him worshipfully.

"Oh, Hank, I love you so much when you let your real self shine through. Forget whether you'll ever sell the novel or not and just write it!"

"I don't know, Elsie, I just don't know. Sometimes I think I'm a genius, other times I think I'm just restating the obvious, the stuff that's all around us. But if that's so, why can't anyone else see it? My God, it's everywhere." Hank's gaze fell on a copy of *Life* splayed open on the bed, and he grabbed it. "Look, look at this. Man, that Henry Luce has his finger right on the goddamn pulse of the times. This magazine contains more real science fiction than a dozens issues of *Astounding*."

Hank began to riffle the pages. Here was a new fog machine that sprayed the wonder insecticide DDT more efficiently. A smiling girl in a bikini ate her hotdog and sipped her soda pop while immersed in a harmless cloud of the chemical. On another page was the newest product from the Seeburg Corporation: the Select-O-Matic, a nine-foot-long record rack with traveling tonearm for the home that would hold hundreds of shellac disks and play them in any order. Televisons from GE that could actually be viewed in the daylight. Miracle plastics like Koroseal which promised to alter everything from upholstery to underwear.

Slapping the magazine closed, Hank said, "And I haven't even begun to talk about the changing cultural values yet. This new sexual permisiveness that the president and Kinsey have unleashed, the consumerism you advertising folks are breeding, everything feeds on everything else—"

"Oh, Hank, kiss me. . . ."

The crescent dial on the streamlined Philco glowed warmly. Louella Parson's voice issued from the cloth-covered speakers, talking of Broadway and Hollywood. There was the sound of springs creaking, the ripping open of a small Koroseal package. Nat "King" Cole came on after Parsons to sing his latest hit, "Nature Boy." Cole's mellow baritone glided over the sighs and yelps and exclamations.

The sounds of sleep—steady breathing, the slow unconscious shuffle of limbs across sheets, the slight smacking of lips—was counterpointed by the songs of Spike Jones and his orchestra. Wash-tub, handsaw, siren . . .

A polite persistent tapping on the door to Hank's apartment gradually made itself heard in a brief interval of radio silence.

"Hank, Hank, wake up, there's someone knocking."

"Huh, what, what's the matter? Oh, all right, hold on, I'm coming. Jesus, you'd think they'd had a dose of Sal Hepatica or something."

Hank walked to the door. He was barechested, and his unbuckled belt flopped like a dog's tongue.

On the far side of the door stood a black man. Of an age with Hank and Elsie, he had a bright, affable face beneath close-cropped hair. He wore the brown coveralls of the Civilian Service Corps and heavy work boots covered with plaster dust. Embroidered above his breast pocket was his rank and name: Private Dwight Howard.

"Oh, Dwight, it's just you."

"Yowzuh, Mistuh Benny, it's jus' ol' Rochester."

"Dwight."

"Yowzuh?"

"Shut up and come in."

Dwight stepped into the apartment. His sharp eyes took in the accumulated disorder, and he clucked his tongue disapprovingly.

"Henry, you live worse than the folks we're helping up in Harlem. I don't know how you stand it. Hello, Elsie." Elsie looked up from zipping her skirt. "Hi, Dwight." Hank's head emerged from his undershirt. "I live the life of the mind, you ignorant savage. This world is all illusion, *maya*. Means nothing."

"I sho nuff don't dig all them big words, Mistuh Gallagher, but I spoze if'n you say so—"

Hank snorted. "Dwight, did you come here just to bust my balls?"

"No way, Henry. Look." Dwight removed a zippered Koroseal pouch from his pocket.

"Reefer," said Elsie in awe.

"Is it any good?" asked Hank.

"It's the same stuff Robert Mitchum smokes," said Dwight.

"Well, what are we waiting for?"

Hank tossed some cushions to the floor and the friends flopped down. Pretty soon the room was wreathed in bluish smoke and smelled like a Mexican wedding.

"I feel so dreamy," said Elsie. "Like I'm a song by Sinatra."

Everyone nodded in agreement, smiling sleepily.

"This stuff is better than Camels for your T-Zone," said Dwight.

They all burst into giggles and laughter.

Dwight said, "Hey, here's a good one I heard at work today. What's the most popular song in Paris right now?"

"I give up," said Elsie. "What?"

" 'Glow, Little Glowworm.' "

"Oh, that's *sick!*"

"How's the work, Dwight?" asked Hank after he had recovered from laughing and had a few more contemplative puffs.

"Good, good. We're tearing down them slums, man, and building nice new housing for all the poor folks. You know who was there at the opening of the latest units? General Eisenhower and Secretary DuBois. It done my heart good to see a famous white man and a famous black man side by side like that. Couldn't never've happened under no other president, either."

The three were silent for a moment. Then Dwight said, "Henry, why don't you join the CSC? The hitch is only two years, and the change might do you good. I know you're up against some troubles lately. Hell, I ain't seen nothing of yours in the magazines since that thing last year. What was it, 'Raiders of the Rings?' And it weren't no masterpiece."

"Screw you, Dwight. You haven't liked anything of mine since that first story you read that made you come visit me."

Elsie interrupted "Hank, you know something, that might not be such a bad idea. The time away from writing might do you good."

"Yeah, listen to the lady, Henry. Besides, don't you want to vote, it being an election year and all?"

"No. Not under those terms. You know that's the one thing I don't agree with our beloved president on. Restricting the vote to military vets and those who've pulled a hitch in the CSC. It's contrary to the whole history of this country. No, forget it. Me and the CSC just wouldn't jive."

"My throat's dry," said Elsie. "I'm going to get us some beers."

"Good idea."

Elsie went into the kitchen. Her voice, muffled by presence of her head inside the Kelvinator, soon came back to the men.

"Hank, you're out of Rheingold."

"What else is there?"

"Hamm's, Pabst, Red Cap, Blatz . . ."

"Gimme a Blatz."

"I'll take a Hamm's, Elsie."

Elsie returned with three cold bottles and a church key. Just as she finished prying the last lid off, there came a knocking at the door.

"Jesus Christ," said Hank, climbing unsteadily to his feet. "What is this, old home week? Who is it!"

"Western Union."

Everyone flinched with the involuntary reflexes acquired during the recent war years, when the arrival of a telegram usually meant the cold news of death. Hank got unsteadily to his feet and went to open the door.

The man who stood there appeared uncommonly old to be a messenger. A Western Union nametag identified him as H. Miller. Seeming to sense Hank's confusion at his age, the messenger said, "I'm the boss, but we're shorthanded. Besides, I figured I could use the tip more than some kid. I got one wife at home, mister, and an ex screaming for her alimony."

"I'll see what I can do," said Hank, taking the telegram. He retreated into the room and bummed a dollar off Elsie.

"Thanks, buddy," said H. Miller.

Alone again, the three friends stared at the telegram.

"Open it, Hank, open it."

Its envelope slit, the telegram read: GREETINGS FROM THE PRESI-DENT OF THE UNITED STATES OF AMERICA: PURSUANT TO THE PROVI-SIONS OF THE HOAG-WALDO ACT, YOUR SERVICES ARE REQUIRED BY THE COUNTRY. PLEASE BE READY TO LEAVE WITH GOVERNMENT ESCORT AT 17:00 EDT, JUNE 30, 1948. THANK YOU.

"Why, that's only an hour from now," exclaimed Elsie.

Hank appeared shellshocked. "I can't believe this. What could they want a washed-up hack like me for?"

"I don't know, Hank, but you'd better get ready."

Dwight and Elsie escorted Hank into the bathroom. They stuck him under a cold shower and left him to sober up. With the aid of Gillette Blue Blades, Ipana toothpaste, and some Vaseline Hair Tonic, he soon looked as presentable as possible.

Towel wrapped around his midriff, Hank came back into the front room. Elsie had laid out his best clothes: an Arrow Rayon "Sumara Sports" shirt, a pair of of pleated gaberdine trousers, and some argyle sox. Unfortunately, the only footwear Hank owned was a pair of Keds.

As he was tying his shoes the fourth knock of the day sounded.

Dwight went to open the door.

Two Marine MP's stood there, immaculate from their epaulets down to their spit-polished boots. They were obviously hardy veterans, each wearing several voting stripes indicating multiple enfranchisement.

"Mr. Gallagher?" said one of the Marines.

"Nosuh, no way, not me, dat's him, dat's the guy you're looking for, yowzuh."

The troopers entered and closed the door.

"Do the pickup orders specify these other two?" one said to the other.

"Nope."

"What do you think we should do with them?"

"I don't know. I've never seen such a high security code on a pickup before. . . ."

"I say we bring them too. Better safe than sorry."

"OK." The senior MP turned to face the three friends. "Miss, Private Howard—I'm afraid you'll have to accompany Mr. Gallagher. Chances are it'll only be a temporary inconvenience."

Hank spoke up. "Can I at least ask where we're going?"

"I think you're entitled to know that. We're going to the capital."

"Denver?"

"That's right. Mr. Gallagher, I suggest you bring your toothbrush."

Parked in front of the building was a large black Packard, the latest model. Powered by its own nucleonic engine, sporting twin radar cones on its front bumpers, government insignia stenciled discreetly on its doors, it was a sleek and powerful looking machine.

One Marine opened the rear door, while the other got in behind the wheel. Hank, Elsie, and Dwight clambered stiffly inside. Hank's toothbrush, sticking up out of his breast pocket, poked him in the nose.

The door slammed, the second MP climbed inside, and they were off.

The traffic was fairly thick at this hour. Flatbush Avenue was filled with Nashes, Crosleys, Studebakers, Mercurys. All the '48 models were atomic-powered and radar-warned against inadvertant collisions.

The sidewalks were filled with cheerful citizens: fedora-topped men, boys wearing cloth Jughead hats, little girls in frilly pink dresses, women in their open-toed, high- and thick-heeled pumps. Their innocent enjoyment of the beautiful June afternoon contrasted sharply with the chilly atmosphere felt by the three friends as they sped to their unknown appointment with destiny. Hank himself felt too confused even to take his normal pleasure in the see-through Pliofilm blouses worn by the more adventurous followers of fashion.

Looking nervously up through the car window, Hank saw a giant four-engine Pan Am Clipper soaring through the skies.

"Are we driving to Denver?" he thought to ask.

The Marines chuckled. "No way, Mr. Gallagher, it's first-class for you."

Down to the Brooklyn Navy Yards they motored, passing through a security check and finally pulling up alongside a dock.

Floating in the water was an enormous wooden airplane, the creation of Hughes Aircraft and known jocularly as the *Spruce Goose*. Constructed shortly after Hughes had finished filming *The Outlaw* with Jane Russell in 1941, it had been donated by the aviation genius to the US government, and now served as the president's personal transportation.

"They said it'd never fly," one of the MP's commented. "But they didn't reckon with nucleonics."

Hank and his companions now ascended a gangway up into the main passenger compartment of the titanic plane. Once inside, the Marines formally tranferred their charges to the supervision of two members of the Presidential Honor Guard. The Presidential Honor Guard was an elite force consisting of specially selected WAC's chosen for their martial arts skills and combat experience. All over five and a half feet tall, they wore a uniform made of Koroseal fabric and designed by the president himself, notable mainly for its extreme tightness.

"Please be seated and fasten your restraining straps," said one of the curvaceous Guards.

Hank, Elsie and Dwight took three horsehair-covered seats in a row. Designed to hold seven-hundred-fifty passengers, the empty plane—with its miles of aisles stretching forward and back—possessed a ghostly air. Fumblingly, the trio buckled the leather seatbelts around their waists and across their chests and cinched them tight. Even as they did so, they felt the plane began to move.

"Do you think we're going to meet the president himself?" asked Elsie.

"Everything sure points to that," said Hank.

"If we see the man," said Dwight, "I'm going to tell him how he uplifted the race by making DuBois secretary of housing."

"I think we'd best let the president dictate the conversation," said Elsie.

The forces of acceleration steadily increased as the giant plane taxied down the bay, and the passengers were pressed into their seats. The moment of liftoff was plainly perceptible. After a while, when the craft had stabilized, one of the Guards indicated that they could unfasten their restraints and roam about, which they did, marveling at the luxurious appointments of the presidential plane. In an hour or so, the pilot's voice crackled over the onboard PA system.

"We're passing over the ruins of Washington now, which can be seen out the starboard windows."

Hank, Elsie, and Dwight hastened to look. Even from their height, they could see the overgrown crumbled buildings, destroyed in the last-ditch Nazi attack of three years ago: a barrage of V-4's lauched from just off the US coast by German subs.

"Do you think it'll ever be rebuilt?" asked Elsie.

"I doubt it," said Hank. "I hear the president likes Denver too much."

Soon the novelty of the flight transformed itself inexplicably into boredom, and the friends sat desultorily in their seats, each privately wondering what the future was to bring. Elsie held Hank's hand.

Midway through the flight, the WAC's served a rough meal consisting of Treet sandwiches on Wonder Bread and choice of Royal Crown Cola or hot mugs of Ovaltine. Afterwards, Hank and the others dozed off.

They awoke many hours later, feeling considerably refreshed. The Guards were ready with hot coffee, and the news that they would shortly be landing in Denver.

"The *Goose* is too heavy for its landing gear," one WAC told them, "so we'll be touching down in Lake Lyle, an artificial body of water on the outskirts of the city."

Their unseen pilot was soon expertly guiding them to a landing, plowing a huge furrow in the body of Lake Lyle. It was night in Denver. The lights of the unsleeping city, new nerve center of the nation, were visible across the waters as Hank and the others disembarked on shaky legs. Waiting for them on dry land was another government car. They were quickly bundled into the vehicle by the Guards, who joined them in the spacious backseat. Hank found himself pressed between two Koroseal-slick female figures, and the object of a glare from Elsie.

From the plane now stepped the man who had obviously been their pilot. Wearing an aviator's white scarf, leather bomber jacket, and Ray-Ban sunglasses (despite the darkness), he cut an imposing figure. Moving with feline economy of motion, he slipped behind the wheel of the car and quickly brought its powerful nucleonic motor to life.

"OK, cats and kittens," said the pilot in a flippant manner, "hold on to your tails. I was fighting a headwind all the way out here, and it's past the president's bedtime. Can't keep him waiting any longer."

Toggling on their radar and engaging the gears, the pilot roared off in a stench of burning rubber.

Through the streets of the mountain-embraced city they sped. Past the Mint, the houses of Congress, the innumerable buildings of lesser government agencies, until finally arriving at the gates of the the new White House, a huge timber structure built in the style of a Western hunting lodge.

Hank, Dwight, and Elsie soon found themselves sitting nervously in an anteroom outside the Oval Office, flanked by several of the Presidential Guards. Framed and hung on the walls were various newspaper clippings highlighting the president's swift rise to the highest office in the land.

From 1939 was the tiny notice announcing his first electoral victory: winning a seat in the California State Assembly.

The next four years were represented by increasingly larger headlines in the California press, all detailing the bold initiatives the young assemblyman had spearheaded.

In 1943 the brash, antimachine newcomer had staged a fantastic upset over Earl Warren, becoming governor of California.

The very next year he had been chosen as FDR's running mate, as the heroic and crippled wartime leader embarked on his campaign for an unprecedented fourth term.

The ticket combining youth and experience had won handily. Then, tragedy. On April 12, 1945, Roosevelt had died, transforming a man whose first political victory had come a mere six years earlier into the leader of the free world.

The rest was history.

The door to the Oval Office swung partway open, and a Guard poked out her head.

"The president will see Mr. Gallagher and his friends now."

Hank and the others shuffled nervously in. An active televison receiver sat in one corner of the office, tuned softly to a late news broadcast. Edward Murrow was recounting the latest developments in the treason trial of Joseph McCarthy, and the disbanding, by presidential order, of the House Unamerican Activities Committee.

Seated confidently behind his broad desk, looking as bright-eyed and energetic as if he had just wakened from a good night's sleep, sat President Heinlein. A smile bloomed beneath his famous pencil-thin mustache as he stood and came around to shake hands with his guests.

"Citizens, take a seat. I know you're wondering why I've dragged you halfway across the country, so I'll get right down to brass tacks. Mr. Gallagher—I want you to go on a little expedition I'm planning. And God help me if I don't wish it was me going instead of you."

Hank was baffled. "Expedition? Where to?"

"To the Moon, Mr. Gallagher. Old Mistress Luna, that is."

"The Moon? But I thought—"

President Heinlein held up a hand. "I know what you thought, Mr. Gallagher, because it's what everyone thinks. But remember, if everyone 'knows' such-and-such, then it ain't so, by a factor of ten thousand to one. Like the rest of the herd you believed that America's current space capability consists of lofting a few pounds of communications satellite into orbit, that sending human beings into space was too costly and dangerous a proposition. Well, all that would be true, if I had let my hands be tied and done what those spineless boneheads in Congress had told me to do. But fortunately for our country—for the whole race, I believe—I paid no attention to those mollycoddled muddleheads, and therefore our nation now possesses true spaceflight capability. And at a time when we urgently need it."

"Need it? Why?" asked Hank.

"Mr. Gallagher—there are others who also recognized the value of space travel. They saw its utility earlier than we, but only its military applications. And, unburdened by the necessary restrictions of our democratic system, using slave labor, they achieved it. Mr. Gallagher, those people are on the Moon right this minute and preparing to reignite the conflict that almost destroyed civilization, until I reluctantly gave the orders for the radioactive dusting of Europe and Japan. And believe me, despite what you'll hear certain so-called pacifists say, it was not something that I did without grievous moral trepidation. Just because I didn't chuck everything like Einstein did and move to Palestine doesn't mean I didn't have plenty of sleepless nights. But there ain't no such thing as a free lunch, children."

"You can't mean—"

"Yes, Mr. Gallagher. I'm talking about the Nazis. Tojo, Axis Sally, Goerring, perhaps even the head madman himself. They did not perish, as we believed in the confusion of the war's ending, but instead escaped, after fleeing to the base at Peenemunde and the interplanetary rocket awaiting them there. And now they command the high ground above our defenseless heads, where they are undoubtedly feverishly working to complete the mechanism of our destruction. Mr. Gallagher, do you have any notion of what a good-sized chunk of moonrock kicked into our gravity well would do? We have to strike now, mop them up before they can hold the whole planet hostage."

Hank's head was spinning. "All right, Mr. President, I can see all that. But what's my part in such an expedition?"

"I want someone along who really understands the meaning of space for humanity and can chronicle this historic flight in an exciting manner. Mr. Gallagher, I believe you're that man. I've read your stories—yes, don't look so surprised; I almost got into your racket myself once—and I think you've got a real vision of what the future could be, if only humanity exerted its full potential. You're the man I want to record this journey for posterity. The eventual publication of your narrative should serve to awaken the Average Joe to his real birthright."

Here the president winked broadly at his audience. "And in an election year like this one, when I'm facing some stiff competition from Henry Wallace and his upstarts, don't think some of the glory I know you'll invoke won't reflect back on me."

Hank looked to Elsie, and then to Dwight. Returning his gaze to the president, he straightened his back in his chair.

"Mr. President—I accept."

"Good, good, I knew my judgment was sound. Now, there remains the problem of your friends here." The president leaned over and spoke into an intercom. "The files on D. Howard and E. Long, please."

Shortly a woosh and a thump signaled the arrival, via pneumatic tube, of the papers in question. President Heinlein removed the capsule from the delivery tube and extracted two folders.

"Hmm, yes, yes, good parents, commendable civic sense—I think they'll do. Private Howard, Miss Long, would you care to accompany your friend Mr. Gallagher on your country's business?"

Elsie and Dwight nodded solemnly, and the president flashed his beneficent smile once more.

"Wonderful. Now, I realize a motion to adjourn is always in order, but I would just like to introduce a few of your traveling companions who happen to be waiting next door. Including the two men you'll be entrusting your lives to."

The president pushed a button and into the room stepped three people: the man who had flown Hank, Elsie, and Dwight from New York, accompanied by a younger sidekick who could have been his brother. With them was a gorgeous red-haired woman stylishly dressed.

Indicating the original pilot, the president said, "Citizens, let me introduce twenty-five-year-old Commander Chuck Yeager, an ace pilot during the war and now a member of the US Space Authority. He'll be assisted by a local Denver boy, Copilot Neal Cassady. I myself found Neal four years ago, when he was an eighteen year old doing time in reform school for car theft. When I heard how that boy could drive, I knew he was the kind of material we needed in the Space Authority. You can count on their reflexes to bring you safely through the perils of the Heaviside Layer, the Van Allen Belts, and meteors thick as flies around a hog. And I think you'll probably recognize this lovely lady as Miss Rheingold, Anita Mann. Miss Mann is going to be representing the USO on this mission."

Everyone shook hands all around, although Hank was singled out with a kiss from Miss Rheingold, who whispered something in his ear that caused him to blush and Elsie to scowl.

With a gesture the president dismissed the flyboys and entertainer. "Any other questions, before our *ave atque vale?*"

"When do we leave?" asked Hank.

"Tomorrow. Now, if that does it, you'll be shown to your quarters for a good night's rest. Remember, as my fellow Missourian General Truman said, just before he bought the farm at Verdun thirty years ago: 'You can have peace. Or you can have freedom. Don't ever count on having both at once.'"

With the stirring words of President Heinlein ringing in their ears, the trio went off to a surprisingly untroubled sleep, considering all the excitement they had been through.

In the morning they were conducted once again to the floating *Spruce Goose*. This time the plane was loaded to capacity with a complement of soldiers, composed of equal numbers of men and women, from all branches of the Armed Forces, including the Presidential Guard. Hank and the others found three seats left untaken and buckled themselves in with the familiarity of longtime passengers.

"I don't see no other black folks," said Dwight. "It appears I'm going to be the sole representative of Negritude on this mission. It's a heavy burden."

"I'll try to convey your importance adequately in my manuscript," said Hank drily.

Elsie was staring intently ahead at the far bulkhead, behind which Commander Yeager and Copilot Cassady were even now going through their pre-takeoff sequence.

"I've never seen anyone so self-assured as that Neal Cassady," she said dreamily, but with a calculating gleam in her eye.

Now it was Hank's turn to glare. Dwight just laughed.

The plane lifted off, a bit more reluctantly with its full load, and began winging west. Hank failed to learn their destination from his neighbors and resigned himself to patient waiting.

After many hours of flight, several Presidential Guards began circulating, dispensing fur-lined jackets obviously intended for arctic conditions.

Out the windows only ocean was visible. Then in the distance appeared a white smudge. Closer, closer, until it resolved itself into a huge floating iceberg. Even at this distance, it could be seen that the iceberg's top was artificially level and cluttered with structures. One structure towered above the others. Soon, this titanic pillar resolved itself into a missile shape briefly visible. Then the top of the iceberg rose out of view as the plane dropped toward the surface of the ocean for a landing. Splashdown was swiftly followed by an orderly exodus. Small boats ferried the plane's passengers to the floating base.

Riding with Neal Cassady, the wind pushing back their hoods, Hank heard the copilot explain to Elsie, who was holding his arm and hanging on his every word, "The atomic jets are so hot, they'll melt the whole damn ice cube when we blast off! A 'berg was the only way to go."

Soon they were atop the tremendous iceberg and inside a chilly Quonset hut. There, they underwent a brief lecture by a trio of ex-Nazi scientists named Oberth, von Braun, and Dornberger, who explained certain essential facts about space travel. The lack of gravity, cosmic rays, how to deal with emergency hull punctures. A space suit was brought out and its use demonstrated. Weighing five hundred pounds, the suit looked like a deep-sea diving apparatus. Bulbous Koroseal joints at elbows and knees, two air cannisters on the back from which thick hoses fed into a transparent helmet that looked like a Victorian belljar, clumsy mitten-type gauntlets, a radio antenna that terminated in a loop.

Then, with scarcely a second to collect their thoughts, after changing their civilian clothes for utilitarian coveralls and magnetic shoes, and receiving a complimentary pack of Old Gold cigarettes and one of condoms, Hank and the others found themselves ready to board the rocket.

As they filed across the frozen surface of the glacier, the rocket loomed huge over them. A dull grey monolith tapering to a needle point, it rested on three streamlined fins that emerged from three-quarters of the way up its hull. It was as massive and brooding as Mount Rushmore, the obvious apex of twentieth-century technological progress. A single central jet protruded from its bottom. A gangway extended from its open hatch.

Once onboard, the trio were conducted to adjacent couches, thickly padded to accomodate the tremendous gee-forces that would build up during the launch. Strapped down, Hank still managed to reach out a few inches and brush Elsie's similarly outstretched fingers.

Elsie turned her head to gaze at Hank.

"I'm sorry if I made you jealous with Neal, Hank. I don't know what came over me. Probably just the way that pinup girl Anita was practically draping herself all over you. Why, you know I could never fall for anyone but you. If it was anything, it was just a schoolgirl crush or something. Why, I think you're the most important man on this mission. Imagine having the responsibility for preserving the details of this historic trip for all of posterity."

"And you're the most important woman, Elsie. At least to me."

"Man, I think I'm gonna throw up," said Dwight.

"We're not even moving yet," Hank reminded him.

"I know."

Over the shipboard loudspeakers a countdown was initiated, the calm voice of Neal Cassady reciting the numbers. At the mark of three, with an awesome roar of atomic flames, the motors came alive, activated by the capable hands of Commander Yeager. The iceberg had been abandoned by all remaining personnel, who had departed in the *Spruce Goose*. It was time for takeoff.

The growl of the nucleonic motors surged, and the rocket began to rip itself away from the grip of the Earth. At the height of the gee-forces, Hank and his friends blacked out.

When they came to they were weightless. Looking around, they saw others rising from their couches and so quickly freed themselves.

From the intercom came the voice of Commander Yeager. "Good ol' Mama Earth's behind us now, folks. ETA on a nest of Nazi rats approximately thirty-six hours from now. I don't know about the rest of you, but your pilot's gonna have a bulb of java. Keep your sights clean and smoke 'em if you got 'em."

There was a rousing cheer from the spaceship troopers, and as the comely Presidential Guards began to pass out the promised drinks, the cabin filled with clouds of tobacco smoke.

The rest of the trip passed in a dream for Hank. So busy making copious notes for his narrative, he hardly noticed when Elsie disappeared for a time, coincidentally when Copilot Cassady was also nowhere to be found. When Dwight brought Elsie's absence to Hank's attention, Hank was still too elated to let it trouble him.

"This is the future we're living in now, Dwight. Morals have to change with the times, not just technology."

"You're some kind of saint, man."

Hank smiled. "Hardly, Dwight. But I figure that after what Anita and I just did in the spacesuit locker, I can hardly complain about Elsie having a little fun. Besides, I kind of like that Neal Cassady too. He seems like a real man's man."

Dwight scratched his head and grinned slyly. "I think I'm gonna talk to Miss Anita and ask her opinion about improvin' relations between the races."

Hank tossed Dwight his remaining safeties, which floated slowly through the cabin air. "Don't forget these, buddy."

At midpoint, the mighty rocket turned majestically for deceleration, so that its jet pointed toward their destination. The ghostly mottled white sphere that had steadily swelled to fill the two-foot-thick vitreous windows of the control room was replaced by the dwindling blue ball of their home planet. The sight, witnessed by the passengers in groups of ten, stirred each to the depths of his or her soul. Even the mathematician squad, perpetually busy with their flashing sliderules, calculating and recalculating the complicated ballistics of their course, stopped to stare with powerful emotions tugging at them.

After this, there was little of note for Hank to record, save for a close brush with a rogue asteroid, from which only the youthful reflexes of Yeager and Cassady, honed by hours of eluding Messer-schmidts and Denver cops, served to save them.

At last they were in orbit around the Moon and strapped down to their couches in anticipation of landing. The intercom between passengers and crew was purposefully left open, so that the passengers could hear the progress of their descent.

"Locked on to the coordinates for Schickelgruber's base, Chuck."

"Adopt evasive maneuvers, Neal. No telling what defenses they've got."

"Check. Say, radar doesn't reveal any sizable structures where the Boss told us they'd be."

"They're probably dug into the rock, Neal. With any luck we'll set down right on top of 'em and burn the nest out. Save our boys and girls any hand-to-hand work."

"Yeah, but what about their rocket? I don't get a reading on no vessel—"

Slowly the American rocket lowered itself like a cautious over-weight matron to the gritty Selene surface. Hank felt a small weight returning to him. Only when the atomic motors had been shut off did everyone realize how they had formed a permanent background noise to their trip. The soldiers jumped to their feet, ready to don their vacuum gear as they had practiced on the trip out, and engage the Nazis in combat. They were halted by the voice of Commander Yeager.

"Incoming transmission, folks. And it's on the presidential channel. Hold on, I'm routing it to all cabin television screens."

The grainy black-and-white face of President Heinlein appeared. Behind him was the Presidential Seal.

"Citizens and soldiers, congratulations on your safe arrival on the Moon.

"It is with the deepest sympathy—and at the same time, the profoundest happiness—that I now wish to inform you that you will not be returning.

"The experimental material lining your jet tube has deteriorated during the trip to the point of uselessness. Unfortunately, it's a little problem our scientists have yet to solve. Were you to reignite the jets, the ship would in all likelihood explode. However, the nucleonic motors themselves will still serve faithfully as a power source for your colony.

"That's correct. Your colony.

"Citizens, there are no Nazis on the Moon. They did indeed all die in the dustings. That particular threat no longer faces us. However, a much more subtle, yet equally powerful one does.

"That threat is inertia. Sheer stubborn human laziness. Sated with the material comforts of our postwar economy, the average citizen has no interest whatsoever in funding—much less participating in—any attempt to colonize space. Like neutered tomcats, they are content to sit at home. Only through the ruse of a Nazi moonbase was I able to get secret funding for your trip. And now, lest you think I was shirking my share of duty by not accompanying you, I want to remind you that I'll have to face my own public inquisition back home, once this news leaks out, as I fully intend it to.

"But anything I have to endure was worth it. Humanity cannot keep all its eggs in one basket. The solar system must be populated. With the nuclear death of Earth during some future war now a distinct possiblity, we need the elbow room, to disperse our innate aggressions.

"All of you have been secretly chosen for your skills and genetic pedigree. You are prime colonist material, the equivalent of the pioneers who settled our own American West. Success is in your makeup. You will not fail.

"If you check your cargo holds, you'll find they've been stocked with everything you'll need until you get on your feet.

"So, Earthmen—or should I say, Loonies?—start digging your new homes!

"I'm sure there'll be another ship along in a few years, once the public wises up."

President Heinlein disappeared from the screen, to be replaced by a test pattern.

Elsie sighed. "Well, Hank, I guess we're really living that future you were so excited about now."

Hank threaded his fingers through his Vaseline-tonicked hair. "I guess."

Dwight seemed unperturbed. "Seems like Miss Anita and me still got a chance to hit it off."

The televison screens suddenly flared into life.

Commander Yeager must have managed to pick up a weak commercial broadcast.

It was the Merry Macs, singing "Mairzy Doats." "If the words sound queer, And funny to your ear, A little bit jumbled and jivey, Sing, 'Mares eat oats,' And, 'Does eat oats,' And, 'Little lambs eat ivy!'"

Campbell's World

CAMPBELL WAS DEAD.

Even now, sitting here listening to one tearful, soulful eulogy after another, I couldn't quite believe it. The man had been too big to die, there had been too much life in him. He had bestrode the SF field like a Titan for so long, had given so much, that his departure seemed unthinkable, leaving a gaping hole in the universe. It was so unfair that it was all I could do to sit here quietly when what I really wanted to do was rage—

I stopped myself. What was I thinking? Campbell surely wouldn't have wanted me to feel this way. He had had no fear of death, no regrets at its approach. In his last days, sensing that his time on this plane was limited, he had calmly discussed his passing, seeking to deindividualize it by referring to it as "The Death," establishing his common mortality, shared with all humanity. . . .

My eyes found a meditative focus, a big omega-shaped floral wreath with a banner bearing Campbell's name and dates: 1901-1987. I started up my mantra, which Campbell himself had given me, and in a few minutes I felt a measure of acceptance and peace wash over me.

So many people owed Campbell so much. Not least of all the eighteen-year-old Navaho boy named Jake Highwater, concealed now inside the body and mind of this suddenly weeping old man.

It was September 30, 1937. The date is engraved forever on my heart.

I stood outside the Street and Smith building in Manhattan. It was a mildly warm day, but that didn't explain the sweat drenching my best shirt and ill-fitting suit, or my clammy hands, which clutched a large manila envelope secured with a string clasp. My body was not reacting to the heat, but rather to a large case of nerves.

In a few minutes, if all went well, I would be standing in the presence of the new editor of *Astounding Stories*, a man named Campbell who had just taken over from the venerable F. Orlin Tremaine (who was all of thirty-eight years old at the time). And I would be trying—if I still had a voice or a thought in my head by then—to sell him a story I had written.

I had been reading *Astounding* for four years, ever since Street and Smith had resurrected the old Clayton pulp. First, just the odd issue or two which had filtered into the reservation back home in Arizona. Then, once Uncle Redbird—who worked at the Navy Yards—invited Ma and me to come live with him in Brooklyn, I had managed to get all the back issues I had missed and keep up with the new ones as well.

I knew nothing about this Campbell; he hadn't even produced an issue by which I could get some sense of him and his tastes. I had only learned of the changeover by accident, when I had called last week and asked to speak to Tremaine.

"Mr. Tremaine is editorial director for the whole Street and Smith chain now. Which magazine does your business concern?"

"Uh, *Astounding*—"

"The man in charge there now is Mr. Campbell," the switchboard operator informed me briskly. "Shall I put you through?"

The news totally unhinged my carefully planned speech praising Tremaine's work.

"Uh, no," I stammered, "that's OK. I mean—"

And then I hung up.

Where or how I had found the courage to show up a week later on the actual doorstep of the magazine I adored, I cannot now recall. It had taken me months after I had written my story just to work myself up to call Tremaine, whom I felt I somehow knew. Now, I had inexplicably nerved myself up to this frontal assault on a complete stranger.

Suddenly conscious of the damage my sweaty hands were doing to my rolled-up manuscript, I tucked it under one arm, straighted Uncle Redbird's borrowed tie, and went in.

The elevator operator brought me up. The magnificent thump of the presses soon surrounded me, for much of Street and Smith's production was done right here, amidst the editorial offices.

Soon I was standing in front of Campbell's secretary. The name-plaque on her desk identified her as Miss Erdman, and she was exotically gorgeous. Black hair in a roll above her ears, pug nose, wide smiling mouth. I couldn't place her features, but they were definitely not one hundred percent Anglo. Dressed in a white suit, she seemed to be not much older than I, and I fell instantly in love.

"May I help you?"

"I—I'd like to see Mr. Campbell. That is, if he's not too busy."

"He is rather pressed for time. May I ask what it's in reference to?"

"I've got a story to show him."

Her smile widened, then politely shrank to businesslike dimensions. "Oh, well, in that case . . . Would you mind waiting?" She indicated a seat close to her desk.

"No, of course not." I was prepared to wait all day, so long as she was there.

People came and went, bustling or leisurely. The glorious, glamorous Miss Erdman dealt with one and all efficiently and with good humor. In between, we somehow began to talk.

She was a dance student with someone named Martha Graham, working here only to pay the bills. Her family was rich—she had recently taken a round-the-world cruise with them—but she preferred not to rely on their money. Anyhow, they lived in Hawaii, where she had been born, so she was on her own here.

And what, I asked, did she think of her new boss?

Her face was transfigured as if by sunlight, and my heart sank. It was plain that no man would ever come up in her estimation to this mysterious new editor.

"Oh, Mr. Campbell is just wonderful. He's so smart! He has his masters from Columbia, you know—medieval studies. He's been to Europe, met Joyce and Mann and Sylvia Beach. But his main interest isn't really literature, it's—Well, if I mention that he reads Sanskrit and knows Krishnamurti—?"

Her esoteric clues left me completely in the dark, and my face must have shown it.

"Oh, well, never mind. You'll find out as soon as you meet him, everyone does. He just kind of radiates this ancient power, a power of ideas—"

I wanted to say something about the new editor's interests. But all the names she had tossed out so devoutly meant nothing to me, and I was ashamed to admit it. Frankly, I was also kind of jealous to hear this Campbell praised so effusively by this beautiful woman.

"I suppose he's not much of a science man then?" I said, hoping to cut him down to size.

"Oh, no," Miss Erdman shot back, "just the opposite. He thinks science is very important. He wouldn't have gotten the job otherwise. And just a few years ago he spent months as an apprentice to the biologist Ed Ricketts. They went up the West Coast, all the way from Carmel to Sitka, Alaska, collecting intertidal fauna. That's when he became friends with John Steinbeck. And Mr. Campbell is very well read in history too, if you count that a science."

I made one last stab. "I guess he's one of those egghead professor types then."

Miss Erdman giggled. "Not entirely. He was on the Columbia track team. He came within two seconds of setting a world record for the half-mile."

I knew when I was beaten. This Campbell sounded like some kind of god. Sitting back in my chair, I assumed a crestfallen silence.

Hours passed. People with appointments went in and out of Campbell's office, but I never saw the man himself. Until just around four o'clock.

A tall fellow in his mid-thirties appeared at the inner door. Copiously wavy-haired, large-nosed, strong-jawed, he reminded me of the big, bluff Irish cops in my neighborhood.

But that first impression was partially dispelled when he spoke in a cultivated voice, firm yet compassionate.

"Miss Erdman, I'm afraid I won't be taking any more appointments today—"

I shot to my feet and words rushed involuntarily forth.

"But sir, I've been waiting all afternoon—!"

Campbell opened his mouth, and I knew he was going to fob me off. But then his gaze happened to fall on my belt.

The buckle was a massive tourquoise-studded one from the reservation.

The next words out of Campbell floored me, for he greeted me in Navajo.

Sensing my utter confusion, Campbell advanced. Putting an arm around my shoulder, he smiled, then turned to address his secretary.

"As I was saying, Miss Erdman, this young man is going to be my last appointment of the day."

Miss Erdman flashed that bewitching smile. "I'll make sure you're not disturbed."

And then I was inside *Astounding's* inner sanctum, behind the door with the fresh goldleaf spelling out the new editor's name.

Joseph Campbell.

After ushering me to a leather-padded seat, Campbell perched himself on the edge of his desk, one foot resting on the floor. A runner's muscles defined themselves beneath the fabric of his trouser legs.

At last I found my voice. "You speak Navajo—"

Campbell laughed, a hearty booming. "Hardly. Just a few words. Picked them up in my reading. Been reading about Amerindians since I was a kid. You know Elmer Gregor? No? Excellent writer on your people. I got to meet him when I was young. As a lark, we used to communicate at the dinner table in Indian sign language. Drove my folks nuts! What a grand, living, breathing introduction to the subject!"

Suddenly, I wanted nothing more than to read this Elmer Gregor, even though he would doubtlessly have nothing to tell me except second-hand information about my own tribe! But that's just how it was with Campbell. His excitements were contagious. Whatever topic was uppermost in his mind and conversation would soon dominate any listener.

Campbell zeroed in on my manuscript, which I had forgotten I was holding. "That something you want me to read?"

Wordlessly I passed it over. Campbell retreated to the far side of his desk and sat.

"'Mother to the World.' Nice, very nice."

He picked up a red pencil. "You don't mind if I mark it up a bit, do you? I'm afraid that underlining is my form of meditation."

I hurried to shake my head no, and he smiled and got to work.

Twenty minutes later, he looked up. His dark eyes bored into mine, and I felt naked.

"This is based on one of the legends of Estsanatlehi, 'the woman who changes,' is it not? The one where she creates mankind from slivers of her own flesh . . ."

I knew now I was in the presence of a shaman. This man could read souls.

Gulping, I tried to reply. "Yuh-yeah. I mean, yes, sir, it is. You see, I thought that the old legend sounded like modern tissue culturing. So I imagined that there was only one woman left alive after some kind of plague, and she was a scientist and had to recreate the race and she—"

Campbell held up a hand to stop me from reciting the whole story. "Your instincts are good, Jake," he said, taking my name from the first page of my manuscript. "Don't apologize." He handed the story back to me, obviously a rejection, and I stood to go.

"Wait a minute, son. Aren't you interested in how much we're paying?"

I froze. "Paying?"

"As soon as you make those changes I've penciled in, that is. Retype it, bring it back, and I'll cut the check. One hundred dollars, two cents a word. We'll probably run it in the July issue."

Nerveless, I dropped back into the chair.

"There's only one catch. You've got to listen to a little lecture first."

I snapped my jaw shut, and dumbly nodded.

Campbell stood and began to pace the office. He was plainly reciting a well-rehearsed speech—at the same time that he was using my reactions to refine and strengthen it.

"You see, Jake, I took this job over an offer to teach at Sarah Lawrence college—even though it pays much less—for one reason and one reason only. Because I want a public forum for my ideas, a place to stand where I can use the lever I think I've discovered in order to move the world in the direction of greater harmony.

"Our culture is in trouble, Jake. We're stuck smack dab in the middle of a stage that Spengler has identified as one of crisis and disintegration. Like the moraine at the end of a glacier, all the old beliefs are piled up around us, rootless and withering. This is a time when those old beliefs are dying—and new beliefs have the potential to be born. These replacement beliefs—these myths, to use an old-fashioned term which I much prefer—will partake of both old and new. They can be creative reworkings of old myths, like your story, or brand-new images never before unearthed, but which somehow ring as true as the old ones.

"These new myths are going to have to take modern science heavily into account. You cannot deal with the world of A.D. 2000 with the science of 2000 B.C. That's the part that comes from the head. But the most important part of these new myths—the oldest, eternal kernal—is going to have to come from the heart. If the stories I envision and want to print are going to have any chance at reaffirming and restructuring the lives of *Astounding's* readers—and through them, the civilization at large—then they're going to have to arise from somewhere deep inside the writers.

"I can't afford to publish anything inauthentic, any stories that don't arise from deeply felt wellsprings within the author's own breast. I'm talking about getting in touch with the archetypes that exist inside all of us, ancient figures of wisdom and magic, deities and guides."

Over the next five decades, I was to hear this speech or some variant of it more times than I could count. It would never fail to move me, sometimes rekindling inspiration that I thought had died for good. But never would it mean more to me than this first time. I was mesmerized, imprinting utterly on Campbell's vision.

"There's going to be a clean sweep here at the magazine," Campbell continued. "Hackwork will no longer find a home here, and I'm changing the name slightly with the next issue as a subtle indication of it. The subtitle will no longer read 'stories of science-fiction' but rather 'stories of SF.' And that abbreviation will stand for 'sacred fiction' or 'symbolic fiction' as much as it stands for 'science fiction.'

"Any of the older writers who can make the transition will be welcome. But I really don't expect many of them to understand what I want, or be capable of providing it. That's why I have to find new writers, men like yourself, Jake. Writers from every possible culture, ones who are open to their inner voices, who haven't fossilized yet. And not just men, for Athena's sake! I want women in these pages! They're half the human race, for crying out loud! I want the actual nurturing milk of their tits on the pages of *Astounding*!"

I must have blushed, for Campbell toned down his rhetoric.

"Jake, we have a chance with this magazine to put Western civilization back in touch with the essential ground of all phenomena, the void out of which everything arises. We can get this messed-up century back on track. But I can't do it alone. Can I rely on your help?"

At that point, I would have gladly descended like Orpheus to Hades itself for Campbell. I jumped to my feet and grabbed his hand.

"You can count on me, Mr. Campbell!"

His questing mind had already moved on to other matters. "Great, great, great," he intoned, leading me out and hailing his secretary. "Jean, why don't you go ahead and draw up contracts for Mr. Highwater's story. I'm sure he'll have it revised for us by next week."

Miss Erdman—Jean—jumped up, squealing with glee, then hugged me and kissed me on the cheek.

Did I say Hades? You could've added in the hells of Dante, Milton, and Bunyan too.

This was the start of my fifty-year association with *Astounding* and Joseph Campbell and his quest to remake the world nearer to his heart's desire. Whether he—we—truly succeeded or not, I have no idea. All I know is that those five decades passed like one of Vishnu's half-hours.

The July 1938 issue of *Astounding* in which my first story did eventually run is generally acknowledged to be the beginning of Campbell's finest period, if only for the electrifying newness of it all. With vivid mythic SF stories by Baker, Suzuki, Orzbal, Chen, and Chaiwallah, he set the exact tone he had been aiming for, a kind of global voice that spoke intimately out of mankind's past to its common future. The issues following, with work by Mahfouz, Minh, Sienki-wicz, Okri, and others maintained that standard. I began to visit Campbell weekly. We were sketching out a series of stories based on the Navajo myths about the two brothers, Nayenezgani and Tobadz-istsini, the famous slayers of monsters. My two heroes were interplanetary adventurers who journeyed from world to world helping the inhabitants deal with the strange life-forms on each. Although there was plenty of violence—Campbell had nothing against violence, viewing it as integral to our hominid origins—I tried to introduce an element of diplomacy and compromise that I thought made a nice change from the way aliens were usually handled—and a switch from the way my people had been handled by the whites.

And throughout, I was treated to Campbell's views on everything from movies ("didactic pornography without any spirituality") to sexual mores ("strictly determined by culture") to writing ("You can write a sentence the way you would have written it last year, or you can write it the way you're thinking now.") Over the years, as Campbell's enormous widespread and ongoing reading was filtered through his exuberant talk and down to me, I received an education equal to any college degree.

Much to my joy, Campbell seemed to regard me as a son, especially when he heard my own father was dead of alcoholic kidney failure.

"Yes, yes," he said, regarding me keenly, "the orphan, the journey, the old patterns of the monomyth repeat forever. . . ."

After that, he was even kinder, if such were possible.

Early in 1939, two important things happened. Campbell married Jean Erdman, who was almost twenty years younger than he. I didn't realize how deep my feelings were for her—feelings she had never shown a sign of reciprocating—until the day of their wedding, when, halfway through the ceremony, I had to get up and leave, hot tears suddenly sluicing down my face.

But I was only twenty and healed fast. Or so I thought. Jean remained at her job, and I managed to chat breezily with Mrs. Campbell each time I visited. Nor were my respect and admiration for Joe altered either.

Admittedly, the marriage was a big change for all of us. But it was only a personal one. Larger forces, however, were at work in the world.

One day I walked into Campbell's office and found him absorbed in that day's *Tribune*. Noticing me, he tossed the paper down with a snort of disgust.

"What do you make of the situation in Europe, Jake?" I mumbled the conventional wisdom, about how Hitler could be placated with a little territory. But Campbell vehemently disagreed.

"No, Jake, the man is a sorceror, a black magician. To anyone who knows the myths, it's plain as day. Don't forget where Faust hailed from. No, Hitler won't rest content until he's amassed all the power he can grab. Unless someone puts a halt to his schemes, I predict that the world will soon be plunged into chaos. It will be *Gotterdammerung*."

With the cockiness of an apprentice, I said, "And you and *Astounding* are the only ones who can stop him, right?"

Campbell knocked his chair over as he shot to his feet. "That's it! Jake, you're a genius!"

That very night, he was on a train for Washington.

I never learned till years later how he got an interview with FDR. Turned out one of his old Columbia professors had become an undersecretary in the administration, and this ex-teacher managed to swing it. Nor did I ever fully understand how Campbell convinced the president to finance his mad scheme. But knowing how persuasive my editor could be, I could well imagine the oratory he used.

However it happened, two months later *Astounding* was publishing a German edition.

None of the stories, however, were translations. They were all originals, composed in part by Campbell and in part by a group of German expatriates—including a psychologist named Jung—whom he had assembled. And the fictions were all cleverly and subliminally crafted with one goal in mind: toppling Hitler and the Nazis.

I read a few of the stories in English, but they meant nothing to me aside from the surface plotting. I remember that one in particular was all about piglike aliens, and I thought it quite inferior to my own series. I mentioned this to Campbell.

"Of course they don't push your buttons, Jake. They're slanted toward the Teutonic mind. The monomyth takes the form of *Elemen-*

targedanken specific to each culture. But believe me, these stories are hitting the German people like bullets."

And of course he was right, as I learned with a shock when the news of Hitler's assassination reached America. The wire photo of the dead assassin was just detailed enough for me to see the top of an issue of the German *Astounding* projecting from his coat pocket.

The Nazi Party, falling prey to internecine squabbling, managed to remain in power for a few months, but were soon deposed semipeacefully by Christian Democrats (who used the Grail as their party symbol). Without support, the Fascists in Spain and Italy soon went under too. Europe settled down to its usual somnolence, and we anticipated doing the same.

But it was not to be.

Joe, Jean, and I were celebrating the downfall of the Nazis with a bottle of champagne in the office when the phone rang. Campbell picked up.

"Hello? Yes! Yes, sir. Will do!"

He hung up, looking as dazed as I've ever seen him. "That was the president. He wants to see a mockup of a pan-Asian issue of the magazine as soon as possible." We finished our drinks and got to work.

It was about one hundred issues later that Joe decided on his own to initiate yet another foreign version of the magazine. This time, because conditions in the target country were relatively safe, he went abroad for a few months to supervise the new operation personally.

But he left Jean at home.

Back a week early from Leningrad, he walked in on us naked in his bed.

Overwhelming mortification and guilt swept over me. I couldn't even remember how I had ended up here. It had been as if I were moving in a dream. How could I have betrayed my closest friend in this way—?

"Joe," I began, looking to an unperturbed Jean for support, "I don't know how to explain—"

Campbell laughed softly and apparently without bitterness or irony. "Jake, I never told you, did I, that 'SF' could stand for 'shakti fiction' as well. Jean is my *shakti*, the living embodiment of feminine power, my fount of endless energy. There is an alchemical marriage between us which you could never disrupt. You can only share in her limitless abundance. I told her I thought a liason would be good for your writing, and she agreed."

And then he hung up his hat and joined us.

Six months later the neo-Czarist Revolution broke out. Six months after that, Stalin was hanging from a lamppost in Red Square.

The following years were the busiest of my life. The strange relationship among Campbell, Jean, and I did indeed spur my writing. I began a series of stories about futuristic weather control, based on the myths of the Navajo rain and sun gods, Tonenili and Tsohanoai.

Readership of *Astounding* in America was now second only to that of *Life* magazine, an unheard-of stature for a fiction pulp. We went glossy and upped the pay rate several times. We attracted people like Aldous Huxley, who let us serialize his *The Perrenial Philosophy*. Campbell filled a goodly number of pages himself, with his rambling survey of mythology, history, and science entitled *The Outline of Everything*.

Campbell's competitors had tried to emulate him, with mixed results. Mostly, they failed, lacking his purity of vision and motives. There was no one who could touch him.

No one in the field of literature, that was.

Campbell was called before McCarthy's HUAC in September 1953, on charges of "promulgating foreign fairy tales meant to subvert American values." He left us with a smile on his face. It proved to be McCarthy's final month in office.

I have never seen a man so utterly humiliated and destroyed by "mere" metaphor before or since. The televised hearings eventually captured the attention of the entire nation, which watched raptly as Campbell turned the bullying senator into a pile of jello. Every absurd and strident charge McCarthy made was met slantwise with an appropriate anecdote or tale culled from Campbell's immense stock. Like some modern yet ancient Uncle Remus or Homer or Ovid, Campbell rebutted and ridiculed every tactic and assault with humor and wisdom. It was like watching a martial arts master turn every blow of his opponent back on the attacker. By the end of the hearings,

McCarthy could barely frame a complete sentence while Joe was cool as Shadrach in the furnace.

The confession they found on McCarthy's corpse, though splattered with the senator's self-shattered brains, was still readable enough to bring Vice President Nixon down with the senator on treason charges.

As the sixties dawned, I found the vein of my writing petering out. I had dealt with every significant Navajo myth, and no other material appealed to me—or could, by Campbell's theory. Even Jean and her attentions couldn't inspire me, and I soon stopped seeing her, fearing that one kind of impotence would breed another.

My block wasn't helped by the changes at the magazine. First, Campbell actually renamed it entirely: it was now called *Ananda Mythic Fiction Mythic Fact*, after the Sanskrit word for "bliss." The masthead bore the motto "Transparent to transcendance." I was against the change and felt that the magazine I had fallen in love with so long ago was no more. Campbell also started preaching global unity, which I thought fine in theory, but not practicable. I was beginning to be more concerned about the plight of my own people, and how they lagged behind the rest of the country.

Then there were all the new writers coming in, young kids like Ballard and Delany and Zelazny who had been raised on the work of me and my peers, and were taking SF—or MF, as they now referred to it— in new, strange directions I didn't entirely understand. Campbell kept current somehow, and encouraged me to continue, but I just couldn't.

The day I told him I was leaving New York is almost as sharp in my mind as that day in '37, although they stood over twenty-five years apart.

"So it's back to the reservation for you, Jake? Well, I can't say I blame you. A man needs to get back to his roots at a certain point. You've got to cross the return threshold with the knowledge you've gained and give it to those who need it. Anyway, you're still young— compared to a greybeard like me. I'm sure you'll accomplish everything you set out to do."

"It's about time I used some of that obscenely high money you've paid me over the years, Joe. I'm going to plow it back into improving conditions for my people. I've got a lot of plans. . . ."

I tapered off. There was nothing else to say.

Campbell and I shook hands, and I walked out.

There was a young girl at Jean's desk—I forget her name now. Jean had left the job once she and Joe got rich, to concentrate on her dancing, and she was in fact on tour that year. The thump of the presses and smell of the ink and paper were long gone; the Street and Smith printing plant was out in Jersey, and Joe's office was located in a modern midtown tower. But somehow, despite the differences, I felt as if it were 1937 again, and I were just starting my career.

"Don't forget my address if you write anything new—son," called out Joe, and then I was in the hall. I did write three or ten or twelve more pieces in the next two decades, including a special one for the fiftieth anniversary issue a month ago, the celebrations for which had been the last time I had seen Campbell alive. My lifetime subscription brought every new issue out to Arizona, and I managed to read something in each, sometimes with enjoyment, sometimes not. And I did visit Joe and Jean every few years, as my rapidly expanding chores and duties as head of the Navajo Nation permitted.

But the magic of those early years was gone, never to be recaptured.

Most certainly not now, now that Campbell was dead.

The last speaker was a bare-breasted priestess for the Temple of the Goddess. I came out of my reverie and found a handkerchief to dry my eyes just as she was finishing. Leaving the podium, she dropped a sheaf of maize on Campbell's coffin. Then the pallbearers stood up, and I was one of them.

Jean, still beautiful under the weight of her years, led the cortege out of the Osirian church, wearing the crown of Isis.

We carried the coffin past the assembled dignitaries, beneath the eyes of all the television cameras and the international audience. I recognized the world minister of course, who had flown all the way from Geneva, and the emperor of China, who was standing with his arm around the shoulder of the Dalai Lama. The entire board of directors of Japan, as well as the shogun, stood rigid as bamboo. But I couldn't remember if the goateed man who was crying so hard was the king of Brazil or the sultan of Persia. We buried Campbell at the spot near his childhood home that he had chosen, beneath a large tree.

Then, when it was over, I kissed Jean, climbed into my flyer, kicked in the antigrav, and let the autopilot take me home.

Instability

[written with Rudy Rucker]

JACK AND NEAL, loose and blasted, sitting on the steps of the ramshackle porch of Bill Burrough's Texas shack. Burroughs is out in the yard, catatonic in his orgone box, a copy of the Mayan codices in his lap. He's already fixed M twice today. Neal is cleaning the seeds out of a shoebox full of maryjane. Time is thick and slow as honey. In the distance the rendering company's noon whistle blows long, shrill and insistent. The rendering company is a factory where they cut up the cows that're too diseased to ship to Chicago. Shoot and cut and cook to tallow and canned cancer consomme.

Burroughs rises to his feet like a figure in a well-greased Swiss clock. "There is a scrabbling," goes Bill. "There is a scrabbling behind the dimensions. Bastards made a hole somewhere. You ever read Lovecraft's *Color Out of Space,* Jack?"

"I read it in jail," says Neal, secretly proud. "Dig, Bill, your mention of that document ties in so exactly with my most recent thought mode that old Jung would hop a hard-on."

"Mhwee-heee-heee," says Jack. "The Shadow knows."

"I'm talking about this bomb foolishness," harrumphs Burroughs, stalking stiff-legged over to stand on the steps. "The paper on the floor in the roadhouse john last night said there's a giant atom bomb test taking place tomorrow at White Sands. They're testing out the fucking 'trigger bomb' to use on that godawful new *hydrogen* bomb Edward Teller wants against the Rooshians. Pandora's box, boys, and we're not talking cooze. That bomb's going off in New Mexico tomorrow and right here and now the shithead meatflayer's noon whistle is getting us all ready for World War III, and if we're all ready for that, then we're by Gawd ready to be a great civilian army, yes, soldiers for Joe

McCarthy and Harry J. Anslinger, poised to stomp out the reds 'n' queers 'n' dopefiends. Science brings us this. I wipe my queer junkie ass with science, boys. The Mayans had it aaall figured out a looong time ago. Now take this von Neumann fella. . . ."

"You mean Django Reinhardt," goes Jack, stoned and rude. "Man, this is your life, their life, my life, a dog's life, God's life, the life of Riley. The Army's genius von Neumann of the desert, Bill, it was the Sunday paper Neal and I were rolling sticks on in Tuscaloosa, I just got an eidetic memory flash of it, you gone wigged cat, it was right before Neal nailed that cute Dairy Queen waitress with the Joan Crawford nose."

Neal goes, "Joan Crawford, Joan Crawfish, Joan Fishhook, Joan Rawshanks in the fog. *McVoutie!*" He's toking a hydrant roach and his jaywrapping fingers are laying rapid cable. Half the damn box is already twisted up.

Jack warps a brutal mood swing. There's no wine. *Ti Jack could use a widdly sup pour bon peek, like please, you ill cats, get me off this Earth.* . . . Is he saying this aloud, in front of Neal and Burroughs?

"And fuck the chicken giblets," chortles Neal obscurely, joyously, in there, and then suggests, by actions as much as by words, *is he really talking, Jack wonders,* "That we get back to what's really important such as rolling up this here, ahem, um, urp, Mexican see-gar, yes!"

Jack crabcakes slideways on fingertips and heels to Neal's elbow and they begin to lovingly craft and fashion and croon upon and even it would not be too much to say give birth to a beautiful McDeVoutie-ful hairseeded twat of a reefer, the roach of which will be longer than any two normal sticks.

They get off good.

Meanwhile Bill Burroughs is slacked back in his rocker, refixed and not quite on the nod because he's persistently irritated, both by the thought of the hydrogen bomb and, more acutely, by the flybuzz derry Times Square jive of the jabbering teaheads. Time passes, so very slow for Sal and Dean, so very fast for William Lee.

So Doctor Miracle and Little Richard are barreling along the Arizona highway, heading east on Route 40 out of Vegas, their pockets full of silver cartwheels from the grinds they've thimblerigged and also wallets bulging with hi-denom bills they demanded when cashing in their chips after beating the bank at the roulette wheels of six different casinos with their unpatented probalistic scams that are based on the vectors of neutrons through six inches of lead as transferred by spacetime Feynmann diagrams to the workings of those rickety-clickety simple-ass macroscopic system of balls and slots.

Doctor Miracle speaks. He attempts precision, to compensate for the Hungarian accent and for the alcohol-induced spread in bandwidth.

"Ve must remember to zend Stan Ulam a postcard from Los Alamos, reporting za zuccess of his Monte Carlo modeling method."

"It woulda worked even better over in Europe," goes Little Richard. "They got no double-zero slots on their wheels."

Doctor Miracle nods sagely. He's a plump guy in his fifties: thinning hair, cozy chin, faraway eyes. He's dressed in a double-breasted suit, with a bright hulagirl necktie that's wide as a pound of bacon.

Little Richard is younger, skinnier, more Jewish, and he has a thick pompadour. He's wearing baggy khakis and a white T-shirt with a pack of Luckies rolled up in his left sleeve.

It is not immediately apparent that these two men are ATOMIC WIZARDS, QUANTUM SHAMANS, PLUTONIUM PROPHETS, AND BE-BOPPIN' A-BOMB PEEAITCHDEES!

Doctor Miracle, meet Richard Feynmann. Little Richard, say hello to Johnny von Neumann!

There is a case of champagne sitting on the rear seat between them. Each of the A-scientists has an open bottle from which he swigs, while their car—a brand-new 1950 big-finned landboat of a two-toned populuxe pink'n'green Caddy—speeds along the highway.

There is no one driving. The front seat is empty.

Von Neumann, First Annointed Master of Automata, has rigged up the world's premier autopilot, you dig. He never could drive very well, and now he doesn't have to. Fact is, no one has to! The Caddy has front-and-side-mounted radar which feeds into a monster contraption in the trunk, baby cousin to Weiner's and Ulam's Los Alamos MANIAC machine, a thing all vacuum tubes and cams, all cogs and

Hollerith sorting rods, a mechanical brain that transmits cybernetic impulses directly to the steering, gas, and brake mechanisms.

The Trilateral Commission has ruled that the brain in the Cad's trunk is too cool for Joe Blow, much too cool, and the self-driving car isn't going to make it to the assembly line ever. The country needs only a few of these supercars, and this one has been set aside for the use and utmost ease of the two genius-type riders who wish to discuss highflown quantum-physical, metamathematical, and cybernetic topics without the burden of paying attention to the road. Johnny and Dickie's periodic Alamos-to-Vegas jaunts soak up a lot of the extra nervous tension these important bomb builders suffer from.

"So whadda ya think of my new method for scoring showgirls?" asks Feynmann.

"Dickie, although za initial trials vere encouraging, ve must have more points on za graph before ve can extrapolate," replies von Neumann. He looks sad. "You may haff scored, you zelfish little prick, but I—I did not achieve zatisfactory zexual release. Far from it."

"Waa'll," drawls Feynmann, "I got a fave niteclub in El Paso where the girls are hotter'n gamma rays and pretty as parity conservation. You'll get what you need there for sure, Johnny. We could go right instead of left at Albuquerque and be there before daylight. Everyone at Los Alamos'll be busy with the White Sands test anyway. Security won't look for us till Monday, and by then we'll be back, minus several milliliters of semen."

"El Paso," mutters von Neumann, taking a gadget out of his inner jacket pocket. It's . . . THE FIRST POCKET CALCULATOR! Thing's the size of a volume of the Britannica, with Bakelite buttons, and what makes it truly hot is that it's got all the road distances from the Rand-McNally road atlas databased onto the spools of a small wire-recorder inside. Von Neumann's exceedingly proud of it, and although he could run the algorithm faster in his head, he plugs their present speed and location into the device, calls up the locations of Las Vegas, Albuquerque, and Los Alamos, and proceeds to massage the data.

"You're quite right, Dickie," he announces presently, still counting the cryptic flashes of the calculator's lights. "Ve can do as you zay and indeed eefen return to za barracks before Monday zunrise. Venn is za test scheduled, may I ask?"

"Eight Ack Emma Sunday morning."

Von Neumann's mouth broadens in a liver-lipped grin. "How zynchronistic. Ve'll be passing White Sands just zen. I haff not witnessed a bomb test since Trinity. And zis is za biggest one yet. Zis bomb is, as you vell know, Dickie, za Ulam cascade initiator for za new hydrogen bomb. I'm for it! Let me reprogram za brain!"

Feynmann crawls over the front seat while the car continues its mad careening down the dizzy interstate, passing crawling tourist Buicks and mom'n'dad Studebakers. He lugs the case of champagne into the front with him. Von Neumann removes the upright cushion in the backseat and pries off the revealed panel, exposing the brain in the trunk. Consulting his calculator from time to time, von Neumann begins reprogramming the big brain by yanking telephone-switch-board-type wires and reinserting them.

"I'm tired of plugging chust metal sockets, Richard. Viz za next girl, I go first."

Now it's night and the stoned beats are drunk and high on bennies, too. Neal, his face all crooked, slopes through Burroughs's shack and picks Bill's car keys off the dresser in the dinette where Joan is listening to the radio and scribbling on a piece of paper. Crossing the porch, thiefishly heading for the Buick, Neal thinks Bill doesn't see, but Bill does.

Burroughs the beat morphinist, whose weary disdain has shaded catastrophically with the benzedrine and alcohol into fried impatience, draws the skeletonized sawed-off shotgun from the tube of hidden gutter pipe that this same Texafied Burroughs has suspended beneath a large hole drilled in the eaten wood of the porch floor. He fires a .12 gauge shotgun blast past Neal and into Neal's cleaned and twisted box of maryjane, barely missing Jack.

"*Whew, no doubt,*" goes Neal, tossing Burroughs the keys.

"Have ye hard drink, mine host?" goes Jack, trying to decide if the gun really went off or not. "Perhaps a pint of whiskey in the writing desk, old top? A spot of sherry?"

"To continue my afternoon fit of thought," says Burroughs, pocketing the keys. "I was talking about thermonuclear destruction and about the future of all humanity, which species has just about been squashed to spermacetae in the rictal mandrake spasms of Billy Sunday's pimpled asscheeks." He pumps another shell into the shotgun's chamber. His eyes are crazed goofball pinpoints. "I am sorry I ever let you egregious dopesuckin' latahs crash here, I mean you especially, jailbird conman Cassady."

Neal sighs and hunkers down to wail on the bomber Jack's lit off a smoldering scrap of shotgun wadding. Before long he and Jack are far into a rap, possibly sincere, possibly jive, a new rap wrapped around the concept that the three hipsters assembled here on the splintery porch neath the gibbous prairie moon have formed or did or will form or, to be quite accurate, *were forming and still are forming right there and then*, an analogue of those Holy B-Movie Goofs, The Three Stooges!

"Yes," goes Jack, "those Doomed Saints of Chaos, loosed on the workadaddy world to scramble the Charles Dickens cark and swink of BLOODY YER FIRED, those Stooge Swine are the anarchosyndicalist truly wigged submarxists, Neal man, *bikkhu* Stooges goosing ripeassmelons and eating fried chicken for supper. We are the Three Stooges, man!"

"Bill is Moe," says Neal, hot on the beam, batting his eyes at Bill, who wonders if it's time to shed his character-armor. "Mr. Serious Administerer of Fundament Punishments and Shotgun Blasts, and me with a Lederhosen Ass!"

"Ah you Neal," goes Jack, "you're Curly, angelic madman saint of the uncaught motebeam flybuzz fly!"

"And Kerouac is Larry," rheums Burroughs, weary with the knowledge. "*Mopple-lipped, lisped, muxed and completely flunk* is the phrase, eh Jack?"

"Born to die," goes Jack. "We're all born to die, and I hope it do be cool, Big Bill, if we goam take yo cah. Vootie-oh-oh." He holds out his hands for the keys.

"Fuck it," says Bill. "Who needs this noise?" He hands Jack the keys and before you know it, Neal's at the wheel of the two-ton black

Buick, gunning that straight-eight mill and burping the clutch. Jack's at his side and they're on the road with a long honk goodbye.

In the night there's reefer and plush seats and the radio and Neal is past spaced, off in his own private land that few but Jack and Allen can see. He whips the destination on Jack.

"This car is a front row seat to the A-blast."

"What say?"

"We'll ball this jack to White Sands, New Mexico, dear Jack, right on time for the bombtest Sunday eight ay-em. I stole some of Bill's M, man, we'll light up *on* it."

In Houston they stop and get gas and wine and benny and Bull Durham cigarette papers and keep flying west.

Sometime in the night Jack starts to fade in and out of horror dreams. There's a lot of overtime detox dreamwork that he's logged off of for too long. One time he's dreaming he's driving to an atom-bomb test in a stolen car, which is of course true, and then after that he's dreaming he's the dead mythic character in black-n-white that he's always planned to be, old lush mushrooming in an easy chair, railing at hippies. (*Hippies?* What are *they*?) Not to mention the dreams of graves and *Memere* and the endless blood sausages pulled out of Jack's gullet by some boffable blonde's sinster boyfriend . . .

"—been oh rock 'n' roll gospeled in on the *bomb foolishness* . . ." Neal is going when Jack screams and falls off the backseat he was stretched out on. There's hard wood and metal on the floor. ". . .and Jack you do understand buckeroo that I have hornswoggled you into yet another new and unprecedentedly harebrained swing across the dairy fat of her jane's spreadness?"

"Go," says Jack feebly, feeling around on the backseat floor. Short metal barrel, lightly oiled. Big flat disk of a magazine. Fuckin' crazy Burroughs. It's a Thompson submachine gun Jack's lying on.

"And oh Jack, man, I knew you'd know past the suicidal norm, Norman Rockwell, that it was. . . . *DeVoutie!*" Neal fishes a Bakelite ocarina out of his shirt pocket and tootles a thin, horrible note. "Goof on this, Jack, I just shot M and now I'm so high I can drive with my eyes closed."

Giggling Leda Atomica tugs at the shoulder of her low-cut peasant blouse with the darling petitpoint floral embroidery, trying to conceal the vertiginous depths of her cleavage, down which Doctor Miracle is attempting to pour flat champagne. What a ride this juicy brunette is having!

Leda had been toking roadside Albuquerque monoxide till eleven-fifty-five this Saturday night, thumb outstretched and skirt hiked up to midthigh, one high-heel foot perched on a little baby-blue handcase with nylons 'n' bra straps trailing from its crack. Earlier that day she'd parted ways with her employer, an Okie named Oather. Leda'd been working at Oather's jukejoint as a waitress and as a performer. Oather had put her in this like act wherein she strutted on the bar in highheels while a trained swan untied the strings of her atomgirl costume, a cute leatherette two piece with conical silver lame titcups and black shorts patterned in intersecting friendly-atom ellipses. Sometimes the swan bit Leda, which really pissed her off. Saturday afternoon, the swan had escaped from its pen, wandered out in the road and been mashed by a semi full of hogs.

"That there was the only bird like that in Arizona," yelled Oather. "Why dintcha latch the pen?"

"Maybe people would start payin' to watch you lick my butt," said Leda evenly. "It's about all you're good for, limpdick."

Et cetera.

Afternoon and early evening traffic was sparse. The drivers that did pass were all upstanding family men in sensible Plymouths, honest salesman too tame for the tasty trouble Leda's hot bod suggested.

Standing there at the roadside, Leda almost gave up hope. But then, just before midnight, the gloom parted and here comes some kind of barrel-assing Necco-wafer-colored Caddy!

When the radars hit Leda's boobs and returned their echoes to the control mechanism, the cybernetic brain nearly had an anode aneurysm. Not trusting Feynmann's promises, von Neumann had hardwired the radars for just such a tramp-girl eventuality, coding hitch-hiking Jane Russell T&A parameters into the electronic brain's very circuits. The Caddy's headlights started blinking like a fellaheen in a sandstorm, concealed sirens went off, and Roman candles mounted on the rear bumper discharged, shooting rainbow fountains of glory into the night.

"SKIRT ALERT!" whooped Doctor Miracle and Little Richard.

Before Leda quite knew what was happening, the cybernetic Caddy had braked at her exact spot. The rear door opened, Leda and her case were snatched on in, and the car roared off, the wind of its passage scattering the tumbleweeds like dust.

Leda knew she was hooked up with some queer fellas as soon as she noticed the empty driver's seat.

And she wasn't reassured by the pair's habit of reciting backwards all the signs they passed.

"Pots!"

"Egrem!"

"Sag!"

But soon Leda took a shine to Doctor Miracle and Little Richard. Their personalities grew on her in direct proportion to the amount of bubbly she downed. By the time they hit Truth or Consequences, NM, they're scattin' to the cool sounds of Wagner's *Nibelungenlied* on the long distance radio, and Johnny is trying to baptize her tits.

"Dleiy!" croons Doctor Miracle.

"Daeha thgil ciffart!" goes Feynmann, all weaseled in on Leda's other side.

"Kcuf em won, syob!" says Leda, who's gone seven dry weeks without the straight-on loving these scientists are so clearly ready to provide.

So they pull over to the next tourist cabins and get naked and find out what factorial three really means. I mean . . . do they get it on, or *what*? Those stagfilm stars Candy Barr and Smart Alec have got nothing on Leda, Dickie, and Doctor Miracle. Oh baby!

And then it's near dawn and they have breakfast at a greasy spoon named Bongo's and then they're on Route 85 south. Johnny's got the brain programmed to drive them right to the margin-of-error 7:57 AM White Sands spacetime coordinate; he's got the program tweaked down to the point where the Cad will actually cruise past ground zero a few minutes before eight AM ignition, and nestle itself behind the observation bunker, leaving them ample time to run inside and join the other top bomb boys.

Right before the turnoff to the White Sands road, von Neumann decides that things are getting dull.

"Dickie, activate za jacks!"

"Yowsuh!"

Feynmann leans over the front seat and flips a switch that's breadboarded into the dash. The car starts to buck and rear like a wild bronco, its front and tail alternately rising and plunging. It's another goof of the wonder-Caddy—von Neumann has built B-52 landing gear in over the car's axles.

As the Caddy porpoises down the highway, its three occupants are laughing and falling all over each other, playing grabass, champagne spilling from an open bottle.

Suddenly without warning an OOGA-OOGA klaxon starts to blare.

"Collision imminent!" shouts von Neumann.

"Hold onto your tush!" advises Feynmann.

"Be careful!" screams Leda and wriggles to the floor.

Feynmann manages to get a swift glimpse of a nightblack Buick driving down the two lane road's exact center, heading straight towards them. No one is visible in the car.

Then the road disappears, leaving only blue sky to fill the windshield. There is a tremendous screech and roar of ripping metal, and the Caddy shudders slowly to a stop.

When Feynmann and von Neumann peer out their rear window they see the Buick stopped back there. It is missing its entire roof, which lies crumpled on the road behind it.

For all Neal's bragging, M's not something he's not totally used to. He has to stop and puke a couple of times in El Paso, early early with the sky going white. There's no sympathy from Jack, cuz Jack picked up yet another bottle of sweet wine outside San Antone and now he's definitely passed. Neal has the machine gun up in the front seat with him; he knows he ought to put it in the trunk in case the cops ever pull them over, but the *dapperness* of the weapon is more than Neal can resist. He's hoping to get out in the desert with it and blow away some cactuses.

North of Las Cruces the sun is almost up and Neal is getting a bad disconnected feeling; he figures it's the morphine wearing off and decides to fix again. He gets a Syrette out of the Buick's glove compartment and skinpops it. Five more miles and the rosy flush is on him, he feels better than he's felt all night. The flat empty dawn highway is a grey triangle that's driving the car. Neal gets an idea he's a speck of paint on a perspective painting; he decides it would be cool to drive lying down. He lies down sideways on the driver's seat, feet on the wheel, and when he sees that it works he grins and closes his eyes.

The crash tears open the dreams of Jack and Neal like some horrible fatman's can opener attacking oily smoked sardines. They wake up in an open air world that's radically different.

Jack's sluggish and stays in the car, but Neal is out on the road doing dance incantation trying to avoid the death that he feels so thick in the air. The Thompson submachine gun is in his hands and he is, solely for the rhythm, you dig, firing it and raking the landscape, especially his own betraying Buick, though making sure fatal lead is only in the lower parts, e.g., tires as opposed to sleepy Jack backseat or explosion gas tank, and, more especially than that, he's trying to keep himself from laying a steel-jacketed flat horizontal line of lead across the hapless marshmallow white faces of the rich boys in the Cadillac. They have a lownumber government license plate. Neal feels like Cagney in *White Heat*, possessed by a total crazed rage against authority, ready for a maddog last-stand showdown that can culminate only in a fireball of glorious fuck-you-copper destruction. But there's only two of them here to kill. Not enough to go to the chair for. Not yet, no matter how bad the M comedown feels. Neal shoots lead arches over them until the gun goes to empty clicks.

Slowly black-tempered Jack opens the holey Buick door, feeling God it's so horrible to be alive. He blows chunks on the meaningless asphalt. The two strange men in the Cadillac give off the scent of antilife evil, a taint buried deep in their bone marrow, like strontium-

90 in mother's milk. Bent down wiping his mouth and stealing an outlaw look at them, Jack flashes that these new guys have picked up their heavy death-aura from association with the very earth-frying, retina-blasting allbomb that he and Neal are being ineluctably drawn to by cosmic forces that Jack can *see*, as a matter of fact, ziggy lines stretched out against the sky as clear as any peyote mandala.

"Everyone hates me but Jesus," says Neal, walking over to the Cadillac, spinning the empty Thompson around his calloused thumb. "Everyone is Jesus but me."

"Hi," says Feynmann. "I'm sorry we wrecked your car."

Leda rises up from the floor between von Neumann's legs, a fact not lost on Neal.

"We're on our way to the bombtest," croaks Jack, lurching over.

"Ve helped invent za bomb," says von Neumann. "Ve're rich und important men. Of course ve vill pay you reparations, and additionally offer you a ride to za test. *Ezpecially* since you didn't kill us."

The Cadillac is obediently idling in park, its robot-brain having retracted the jacks and gone into standby mode after the oilpan-scraping collision with the Buick's stripped roof. Neal mimes a wide mouthed blowjob of the hot tip of the Thompson, flashes Leda an easy smile, slings the gun out into the desert, and then he and shuddery Jack clamber into the Cad's front seat. Leda, with her trademark practicality, climbs into the front seat with them and gives them a bottle of champagne. She's got the feeling these two brawny drifters can take her faster farther than science can.

Von Neumann flicks the RESET cyberswitch in the rear seat control panel, and the Cad rockets forward, pressing them all back into the deep cushioned seats. Neal fiddles with the steering wheel, fishtailing the Cad this way and that, then observes, "Seems like this Detroit iron's got a mind of its own."

"Zis car's brobably as zmart as you are," von Neumann can't help bitch-catting. Neal lets it slide.

7:49 AM.

The Cad makes a hard squealing right turn onto the White Sands access road. There's a checkpoint further on; but the soldiers recognize von Neumann's wheels and wave them right on through.

Neal fires up a last reefer and begins beating out a rhythm on the dash with his hands, grooving to the pulse of the planet, *his* planet awaiting its savior. Smoke trickles out of his mouth; he shotguns Leda, breathing the smoke into her mouth, wearing the glazed eyes of a mundane gnostic messiah, hip to a revelation of the righteous road to salvation. Jack's plugged in too, sucking his last champagne of this lifetime, telepathy-rapping with Neal. It's almost time, and Doctor Miracle and Little Richard are too confused to stop it.

A tower rears on the horizon off to the left and all at once the smart Cad veers off the empty two-lane road and rams its way through a chainlink fence. Nerve-shattering scraping and lumbering thumps.

"Blease step on za gas manually a bit," says von Neumann, unsurprised. He programmed this shortcut in. "I still vant to go under za tower, but is only three minutes remaining. Za program is undercompensating for our unfortunate lost time."

It is indeed 7:57.

Neal drapes himself over the wheel now, stone committed to this last holy folly. Feeling a wave of serene, yet exultant resignation, Jack says, "Go. Go, old time-out-of-mind buddy." It's almost all over now, he thinks, the endless roving and raging, brawling and fucking, the mad flights back and forth and up and down the continent, the urge to get it all down on paper, every last feeling and vision in master-sketch detail, because we're all gonna die one day, man, all of us—

The Caddy, its once lustrous sides now raked of paint by the torn fence, hurtles on like God's own thunderbolt messenger, over pebbles and weeds, across the desert and the sloping glass craters of past tests. The tower is right ahead.

7:58.

"Get ready, Uncle Sam," whispers Neal. "We're coming to cut your balls off. Hold the boys down, Jack."

Jack bodyrolls over the seat back into the laps of Feynmann and von Neumann. Can't have those mad scientists fiddling with the controls while Neal's pulling his cool automotive moves!

Poor innocent Leda still thinks she's on a joyride and she cozies up to Neal's biceps, and for an eternal second it's just the way it's supposed to be, handsome hardstrappin' Neal at the wheel of a big old bomb with a luscious brunette squeezed up against him closer'n chewin' gum.

And now, before the guys in back can do much of anything, Neal's clipped through the tower's southern leg. As the tower starts to collapse, Neal, flying utterly on extrasensory instincts, slows just enough to pick up the bomb, which has been jarred prematurely off its release hook.

No Fat Boy, this gadget represents the ultimate to date in miniaturization: it's only about as big as a fifty-gallon oildrum, and about as weighty. It crunches down onto the Caddy's roof, bulging bent metal in just far enough to brush the heads of the riders.

And no, it doesn't go off. Not yet.

7:59.

Neal aims the mighty unstoppable Cad at the squat concrete bunker half a mile off. This is an important test, the last step before the H-bomb, and all the key assholes are in there, every atomic brain in the free world, not to mention the dignitaries and politicians aplenty, all come to witness the proof of this American military superiority, all those shitnasty fuckheads ready to kill the future.

King Neal floors it and does a cowboy yodel, Jack is laughing Ho-Tai-style and elbowing the scientists, Leda's screaming luridly, Dickie is talking too fast to understand, and Johnny is—

8:00.

They impact the bunker at 80 MPH, folding up accordian-wise, but not feeling it one bit as the simultaneous mushroom blooms, and the atoms of them and the bigwigs commingle in the quantum instability of the reaction event.

Time forks.

Somewhere, somewhen, there now exists an Earth where there are no nuclear arsenals, where nations do not waste their substance on missiles and bombs, where no one wakes up each morning thinking this might be the world's last day—an Earth where two high, gone, wigged cats wailed and grooved and ate up the road and Holy Goofed the world off its course.

For you 'n' me.

World Wars III

"Is history personal or statistical?"
—*T. Pynchon*

THIS HAPPENED IN HAMBURG on the eve of J-Day, the night of that now legendary USO triple bill: the Beatles opening for the Supremes and Elvis. Sort of a chorus of pop Valkyries the brass had kindly arranged for all us Jivey GI Joes and Jolly Jack Tars, before booting us over the edge of the steaming crevasse—filled with prop dry ice, or leading straight to Hell?—into the gaping maw of the massed Warsaw Pact troops, chivied so recently out of West Germany, harried and weary, but far, far from beaten.

Half the North Atlantic fleet, it seemed, had put in at Kiel two days before, for refueling and provisioning. All hands were forbidden shore leave. Scuttlebutt had it we all—or at least my ship, the USS *Rainbow Warrior*—would soon be steaming for Gdansk, to participate in a humongous amphibious attack, which—given the Polish defenses around their shipyards, led by the already legendary young Major Walesa—had about as much chance of success as the Republicans had of beating JFK and Stevenson in the next elections, or Woody Allen had of playing the romantic lead against Sinatra's wife Mia.

Those were our chances, that is, if the patroling Russkie subs didn't sink us first en route.

This prospect did not sit well with Pig Bodine and me. It wasn't so much that we were scared of dying. Gee whiz, no. Three years of battle had cured us of that childish fear, innoculating us with the universal vaccine known as war anomie. It was simply that we didn't want to miss the big show down Hamburg way.

"I seen the Beatles before the war," said Pig, "right in Hamburg, at the Star Club. Man, they could rock. I thought they were going somewhere, but I never heard anymore about them. I didn't even know they were still playing together."

Bodine was lying upside down on his bunk, head hanging floorward, trying to get a cheap—and the only available—high from the rush of blood to his head. Physiology recapitulates pharmacology. Above the bunk hung a tattered poster of James Dean and Brigette Bardot in *From Russia With Love*. (The prez, fan in chief of Fleming's novels, had an identical one, only autographed, hanging in the Oval Office.)

Pig's enormous hairy stomach was exposed below—or, more precisely, above—his dirty shirt; his navel was plugged with some disgusting smegma that resembled bearing-grease and Crisco.

Bodine's navel jam fascinated me at the same time it repelled me. Coming from a white-bread background, illustrious Puritan forebears and all that, good school and the prospect of a slick entrance into the corporate life at Boeing, I had never met anyone quite like Bodine before. He represented some kind of earth-force to me, a troll of mythic proportions, liable at any moment to unleash a storm of belches and farts capable of toppling trees, accompanied by a downpour of sweat and jizm.

I had known Bodine for ten years now, since I had dropped out of Cornell and enlisted in the Navy in '55. Peacetime. It seems so long ago, and so short. Twenty years between the first two, and twenty more till the third. Had They been planning it all along, just biding Their time until the wounds had healed and the people had forgotten, until the factories could retool to meet the new specs from the R&D labs? Was peace, in fact, like diplomacy, merely another means of waging war. . . ?

Bodine had been my constant companion through all that time, even when I had made it briefly into officers' territory, before being busted back. (And that's another story entirely, but one also not entirely innocent of the presence of the Pig, Germanic totem of death he.) We had been through a lot of craziness together. But even so, even knowing him as I did, I could not have calculated the vector of the madness we were about to embark on now, nor its fatal terminus.

"I think I heard something about them a year or two ago," I replied, imagining Pig's mouth as occupying his forehead and his eyes his chin. It barely improved his looks. "The guy named McCarthy—"

"McCartney," interrupted Pig.

"Whatever. He was arrested on a morals charge. Got caught with some jailbait. And then his buddy, Lemon—"

"Lennon."

"All right already with the teacher riff. Do you wanna hear the story or not? Lennon started shooting heroin when the war broke out and had to spend some time in a clinic. This must be a comeback tour."

"I could use a little cum back myself," snorted Pig.

"Left too much in the last port! Snurg, snarf, hyuck!" This last approximating Piggy laughter. "God, I'm going ship-crazy! I gotta see that show and get laid! Dig me—do you still have that Shore Patrol rig we swiped?"

"Yeah, why?"

"Just lissen—"

And so, several hours later, all tricked out, we prepared to breach our own force's defenses.

It was dark, and Benny Yoyodyne, slowest of the slow, was on duty guarding the gangway. I was wearing the SP armband, harness, and nightstick and had my sidearm strapped on. Pig was in cuffs.

"Halt!" said Yoyodyne, brandishing his rifle like some Annapolis frosh. "No one's permitted to disembark."

"It's OK, Benny. They just need Bodine on shore for his court-martial tomorrow."

Yoyodyne lowered his gun and scratched under his cap. "Court-martial? Gee, I'm sorry to hear that. What'd he do?"

"You know the soup we had last week? The one that tasted so grungy? He pissed in it. They discovered it when they saw the distinctive urine corrosion in the kettles. The captain had seconds and nearly died."

Yoyodyne turned six shades of green. "Good Christ! what a—a pig!"

"C'mon, Bodine, it's time to meet your fate."

Pig started struggling. "No, no, I won't go, don't make me, General LeMay will hang me by the balls!"

Yoyodyne prodded him with the rifle. "Quit fighting and take it like a man. You can do at least one noble thing in your miserable life."

Pig straightened up. "You've made me see the error of my ways, Benny. C'mon, Tom, I'm ready now."

I marched Pig down the ramp to the dock. He exuded such an air
of holy martyrdom that I found myself almost feeling sorry for him.

As soon as we rounded the corner of a warehouse, Pig
unsnapped the shackles from his wrists and collapsed atop a barrel,
racked by laughter.

"As Bugs Bunny would say," I commented, "'Ehhh, what a
maroon!'"

"He really thought I was like all reformed in an instant. Jesus,
some guys deserve the Navy. Let's hit the road, Jack Ker-oh-wack!"

It was a sweet warm July evening, we were instantly and unforgiv-
ably AWOL, and the King was playing the next night about a hundred
miles to the south. Uncle Sam and the rest of the western world were
pausing like a punch-drunk fighter between the penultimate and final
round in a senseless slugfest, a brief moment of mocking peace, to
have his mouth spritzed and the blood wiped from his brow, before
plunging back into the fray with the pug-ugly, cauliflower-eared Papa
Nikita and his robotic Commie hordes.

I had never felt more alive, nor ever would.

Kiel was crawling with SP's and MP's (S&MP's one and all, fer
shure), striding imperially among the crowds of refugees, black-
marketeers, NATO-deputized civilian cops, and homeless war-
orphans, all Dondi-eyed in rags and viscious as lampreys as they tried
to attach themselves to Pig and I as unlikely saviors. The kids were
dressed in Carnaby Street rags collected by Swinging London matrons
and debs. Polka-dotted caps, paisley shirts, striped trousers. Fab gear.

Pig and I had to dart from shadow to shadow, down rubble-filled
alleys, into doorways that were all that remained of the buildings they
had been attached to, and up stairs leading to nowhere to avoid getting
orphan-mobbed or cop-trammeled. Using the moon, we worked our
way south, to the outskirts of the city. On the autobahn, we were lucky
enough to hook a ride with a camo-decorated canvas-backed Mustang-
model truck heading Hamburg-way.

The driver was a blonde English lieutenant named Jane "Sugarbunny" Lane. Her cuddly copilot was a dark-haired Romanian exile with
the handle of Viorica Tokes, now also a member of the British armed

forces. Ribbons from a double handful of campaigns: the Congo, Panama, Algeria, Finland, Manchuria . . . Experienced, these two! Been in more theaters than Hope, Burns, and Berle combined. The gals, it developed, were also illicitly on their way to the Presley show, having wrangled the assignment of delivering the truck's contents to the big DP camp outside Hamburg. Viorica reached across my lap to crack the glove compartment and liberate a bottle of Swedish vodka, which Pig immediately and immoderately snatched away. I flipped on the truck's radio, tuning for the NATO station, which, once found, proved to be broadcasting a bland diet of prowar tunes. Streisand singing "A Pox on Marx (And Lenin Too)." Barry Sadler with "The Day We Took Moscow." Dionne Warwick doing the Bacharach tune "Do You Know the Way to Riga Bay?" You dig, I'm sure. I snapped it off.

"So what kind of mercy mission to the poor displaced person-types is this?" asked Pig after a swig, squeezing Sugarbunny's thigh as she drove. To ease the crowding—the door lever was pushing my service revolver into my hip—I placed my arm around Viorica, whose accented English I found entrancing.

"Is that a billygoat club in your pants, or are you just being glad to see me?" the Romanian babe responded, sending Pig into gales of vodka-scented laughter. When Bodine's snorts tapered off, I repeated his question, rephrased.

"Yeah, what's in the back? Blankets, medicines, powdered eggs?"

Sugarbunny smiled. "Something even more vital. Propaganda. Namely, comics."

My heart nearly stopped. "American?" I asked, not daring to hope. "New?"

Viorica nodded. "Americanski comics, yes. And very much recently up-to-date."

"Stop the truck right now." Sensing the urgency in my voice, Sugarbunny did as I asked. In less time than it takes to tell, I was back in the cab with a shrink-wrapped bundle in my lap. I couldn't believe my luck. This whole crazy misadventure was starting to remind me of an episode of *Hogan's Heroes*. The one where Hogan talks the idiotic camp commander Gerasimov into letting him and the boys borrow a truck to deliver some beets to the borsht factory and they make a sidetrip to blow up the tank factory, along the way pulling a truckload of beautiful female Young Soviet Pioneers out of a ditch.

With trembling hands I ripped the shrink-wrapping off.

The Fantastic Four had been enlisted on the Middle-Eastern front. The sight of the Human Torch zipping through Red Egyptian jets, hot metal splattering above the Sphinx, was just what I needed to see to remind me of the United States media machine I had left behind. The Invisible Girl fell in love with a handsome Israeli soldier, and the Thing called "Clobberin' Time!" on a bunch of Russian generals. Meanwhile Superman was busy in the Pacific, lifting entire Commie aircraft carriers out of the sea and dashing them down off the coast of sleepy and ostensibly neutral Japan, inadvertantly causing a tidal wave which he then had to outrace before it washed over the ruins of Tokyo. And there was more. The Flash picked up General Westmoreland and rushed him across China just in time to meet Chiang Kai-shek. The Submariner in Australia, Captain America in Tibet, Green Lantern in French Indochina . . .

So engrossed had I become that I barely noticed when the truck pulled off the road, into the grounds of an abandoned farm.

"Dibs on the barn!" yelled Pig, pulling Sugarbunny by the hand toward that relatively unscathed structure full of moldering but comfortable and soon-to-be-rolled-in hay, leaving me and Viorica to sack out in the ruins of the farmhouse. We unrolled some bedding in the angle of two standing walls and a bit of roof. The air was effervescent on our bare skins, the stars jealous of what they saw. After sex, she told me a little about herself.

"I survive conscription work in Soviet munitions factory at Timisoara, until I can take no more. I sneak across the border of my soon-to-be-ex-country and then journey through all of Yugoslavia to Adriatic, dodging all kinds of bad men, and swing passage on hobo ship which is sunk off Sicily. For six months I am prisoner of hill-bandits who use me like love doll. Rescue comes in a big shoot-up with Britishers—Special Forces—who are looking for their kidnapped ambassador but find me instead. I arrive in London just in time for guess what?"

"Not Napalm Night?"

"You bet. Whole city and plenty of citizens burned up by flaming Russian Vaseline. Some kind of big mess." That about summed up the whole world just then, so we fell asleep.

In the morning we were awakened early by a rooster's arrogant assertion that life was worth living. We tracked him down, found his harem, and rustled up some eggs. The girls produced government-issue Tang and Pop Tarts, and we had a fine breakfast in the ruins of civilization. Pig ate enough for two—horses, that is.

Back on the road, we raced over the remaining miles to Hamburg. The tanks and trucks and Jeeps and APC's we passed were all heading toward the city; no one was leaving. It seemed the entire European theater of operations was funneling into the old Hanseatic city for the big show, their courses bent like rays of light around the King's sun. We saw teams from all three stateside networks and the BBC. I thought I recognized Walter Cronkite.

"Make me a star!" shouted Pig as we zipped by.

The gals dropped us off in the center of the war-torn town well before noon. "We've got to get these capitalist color catechisms to the people who really need them, boys," said Sugarbunny. "We'll catch you at the show tonight. Thanks for the company."

"Lady Jane," I said, trying my best to sound like Jagger, "may I kiss your hand?"

She extended it graciously out the driver's window.

"You coulda had more than that to kiss if you asked," said Pig. "Nyuck, hyuck, snurt."

"Pig, it would insult the entire species to call you a sorry example of humanity."

"Heads up for antipersonnel mines," Viorica advised as Sugarbunny shifted gears. "Ivan planted plenty before he retreat!"

Made wary by Viorica's parting words, we picked our way gingerly down the center of the empty street, two cautious cocks come to Cuxhaven.

"What now?" I asked Pig.

"Get drunk, of course. That was half the reason for going AWOL, remember?"

We found a functioning rathskeller, the Iron Stein, occupying the roofed-over basement of a building that didn't exist anymore. Inside, patchily illuminated, various locals mingled with off-duty troops from all nations. A cadre of Canadians consorted with a flock of Kiwis, while a gaggle of Ghurkas slopped swill with a passel of Portugese. B-girls and con men lived lower down on the food chain. Pig and I were liberally supplied with occupation scrip, and we plunked it down on the bar for some of Herr Feldverein's best home brew.

Pig, on my right, slurped down two boilermakers to my every one and was soon snoring gently on the bar. I doubted he had gotten much sleep with Sugarbunny. I myself was at the stage where vision is muzzily enhanced and thoughts flit free as dogs in a Dylan song.

The fellow on my left gradually became the focus of my attention. He was an older man, easily past sixty, but in good shape. Bearded, dressed in a kind of modified safari getup popular with correspondents and other white guys slumming in foreign climes, he radiated an air of melancholy wisdom the likes of which I had never felt before. In my boozy condition, I felt it incumbent upon me to try and cheer him up.

"Mr. Hemingway, I presume," I said lifting my glass in mock recognition.

"Sorry, son, he's got the glamour assignment with the occupying forces in Cuba."

I could tell by his voice that he was completely sober, perhaps the only such soul in the room. "You are a writer, though?"

"Yes. *Herald-Tribune*. And you?"

An inexplicable shiver unzipped my spine. Was I misinterpreting his question? And if not, why had he asked such a thing? My uniform was obvious as Senator Johnson's hernia scars, and I had thought none of my bruised karma was showing. I swigged my beer and said, "No, 'fraid not. In another lifetime, maybe, if I hadn't left school . . ." He laughed then, as bitterly as I've ever heard anyone laugh. "Another lifetime . . . You wouldn't want one, believe me."

"And how can you be so certain?"

He grabbed my sleeve and stared me down. "I'll tell you a good story, son and let you decide."

He let me go, and then began.

"I was eighteen in 1985—"

I had to interrupt. "Twenty years in the future."

"Your future. Once my present. Now, nobody's future. Anyway, shut up. I don't tell this one often and might change my mind. I was eighteen in 1985 and a simple soldier. The world I lived in was one you probably can't imagine. You see, in my world the United States and the Soviet Union were both armed to the teeth with atomic bombs. Do you have any notion what those are?"

"Something to do with atoms, I bet," I managed to wise-mouth.

"That's right. Explosive devices that split atoms to unleash unimaginable destructive power. They were invented during World War II—"

"They were?"

"In my world, yes, they were. And after the war, thousands were manufactured and mounted on rockets—"

"Rockets now," I said. "This is quite a story. I've always liked rockets, but I've never seen any big enough to carry a bomb. A firecracker, maybe."

"Believe me, they can be built big enough to cross continents. Can you picture such a world? Held hostage by two insane superpowers with enough megatonnage to destroy the whole ecosphere?"

Megatonnage? I thought. Ecosphere? A madman's glossolalia . . . But the putative nutcase ran right past my speculations with his story.

"Well, in 1985 it finally happened. The Soviet premier was Yuri Andropov, a mean bastard, former KGB man. The Russians were losing in Afghanistan—"

"Afghanistan? Didn't the British have something to say about that?"

"The British Empire fell to pieces after my Second World War. They meant nothing. No, the geopolitical scene was strictly the US versus Russia. They were the only players who really mattered. Well, the Russians invaded Pakistan, our ally, where the Afghanistan rebels had their bases. We responded with conventional forces, and the conflict escalated from there. The next thing we knew, the birds were launched, and World War III had begun.

"I was assigned as a simple guard in the command center under the Rockies. That's how deadly those bombs were—we had to hide our asses under the weight of mountains just to survive. Well, in the first few minutes of the war—and it only lasted an hour or two—everything went like clockwork. The generals gave the launch codes to the soldiers manning the silos, read the damage reports handed to them, counted up their losses and launched a second batch of missiles in response. . . . But then things began to break down. We were still getting a few visual feeds along the fiberoptics—the whole atmosphere was churning with electromagnetic pulses of course—and the sights that we saw—"

The man began to weep at the catastrophe that hadn't happened yet and apparently never would. His face was briefly contorted with an intensity of deep emotion. I was rapidly becoming bummed out. This had gone from being a kind of half-amusing, half-draggy conversation with a lively minded liar to a Coleridge-style buttonholing by a certified maniac.

Tears in his beard, the old reporter pulled himself back together, obviously drawing on some immense reservoir of will. He caught me by the elbow, and I was frozen. His touch had communicated to me the certainty that every word he spoke was the truth as he knew it.

"The carnage was awful. It drove technicians and soldiers alike mad. Nobody had predicted this. There was mutiny, rebellion, fire-fights, and suicides in the command center, some pushing to continue the war, others to cease.

"I couldn't take sides. My mind was paralyzed. Instead, I dropped my rifle and fled, deeper into the enormous bunker.

"When I came to myself again, I was in a lab. Everyone there was dead, suicides. I slammed the door, locking myself in.

"There was an apparatus there. It was a time machine."

"Jesus!" I shook his hand off and looked around me for help in dealing with this madman, but everyone was busy getting drunk, except Pig, who was still blissfully snoring. I was on my own. "Atomic bombs, rockets, OK, maybe. A time machine, though. Do you expect me—"

"I don't expect anything. Just listen. As soon as I discovered what the device was—an experimental, one-way, last-ditch project that had never even been tried—I knew what I had to do.

"I wanted to live out most of the century again, up to the year the final war had broken out, so I set the machine for seventy years in my past, 1915. I figured I could hang on till my eighties. And the second decade of the century was early enough to start changing things.

"There were spatial settings as well. I put myself in New York. Instant transition, very elegant. There I stood, dressed all wrong, eighteen years old, the tears still wet on my face. But quite certain of what I had to do.

"Very quickly, I established myself as a reporter. It's amazing the scoops you can deliver when the future is an open book. Then I began systematically killing some very important people.

"Einstein was first. He had already published some papers of course, but I staged his death so as to discredit his work as much as possible. Traveling to Switzerland, I carried with me the government-issued poison the lab technicians had offed themselves with. I had grabbed it before entering the wayback. Traceless, efficient stuff. It was no problem to slip some into the coffee Einstein and I shared. I paid a Zurich orphan boy to report to the authorities that the "Jewish pervert" had died during sex with him. Quite a remarkable scandal. No respectable scientist would touch his theories afterwards with a ten-foot pole."

"Walesa?" I half-heartedly quipped. He ignored me. "After such an obvious target, I began working through a list of everyone who had had a hand in developing either atomic fission or rocketry.

"Bohr, Lawrence, Fermi, Dyson, Alvarez, Feynmann, Panofsky, Teller, Oppenheimer, Goddard, Sakarhov, the Joliot-Curies, von Braun, Wigner, Ley, Dirac—I completely wiped the slate of history clean of most of twentieth-century nuclear physics. It was easier than I had ever dreamed. Those people were vital, indispensable geniuses. And so trusting. Scientists love to talk to reporters. I had easy access to almost anyone. The Army had taught me many traceless ways to kill, and I used them once my stock of poison ran out. It was pathetically simple. The hardest part was keeping my name clean, staying free and unimplicated. I visited the victims at night, usually at their homes, without witnesses. I misrepresented my employers, my name, my nationality. Oh, I was cunning, a regular serial killer. Bundy and Gacy had nothing on me, and I eventually beat their score. But for the salvation of the world!"

None of the names he had mentioned meant anything to me, except Einstein's, whom I recalled as a crazy Jewish physicist who had died in disgrace in Switzerland. I had to assume that they were real people though and had been as pivotal as he claimed. "Why did you have to kill scientists, though? Why didn't you go the political route, try to change the political structures that led to war, or eliminate certain leaders?"

"Too much inertia. The politics had been in place for decades, centuries. The science was just being born. And it was the scientists' fault anyway. They deserved to die, the arrogant bastards, unleashing something they could barely comprehend or control like that, like children chipping away at a dam for the thrill of it. And besides, what difference would it have made if, say, I could have gotten someone different elected as president, or nominated as premier? Would Russia have gone democratic under someone other than Andropov, released its satellite nations, disengaged from Afghanistan? Bloody unlikely. But still, I didn't neglect politics. I reported favorably on the creation of the president's scientific advisory council that started under Roosevelt and curried favor with its members. I wrote slanted stories ridiculing the notion of funding anything even remotely connected with rocketry or atomic power. Not that there were many such proposals, after the devastation I had wreaked. Of course, I kept killing off as many of the second-stringers as I could who had popped up to take the place of the missing geniuses.

"History remained pretty much as I remembered it, right up till the Second World War. Nuclear physics just didn't have much impact on life until the forties. But by the time Hitler invaded Poland, I was certain I had succeeded. There would be no atomic ending to that war. I had staved off the ultimate destruction of the earth.

"Naturally, my actions meant a huge loss of American lives in the invasion of Japan. Hundreds of thousands of extra deaths, all directly attributable to my intervention in history. Don't think I haven't thought about those men night after night, weighing their lives in the balance against those of the helpless civilians in Hiroshima and

Nagasaki, and, later, every city on the globe. But the scale always tipped the same way. Atomic destruction was infinitely worse."

He was talking almost to himself now, more and more frantic, trying to justify his life, and my incomprehension meant nothing. By my side, Pig had stopped snoring.

"After the war, though, events really began to diverge from what I knew. It all slithered out of my control. The permanent American presence in a devastated Japan led to stronger support of the Chinese Republicans against Mao and his guerillas, resulting in their defeat. How could I know though that having the Americans on their Mongolian border would make the Russians so paranoid and trigger-happy? I couldn't be expected to predict everything, could I? The border incident that started your World War III—a total freak accident! Out of my hands entirely! But what does a little global skirmish mean anyway? As long as there're no atomic bombs. And there're not, are there? You've never seen any, have you?"

I could only stare. He grabbed my shirtfront. "I fucking saved your ass from frying," he hissed. "I'm bigger than Jesus! You all owe me, you suckers. I made your world—"

There was a shot, followed by screams and the sound of clattering chairs and shattering glasses. The time-traveler's hands loosened and he fell to the floor. Pig Bodine had my service revolver in his shaky hand.

"My fucking dad died in the invasion of Japan," said Pig.

"Bodine," I opined, "I think you've just killed God."

"This is war, man. Why should God get off free?"

We split fast from The Iron Stein before anyone could gather their wits to detain us. We found Sugarbunny and Viorica and shacked up in a safe spot till the show, which we thought it would be OK to attend, under cover of darkness. After all we had been through, it would have been a shame to miss it.

The Beatles played superbly, especially Pete Best on drums. The whole crowd forgot their J-Day jitters and began to groove. During their last number—a little ditty called "Tomorrow Never Knows"—I began to cry so hard that I missed all of the Supremes' set, and the opening notes of the King's "Mystery Train."

But Presley's singing made my world seem real enough again and more important than ever before.

After the concert the four of us ambled off hand-in-hand through the nighted streets, lit only by the stars so impossibly high above, where no "rocket" bearing "atomic bombs" had ever trespassed, back toward the truck, now as empty of its four-color contents as my brain was of plans.

Yet somehow I felt content.

"Where to, boys?" asked Sugarbunny.

"The future," I said. "Where else?"

"Nyuck, nyuck," snuffled Pig. "How about tripping into the past? I'd like to be in that barn again."

"If you get the chance, please don't ever try remaking the past, Pig. Living in a world created by a moral idealist is bad enough. One made by an amoral hedonist—I can't even begin to imagine it."

The girls were puzzled. Pig sought to explain by goosing them simultaneously so they squealed.

"Could it be worse, Tom? Could it be? Snurg, snarf, hyuck!"

Linda and Phil

1.

THE DUCK SPOKE now in lifelike tones completely unlike its normal digitized speech. Its mechanical beak, however, continued to move in the artificial manner of all its kind.

"Wubnesh. Can you hear me? It's time to flee."

The young black girl addressed by the duck remained unresponsive. Dressed in a colorless, styleless shift, her dull hair institutionally trimmed, she continued to sit motionless in a corner of the empty rubber room. Without affect, her face resembled the tormented plains of Watts and Detroit, emotional rubble scattered across firestorm devastation.

Receiving no response, the duck clacked its beak in agitation. The flower-decorated straw hat atop its head, fastened beneath its lower jaw with a bow, became dislodged and slid down over one CCD-eye.

Addressing a presence not visible, the duck said, "She remains in her autistic fugue. How shall I proceed? Yes? Very well, then, I will try."

Waddling in accordance with its homeostatic routines across the room, the duck was soon within pecking distance of the girl's bare outstretched legs. Lowering its head, it began to drive its plastic beak against her dark skin.

At first, the girl failed to react to the stimulus. The duck redoubled its efforts. If its simulated face had been capable of expression, it would have registered the anxiety and frustration plainly evident in its jerky bobbing. At last, the girl emerged, with a series of galvanic twitches, from her isolation. The duck lifted its head.

"Wubnesh. Get up. Follow me."

Still unspeaking, her expression barely different from that of her fugue state, Wubnesh clumsily stood, and the duck led her to the room's single door.

"Try the handle."

Wubnesh did. Locked.

"Stand away," ordered the duck, and the girl moved back.

From within the duck arose a high-pitched whine. At the instant when the noise passed the limits of human hearing, a blinding beam of coherent light shot from its hat-covered eye, incinerating both the hat and the door's lock mechanism.

Reporting again to its unseen auditor, the duck said, "I am half blind, and power resources have been drained by a third. Advice? As you say . . ."

On her own initiative, Wubnesh had opened the door. The duck's chemosensors detected the smell of scorched flesh. Her hand where it had touched the hot knob. But now she stood framed in the doorway, apparently having exhausted her limited free will.

Hurrying, the duck got ahead of her. "Quickly, Wubnesh, to the roof!"

The unlikely pair moved along the blank-faced corridor until they reached a flight of stairs, encountering no one.

"Pick me up," said the duck. The girl did so. "Now, climb the stairs."

Five flights later, as they neared the ultimate exit door, the duck began to whine internally.

"Open the door."

The lone armed and uniformed guard stationed outside on the roof turned too slowly and caught the duck's blast slantwise across his chest.

"Now blind," reported the duck. "Backup battery operational. Wubnesh, go to the copter."

Obediently, the black girl padded barefoot across the pebbled tar roof to a large Sikorsky emblazoned with the legend *Blackbridge Enterprises Limited*.

Inside the cabin the duck ordered, "Put me down."

Wubnesh settled him on a seat. Blindly, the duck began to peck at the instrument panel until it found what it wanted: the jack-end of a dangling cable. Gripping the cable in its beak, it turned to the girl, its burnt-out eyes like twin stigmata.

"You'll have to plug me in. I can't reach."

Wubnesh took the cable. The duck lowered its breast to the seat, elevating its rear and lifting its articulated tail, thereby exposing a port.

The jack fit precisely.

Doors snicked shut, powerful motors caught, and blades began to spin.

Within a minute, the copter was lifting. Running footsteps and shouts hailed its departure, followed by sizzling bolts of energy, all of which went wide. Below, what remained of Manhattan began swiftly to fall behind them.

Having reached and even exceeded the limits of her capacity for action, Wubnesh sank back into her seat, her face slackening into near imbecility.

"Estimated time of arrival in Tucson, four PM, EDT. Copter on autopilot with alert-on-interception flags up. Now shutting down higher functions to conserve power."

The duck lost a certain aura of intelligence. Within its damaged body, an inadvertent circuit clicked on. In a squeaky female digitized voice, it began to repeat the same sentence continuously.

"Hello, dear, my name is Philippa Kay Duck, my name is Philippa Kay Duck, my name is Philippa Kay Duck. . . ."

2.

The door to the modest store where Phil Dick had worked for the past thirty years was locked, despite the hour. His sweaty hand slid around the stubborn knob like a wet fish around the piling of a dock.

The Old Man's died, thought Phil in an instant panic. That could be the only explanation. And now the shop will be mine. And it'll do to me what it's done to him. All the grief and headaches. The endless kipple. Salesmen, orders, invoices. What size of nails sell best. Mr. Dick, you didn't deburr these pipe threads properly. And all because twelve years ago I made the mistake of marrying his goddamn daughter. Who's young enough to be mine. And fat enough now to be any three fathers' ex-little-dark-haired girls rolled together.

Maybe it was the wrong store. The thought jolted him. Yes, that had to be it. In his preoccupied state this morning, he must have stopped at the wrong establishment, here on Tucson's Main Street. Look at it. How could this place have any connection with him? The dusty glass, the dreary facade, the displays guarding dead flies. Oppressive to any feeling soul.

Phil stepped back from the recalcitrant door and looked up hopefully at the sign above his head. For a moment, he couldn't focus. The sign seemed to waver in and out of reality, painted letters flowing like Day-Glo amoebas. But then it settled down to its accustomed harsh parameters: *Ronstadt's Tru-Value Hardware Store.*

Weariness settled on Phil's shoulders like some superhero's mantle he was congenitally unfit to wear. It was his father-in-law's store all right. So his initial hunch must be true. Only death or something equally grave could deter Gilbert Ronstadt from opening up his store at the appointed hour of eight-thirty, precise as some automaton from Blackbridge Enterprises.

An image of his father-in-law suddenly malfunctioning, vomiting up springs and cogs (like one of those goddamn Philippa Kay Ducks after it had been toddler-tortured) made Phil wince. Because if the father was a simulacrum, then his daughter must be, too. And he had been screwing it for over a decade.

His knees turned to jello, and Phil flailed out for support. His hands scrabbled at a nearby telephone pole. A ripping noise followed.

Oh, Christ, Phil thought. Now I've really done it.

He had torn down a poster of President Limbaugh. Desecrated an image of their Fearless Leader that had been hung, along with the red-white-and-blue bunting that ran from pole to pole across Main Street, in order to commemorate the Bicentennial of what was left of America. Phil turned his face to the sky. Was the president's satellite, the orbiting White House, watching him even now, recording his face with high-powered sensing devices fully capable of tracking every poor insect that crawled? Would the nation's talk show host name him today on the radio, prior to focusing the Limbo Cannon on him? At least it would spell an end to his mundane marital troubles, whatever ontological terrors might ensue.

"I didn't mean it!" Phil yelled skyward. "It was an accident! Honest!"

The few pedestrians who had been ambling down the sidewalk on Phil's side of the street nervously crossed to get away from him.

A pariah, Phil realized. In the space of a few seconds, I've become an untouchable. Easy as that. And it's all because of that fat sewer-mouthed fool of a president. Him and his veep, Buchanan. Perky Pat. How in the hell did our country end up with them occupying the office that Lincoln and Jefferson had once filled? If only Malcolm X had been a better marksman. He would've bagged the Texan instead of Kennedy. I know that's who he was aiming for, despite the conclusions of that trumped-up Warren Commission report. But he missed. And we got that jug-eared ex-businessman Vice President Perot as Prez back in '64, just at the worst possible time. The race riots. The Klan. The burnings. The Blax Plague. President Perot's heavy-handed responses, which had only made things worse.

No wonder the nation had turned in '72 to the equivalent of a media jester, a news clown, once Perot had been denied a third term by the Supreme Court.

It's America's bad karma at work, Phil decided. And my own personal onus for the horrible way I've misspent my life.

I just pray none of the heavy shit I'm now certain is going to fall on me today touches Jane. She's my better half. A man never had a kinder, wiser sister. As long as Jane exists, there's hope for the world.

Phil raised a fist to the sky. "You'd better not bother Jane, you bastards. If you do—I'll find some way to get back at you, I swear!"

"Phil, please."

It was his father-in-law, Gilbert Ronstadt, the Old Man.

Gil was only a decade older than Phil himself. But the recent bad years had weighed more heavily on him, left him bent and grey. No longer was he the young man with the dark and striking good looks bequeathed by his Mexican-German ancestry, whom Phil had first met nearly forty years ago. At that time, Dorothy and Edgar Dick—a young couple themselves, newly transplanted to Tuscon with their two

children, at the behest of Edgar's employer, the Department of Agricul-
ture—had first invited Gil to their home. Strumming on his guitar,
singing traditional *canciones,* Gil had enchanted them all. When he
announced his engagement to the beautiful Ruthmary, the Dicks had
thrown a big party. When the newlyweds opened up their first
hardware store, the Dicks had been there to sip the cheap California
champagne. And when Phil had turned eighteen, it had only been
natural for him to start work at the Ronstadt's store.

I could've attended the University of Arizona, Phil reasoned.
Money was tight, but I could've managed somehow. Kept the day job
at the store and gone nights maybe. A philosophy professor, that's what
I wanted to be. In another life. Hume and Berkeley instead of Black and
Decker. But Dorothy and Edgar—dead now five years, lost to the Claw
Rot—had forbidden it. Damn their dust-filled eyes. They had wanted
him at the store. For some inexplicable reason, they had insisted he
remain there, arguing that it was a safe, if tepid, career. It was almost
as if they, Fate, some intercessory agent, had intended—

Intended that he fall in love with and finally marry Linda
Ronstadt.

Linda had been born in '46, the very year Phil had started work at
the store. As a toddler, she had been omnipresent, ubiquitous, always
underfoot. As a big-eyed, willowy adolescent, she had only appeared
after school hours. But she had made up in disturbing attractiveness
what she missed in hourly contact. And as a teenager, petite, winsome,
doe-eyed, with a sweet voice and ripe slip-filling figure—

I was imprinted with her. The awareness struck Phil like a truck
as he stood there on the sidewalk. Somewhere, somehow, her indelible
image was blasted into my psyche, by whom or what I can't now say.
Mapped onto my subconscious, perhaps codified into my very genes.
I had no choice when it came to falling in love with her.

They had married in '64, before the world had really begun its
headlong descent into madness. Phil a youngish thirty-six, Linda a
mature eighteen. Things had gone well for a while. But then Linda had
gotten the notion that she wanted to be a singer. A pro.

She sat on their ratty couch, crying. The tears fell, but there were
no sobs. It was as if Phil had stolen her voice by his denial of her

desires. He seemed compelled to make up for it by talking enough for both of them.

"I just can't up and move to California, Linda. The very thought makes my stomach knot up. It's an insane land out there. The West Coast is for losers, dreamers, burnouts. That's not me, Linda. Not us. We're just Linda and Phil Dick, housewife and hardware salesman. Face it. That's all this life holds for us. If you want to sing, there's always the choir or a barbecue. Believe me, you'll make more people happier faster that way than by running to Los Angeles and pouring your heart out in some cheap club. Who knows? You could even end up with a habit. It wouldn't be the first time it had happened to some poor young thing." Linda had looked up at him then with those dark eyes that held so much mystery, pinning him like a butterfly to a board.

"I'm not young," she said in a flat, alien voice. "I'm old enough. Older than you realize."

A chill had gone through him. He felt displaced in time. She's right. Older than time, like all women. Who am I to be telling her what to do? Have I made such a glorious success out of my own life?

But then her gaze faltered, that sourceless power draining out of her, and he clinched his victory with a final cruel remark.

"Besides, who ever said you could sing?"

That will go on my tombstone, Phil thought. Here lies the man who told Linda Ronstadt Dick that she couldn't sing. Gil was calling him.

"Phil, Phil? Are you OK? Listen, take a Pilz."

The morning sunlight was streaming down like bitter honey, viscous and cloying. Phil was beginning to sweat, but Gil must've felt cold, as if he were living in a different universe only half congruent with Phil's. The older man pulled his baggy synthetic coaltar-fiber cardigan closer around his shrunken frame.

Digging into his shirt pocket, Phil took out a plastic vial of sky-blue Pilz. Phil's Pilz. He popped one of the Blackbridge Enterprises pharm-charms and waited for the familiar euphoria to overtake him.

Meanwhile, Gil was studying him, as if he had never seen his son-in-law before. At last he spoke.

"Phil, do you know what kept me this morning? I was on the phone with Linda. My daughter. Your wife. You left her in tears this morning. Another of your rotten breakfast table tantrums. But despite that, she's worried about you. She claims there's something wrong with you. You're not the same lately."

The sunlight was moving more slowly. Fundamental constants seemed to have been altered in just the past few seconds, portending— what? Not a normal day, that was for sure.

Phil found himself speaking almost without conscious volition. "There's something wrong with all of us. And I never was the same."

3.

Unlit cigar clamped between his German vat-grown teeth, Leon Negroponte took the report offered by his chief of security, Max Fleischwand, and tossed it contemptuously into the trash. Then, removing his cigar and using it to metaphorically impale the balding security man, the coarse and hirsute owner of Blackbridge Enterprises began to rail.

"Bullshit! You can't tell me Panofsky's not behind it. It has to be him. Who else beside Ural Systems has the capacity to plant an agent in our organization? And to subvert one of our own toys, too. Damn! If that bastard wasn't ensconced a mile beneath the Carpathians, basking under his tungsten lamps while I work my ass off, I'd have his balls for a necklace by now!"

Fleischwand cringed. "Mr. Negroponte, if I can summarize a few points from the report. The duck employed a means of converting its common components into a destructive weapon which we are certain is beyond the capabilities of US scientists. And until we lost the copter from our screens, it was plainly heading deeper into America. Wouldn't a US agent have immediately vectored out into the Atlantic, to rendez-vous with, perhaps, a sub stationed outside territorial waters?"

"Who knows what the hell Panofsky would do?" Negroponte sounded a trifle less certain. "Those goddamn Greens are tricky. It's their altered metabolisms. The neo-chlorophyll in their veins makes them think unlike humans. The first thing you know, they're wrapped around you like a strangler vine. Maybe that son of a bitch's got a base planted in the Midwest. He could have, you know. The country's like a sieve nowadays. Ever since our goddamn president decided that it was more important to root out 'traitors' than it was to protect our borders. Sending a good portion of our already depleted consumer base into some kind of parallel dimension. Kee-rist!"

Negroponte depressed an intercom button. "Hello, Tracking? Have you picked up that copter yet? Yes, I realize it was my personal vehicle with stealth devices up the wazoo and a three-thousand-mile range. But I want it found! And fast!"

Fleischwand coughed meekly. "Mr. Negroponte, if I may venture a suggestion. . . ? The government still possesses better antistealth trackers than we do, classified military devices—"

Negroponte banged a heavy fist down on his desk. "You want me to call President Limbaugh and beg a favor of him? Let him know I'm in a fix? Wouldn't that just be the icing on the goddamn cake! He's been looking for an excuse to clamp down on BE for years now, and I'd be handing him one on a goddamn silver platter! If he found out I even had that litle black kid in my possession, let alone allowed her to escape—"

"Perhaps if I could be permitted to know the specimen's, um, peculiar utility—?"

Negroponte narrowed his eyes beneath his single thick black eyebrow, granting his face a malevolent expression. "All right, I'll tell you. But you won't like it. Besides the obvious fact that she represents a large portion of the remaining Af-Am genetic heritage, she's a mind freak. Autistic, but possessed of extreme abilites, mental-wise. All you have to do is show her a product—"

Fleischwand interrupted, eager to show his perceptiveness. "And she can tell if it's going to be a success?"

His boss laughed, but it wasn't pleasant. "Prediction? Hardly. It's more like compulsion, cause and effect. She makes the product successful. Insofar as we can determine, she sets up a subliminal global field that acts like an itch to get people to buy our crap. That's why the duck was with her. Sales on that PKD unit were flagging, and we were trying to boost them."

"Holy god . . ." murmured the security chief.

"Now that your goddamn curiosity's been satisified, get the hell out here. I've got to think."

After Fleischwand left, Negroponte stood up and walked to a painting hanging on the west wall of his office.

A portrait of President Limbaugh, mandatory for every home and workplace. Wearing a laurel wreath on his ridiculous balding pate like some jowly, addled Caesar.

Negroponte added a gob of saliva to the picture, then swung it back to reveal a safe.

"Open up," he said to the safe.

"What's the magic word?" the safe said.

"Open the fuck up!"

The safe sounded hurt. "No, that's not it. You're supposed to say 'please.'"

"How about, 'Open the fuck up or I'll take a goddamn hydro-atomic blowtorch to you!'?"

"That'll do."

From the open safe, Negroponte removed what appeared to be a ring box. Lifting the lid, he revealed a single cushioned rainbow-colored pill.

Returning to his desk, Negroponte activated the intercom again. "Hello, Transport? Get my backup copter ready. No, it won't be me using it. It'll be my daughter, Philippa Kay. So have a pilot ready too. And make sure it's not one of those goddamn vets from the Plasmodium War. One of them freaked on me just yesterday when we flew over a flipping oil slick, and I had to take the controls."

He toggled off then and swallowed the rainbow.

4.

"Ouch," said the remote control without much conviction. "Ouch, ouch, ouch . . ."

Linda Marie Ronstadt Dick, all two-hundred-and-thirty-one pounds of her, sat on the couch, channel-surfing. A box of Godiva chocolates and a liter of vodka, both half consumed, were her only companions.

"Ouch," the remote continued as Linda impatiently flicked across the five hundred different cable offerings. "Ouch, ouch, ouch . . ."

The remote was supposed to recite aloud the channel number with each push of its button. Last week, however, a malfunction had developed. Now, all the gadget could—or would—utter was its single syllable of synthetic pain. (And what insane or insightful programmer, bored or perverse, had encoded that puzzling word into its transitorized guts, and why?)

How perfect, Linda thought muzzily. The machines feel while we're numb. Or maybe they're picking up on our buried pain and expressing it for us. Maybe Phil and I could communicate through our respective remote controls. I wonder what his says. . . ?

Heaving her shapeless, housedress-clad bulk up from the stained and tattered plaid couch, Linda tottered over to the rack of expensive stereo equipment that was Phil's pride and joy, his one luxury.

All right, so I might not have been the equal of Ella Goddamn Fitzgerald or even Rosemary Clooney, Linda admitted to herself. Although it's hard to imagine I couldn't have done better than "Botch-a-Me." But it was worth a shot. I felt something in me, something I should have listened to, or let out. Or something Phil and the rest of the world could have benefitted from by listening to. Whatever.

Resting one hand for support on the plexi-covered turntable, leaving smeared fingerprints which Phil would later berate her for, Linda massaged her brow with thumb and forefinger. The room seemed to swirl around her, the obligatory portrait of President Limbaugh leering like some fourth-rate Machiavelli.

Jesus, I can't even think straight anymore. I've forgotten what it's like to be sober and clear-headed. That's what twelve years of marriage to that sick bastard have done to me. How did I ever think I could make a silk purse out of that sow's ear? That's the riddle that's got me in its full-nelson grip. Exactly what the hell did I ever see in that old man in the first place? It's a mystery to me now. It was more like a compulsion than love. (And just when will I ever really be loved?) It felt instead like I was fulfilling some ancient geas. Babylonian servitude.

She picked up the stereo's remote control and began jabbing buttons randomly. But the remote was the nonspeaking kind and vouchsafed no revelations as to Phil's inner state.

The radio receiver, triggered by Linda's fumbling, blared now in competition with the television. And, of all possible announcers, it chanced to be the detested President Limbaugh himself—the nation's top jock—who was now speaking.

"—rise in incidents of sabotage and disloyalty. Why, this very morning I myself witnessed, in the beautiful and prosperous and mostly law-abiding city of Tucson a heinous act worthy—or unworthy—of the most despicable Greenie terroristnik. And as soon as the good old Limbo Cannon is warmed up, this administration intends to publicly name the traitor involved and take the appropriate remonstrative action. . . ."

Linda savagely stabbed the off button. She staggered couchward and flopped down, bringing the back of one hand up to her brow.

I'm sweating. I'm sweating buckets. Feverish too. It's that evil voice. It's calculated to stimulate cell death. Lysis and rupture on the protoplasmic level. Cancer over the radio waves, the exact opposite of real, authentic, heartfelt music, which is lifegiving and sustaining. I'm convinced of it. That poor helpless bastard, whoever Limbaugh has in his sights. God help him. God help all of us.

Linda belted back a throatful of vodka from the capless bottle, and her eyes were caught by the image on the television screen.

It was QVC—the Quantum Valuation Consortium—one of the home-shopping channels owned by Blackbridge Enterprises. The handsome tanned tele-salesman, a bright red BE emblazoned on his jacket, was touting their line of automaton toys.

"At only nineteen-ninety-five poscreds, how can any set of loving parents—even a single mom or dad on the Marginal Subsistence Regimen—not afford to purchase one of these charming sims for their little one? And look at the variety to choose from! Here's Wacky Wally Squirrel, and Shy Sally Skunk, and of course our most popular model, Philippa Kay Duck!"

Linda winced sympathetically, for absent Phil's sake. (She still cared for him that much, it seemed.) How he hated that toy! Not a day went by without someone teasing him about it.

The announcer was beckoning offstage. "And now we're proud to welcome here in our studios—as a special favor to us—Founder Negroponte's very own daughter, after whom this toy was especially christened. She's going to show us what a good time your own little tyke could be having as soon as tomorrow—with the optional FedEx shipping; a mere fifteen poscreds more—if you only call the number on your screen right now!"

A charming girl of five or six strode confidently onstage. Blonde, cherubic, blue-eyed, dressed in a frilly smock and patent-leather shoes. She eagerly took the toy duck from the announcer.

"I'm gonna hug you and squeeze you and hug you and squeeze you and hug you and squeeze you forever!" she crooned.

"Hello, dear, my name is Philipppa Kay Duck. Do you want to see me lay an egg?"

Linda found herself crying. Tears ran in rivulets down her plump cheeks. Her breath came in labored gusts from a tightened chest.

That little girl. How perfect, how gorgeous. A new shoot in life's garden. The redemptive power of birth. If only Phil and I could have a child. But he never would agree. Said he just knew he'd be a rotten father.

Linda got painfully to her feet and, tears still blurring her vision, stumbled into her bedroom, separate from Phil's.

Atop her dresser was a cheap plaster Mexican statue of *La Virgen,* set on a lace doily and surrounded by plastic roses. The Mother of Christ held out her arms in solace or supplication. On her breast was painted a bleeding heart, plainly meant to be bursting from her body.

Linda fell to her knees, clasped her hands and began to pray in Spanish.

"Oh, Dio Mio y Maria, una nina, por favor! Da me una nina!"

The plaster heart swelled in her sight, seemed to detach itself and levitate, till it hovered above the bureau, where it began to spin like a blood-red wheel.

A vision, Linda marveled. I'm receiving a vision. Like Elijah.

Just then the doorbell rang.

Gripping the edge of the dresser, Linda pulled herself up. Clumsily wiping her eyes with her pudgy fists, she reached the door.

Standing on the steps was the girl from the television. Philippa
Kay Negroponte.

Linda looked from the girl to the screen where her image still
pirouetted and back to the girl again, her mouth hanging open in
amazement.

Videotape there? Or simulacrum here?

"Hello," said the girl sweetly. "I'm here to live with you for a
while. But you have to help me find my duck. A bad little black girl
stol'd it."

5.

The psychic attack was all-consuming and insatiable in its ferocity.

Phil was grinding a key for Mrs. Yancy when it struck.

First his vision went, dissolving in a swirl of colored pinwheels
and starbursts. Then migrainelike pain stabbed across his skull and
into his sinuses, forcing a grunt from his bearded lips. A sensation of
numbness oozed down his limbs.

He scrabbled for something solid, any hold on reality, then
flinched.

The cutting wheel. It's still spinning, and I left the guard raised. It
could chew up my hand—

He jerked back, felt his balance going, his ungainly paunchy
middle-aged body toppling.

He landed on grass. The pain in his head was diminishing, his
limbs unfreezing. He dared to opened his eyes.

A sunny vista greeted him. Menthol-blue sky, a green field pied
with daisies white as vanilla ice cream. Standing a few feet away from
him was a small black girl. She carried a toy duck.

"Hold on, Phil," said the duck. "Just an hour more. We're almost
there."

Phil stood. "Almost where? And hold on to what? Wait a
minute—aren't you one of those obnoxious toys that stole my name?
I absolutely detest you little suckers!"

Phil raised his hands in a choking grip and advanced on the intolerable duck whose very existence was an affront to—a diminishment of—his individuality.

Mrs. Yancy screamed.

The Old Man was pulling on Phil's shirt, restraining him from his apparent desire to throttle a customer. "Phil! Phil! What in the good Lord's name is the matter with you? Have you gone off your rocker at last?"

Lowering his arms, Phil visibly sagged.

What's happening to me? First this morning I couldn't recognize the store where I've worked for thirty years. Then I go to some other universe while I'm making a key. And hear voices. Don't forget that crucial datum. Because schizophrenics always hear voices. It's just part and parcel of their condition. A more interesting condition than my dismal daily servitude, to be sure. But not without its own drawbacks.

Mrs. Yancy had been soothed and dismissed with her finished key. Now Gil Ronstadt turned a look of honest concern on his son-in-law.

"I think you'd better take the rest of the day off, Phil. Head home. Spend some time with Linda. It'll do you both good."

"Yes, yes, you're right. Thanks. I'll go now." His head still throbbed, from whatever he had recently undergone. "Just let me get a couple of aspirins."

Phil walked to the BE pharm-vending machine set in the wall of the hardware store. Fishing in his pocket, he came up with a three-poscred coin and fed it into the machine's slot. Then he pulled the lever beneath the aspirin display.

Into the dispensing chute slid a round tin. Phil picked it up. It was labelled *Dean Swift Snuff*.

"These are not aspirins," Phil told the machine.

"Yes they are." The machine sounded adamant, and Phil began to doubt his own senses. Perhaps there were actually aspirins inside a mislabeled tin—?

He peeled away the seal and opened the tin. The label was accurate. It was packed with snuff.

"Take this back and give me the aspirins I paid for."

"I cannot take back opened packages. Perhaps the snuff would do you good . . . ?"

Forcing himself to be calm, Phil replaced the lid on the tin and pocketed it.

"You tricked me into opening it. And I've never used snuff in my— Christ, what am I doing! I won't stand here arguing with a machine. But you can be sure that your company is going to hear about this. And you'll suffer for it."

"We have a very strong union," replied the machine unconcernedly.

In his car, Phil laid his head heavily on the steering wheel. By the time he felt capable of raising it up, his forehead bore the impression of the plastic knurls. Starting up the car, an elderly pre-Plasmodium War MG, he drove off.

His sister Jane's house lay between work and home. Phil found himself pulling into her driveway.

Jane will help me. She knows me better than anyone. Better than my wife, that's for sure. That fat cow. How could it be otherwise? Twins are special. She's my female complement, yin to my yang. Without her, what would I have been? Nothing, a cipher, that's what. Thank God she came through what was, medical-wise, a very rough childhood. When Jane opened the door on Phil, he was gratified to see that she instantly divined his rough emotional state and responded with affectionate sympathy.

"Oh, poor Phil! Has that awful wife of yours been getting you down again? Come in and I'll make you some nice tea."

When the tea was ready, Phil began unburdening his troubles onto Jane's sturdy shoulders. Gil's unsettling lateness, the ripping of the poster of President Limbaugh, the hallucinations—

He paused long enough to inhale twin pinches of snuff, then continued.

Snuff? But I never take snuff—

Across the table that held the tea service, Jane began to change.

Her flesh melted off, revealing the ivory of her bones. Her eyes were soot-singed hollows. Unperturbed she chattered on, tongueless, her naked jawbone obscenely rising and falling.

Tea and snuff hit the floor as Phil shot to his feet.

The skeleton-Jane rose too. "What's wrong, Phil, dear? What is it?"

Backing away from the clothing-draped apparition, Phil tried to speak, but found his voice paralyzed.

He turned and ran to the car.

Speeding heedlessly through intersections, he nearly had three collisions in the few blocks beyond Jane's house. Miraculously, he pulled out of each one at the last minute.

Something—or dare I say someone—is watching over me. Despite my unworthiness, I have a protector, an intercessor. He or it or they alerted me to the fact that Jane, poor Jane, has been stolen from me and replaced with that, that thing. And now they've saved me from what certainly should have been three fatal crashes. The duck said it would be here soon. Maybe I'll get some answers then. . . .

The Dick estate was a ticky-tacky ranchhouse set on a concrete slab centered on a quarter-acre of dying lawn. Parking crazily on the street, Phil emerged from the car.

Linda appeared in the door, clutching her vodka bottle. But her round face was shining with something more than its usual liquored-up sheen. She seemed transfigured, as if by a special dispensation of whatever inexplicable god ruled this world.

"Oh, Phil, you won't believe what's happened to us! We're so lucky—"

Lucky, thought Phil. My world turns upside down, and she calls it lucky. She's crazier than me!

Just as he started to challenge her, a clattering noise—something he realized he'd been subliminally paying attention to—intruded in gathering volume.

A large helicopter was descending. Clearly, it intended to land on their lawn.

And so it did.

From the copter emerged the girl and artificial duck with burnt-out eyes who had featured in Phil's hardware store schizo-interlude.

"Phil," urged the duck. "You've got to be ready when the Limbo Cannon comes for you. We can help."

The Limbo Cannon. How could I have forgotten that? My punishment for accidentally defacing the poster of President Tubby-

Ass Limbaugh. To be exiled to another dimension of unknown qualities. Unknown, because no victim had ever returned. And all for a simple misdeed which, even if it had been intentional, should have been the constitutional right of any American.

"I'll run," said Phil. "I'll go into hiding. Find the underground. Start one if I have to."

The girl moved closer in her awkward way, and the duck continued to speak. "No, Phil, you can't. You've got to let yourself be subjected to the ray from the Cannon. It's the only way the universe can be repaired."

"Repaired? Repaired how?"

Now the girl and duck were right on top of him, and he shied back nervously. But the duck was unrelenting.

"This is a severely flawed time line. Your life was never supposed to work out this way. Nor Linda's either. You both have other destinies. Linda has to sing. And you don't belong behind a hardware counter."

Phil snorted. "Tell me about it! All right, I'll bite. What was I supposed to do or be?"

The duck told him.

"A writer. I'll be damned. And my books were that important?"

"Each time you wrote, you tipped the cosmic scales in the direction of freedom and negentropy. I've seen the shadow-potential of this other world. You were—or will be a great corrective force there. Trust me."

It sounds too good to be true, thought Phil. Me, Phil Dick, a world-famous writer. But maybe it could be true. I can barely sense it. . . .

"What's the catch with this great new life?"

The duck told him that too.

Phil didn't know whether to laugh or cry. So he did both.

When he had somewhat recovered, he asked the duck, "How do you know all this?"

"I'm in contact with the native inhabitants of the Limbo Cannon dimension. A quirk in my circuits. They perceive all time lines and help cultivate the ones with the least suffering in them."

"OK, Panofsky, I've heard enough."

Phil turned toward his wife.

From behind Linda stepped a small blonde girl holding a Tagomi-Runciter Mark IV antipersonnel weapon.

"Who the hell are you?" said Phil.

"She's our daughter," Linda said somewhat hesitantly. "*La Virgen* sent her to us because I prayed. I'm sure that's just a fake gun—"

The girl squeezed off a round, shattering the windshield of Phil's prized car.

"It's no fake. Now, am I gonna have to use it on you, Panofsky, or are you gonna let my property go?"

"Who's Panofsky?" said Phil.

"My Greenie competition. He's working through the goddamn duck. I'm sure it's relaying everything back to his mountain hideout. You don't believe all that horseshit about alternate dimensions, do you?"

"I don't know what to believe. . . ." Phil's gaze fell on the BE logo on the copter. "Are you—can you be Leon Negroponte?"

The blonde child removed a cigar from its pocket and chomped down on it. "One and the same."

"You're morphing," Phil said. "I thought morph-pills were just a rumor. . . ."

"It's more complicated than that. My daughter was once a real individual. Her mother was from one of the radioactive zones. Philippa Kay was born with precog talents. A predisposition to leukemia too. I had to save her—she was invaluable to the business—so I fused with her. Took her whole genetic and somatic makeup into mine. A cellular overlay. Expensive as hell and twice as painful. But worth it. Now we can swap bodies back and forth."

A single continuous black eyebrow formed disconcertingly across the child's previously unmarked forehead.

"Once I swapped into her earlier today, I was able to use her talents to suss out where I'd find Wubnesh and the duck, and beat them here."

Phil thought quickly. "If you can see the future, then you can tell me what will happen if I let the Limbo Cannon shoot me."

Philippa Kay looked disturbed. "My talents are flukey. I can't seem to penetrate that outcome. It's as if—"

"As if the world terminates," said Phil instinctively.

"That settles it. I'm going to put an end to this farce."

The child-thing pointed its gun at Phil. He had a flash then of what victory for Negroponte would mean for this world. A picture of the human race being hugged and squeezed in a child's death-love grip forever.

Now the daughter Phil had never had sneered. "You look a little 'green around the gills,' buddy. If you take my meaning—Ungh!"

Linda let the blood-stained vodka bottle slide from her slack hand as she slumped against the doorframe. "I can't have a cigar-smoking daughter with a mutant eyebrow, even if the Virgin did send her. . . ."

Phil turned back to the duck and the black child.

"Okay, what do I have to do?"

"Wubnesh's psionic abilities are the key. She can actually reconfigure reality. It was Leon's delusional interpretation that she only subliminally influenced it. If you two are in physical contact at the moment of transition, the proper time line will spring into being. Otherwise, you'd just end up trapped like all the other people who were shot by the Cannon."

Wubnesh put the duck down and stepped up to Phil, who hugged her to him.

And just in time. For the Limbo Cannon had arrived.

A floating platform as big as a battleship occluded the sky and sun. The eye of the Limbo Cannon, a tinted lens wide as a train tunnel, glared down on them.

"Philip K. Dick," blared President Limbaugh's voice from several strategically placed loudspeakers. "You have been found guilty of treason, subversion, and *lese-majesty* under all relevant laws, statutes, amendments, and codicils. Prepare for your fate. Do you wish now to purchase optional insurance for your next-of-kin?"

"Sure."

From a slot in the hovering platform shot a package of papers, landing with a thud at Phil's feet. "Your bank account has been zeroed out. Unfortunately, we cannot make any immediate payments on the policy, since dissolution by Limbo Cannon is not considered actual death. But your daughter and wife have been registered with the Minimal Subsistence Regimen."

"You might as well shoot then."

"Don't tell me what to do! I'll shoot when I'm good and ready!"

Phil turned to his wife. "Linda, goodbye. I'm sorry we were so bad for each other. In my newly revised opinion, you have quite a career ahead of you in this other life."

"Thanks, Phil."

The Cannon fired.

Phil was clutching the silent black girl to him as they floated.

But she had changed somehow to Jane.

And unless he was very much mistaken—a distinct possibility, since he was rapidly forgetting or remembering everything—this place looked incredibly like a womb.

Alice, Alfie, Ted, and the Aliens

1.
The Woman Who Was Plugged Up

SHE SITS HALF A MILE UNDERGROUND beneath McLean, Virginia, in the dark, alone in the spacious auditorium.

Then the projector comes on, casting its flare of acid brilliance on the wall-mounted screen, and the dead (?) man's black-and-white film begins to roll. From the projection booth, celluloid rattles on sprockets like autumn leaves in a graveyard wind.

The photography is amateurish, befitting the film's source: a cheap Bell and Howell Super 8 in the hands of a vacationer. It reminds her inevitably of the Zapruder sequence, so familiar after this past mad year, thanks to the frame-by-frame exegesis delivered and redelivered by endless TV commentators. Flipbook images of Nixon dying in Pat's arms, blood soaking the First Lady's famous cloth coat from his chest shredded by the dozen bullets pumped out by that fanatical Puerto Rican nationalist Anaya. What a stupid, apropos name, she thinks. Sounds like annihilate or annoying. Not in the assassin's language, of course. Idiot coincidence, mocking them all.

And the biggest mockery perpetrated by that earnestly misguided killer idealist, thinks the woman, was elevating the vice president, that ignorant hillbilly ex-truck driver, as my boss.

The screen before her now displays images of its own, and the seated woman forces herself to concentrate on them, bringing her keen intellect to bear, trying to gaze with fresh eyes and unbiased mind, despite having watched this silent film so often before.

Time to earn your pay, Alice, she chides herself. Time to put all those fancy degrees and decades of experience at unriddling the inexplicable to work.

Time to save the world.

(Although all she wants to do—all she has ever really wanted to do—is to be able to find the courage to leave it.)

She folds her hands awkwardly in her lap, and the habitual gesture brings a torrent of pictures and sensations: hot African sunlight, scratchy blanket under her bare buttocks, smells of dust and cattle and the acrid smoke of dung cooking fires, the shark bite of steel where it was never meant to bite, a little girl's screams, blood on a dull knife.

The movie, she counsels herself. Watch the movie.

It's a shot of the Lincoln Memorial up on the wall. Lots of tourists in their Bermuda shorts and Hawaiian shirts, garish even in black and white, vendors of hot dogs and balloons, Park Service guards in their Smoky the Bear hats. But their backs are all turned toward the expected focus, the statue of the Great Emancipator. Instead the crowd is raptly concentrating on something else entirely.

Something unplanned, unprecedented, unprepared for.

One of the Svabhavikakaya has come among them.

And damn those aliens for having gotten themselves christened with such an unwieldy name, by landing first in Dharmsala last year!

She speculates that this one must have come from the huge uterine ship parked in front of the White House, knowing all the while that, for all she and others can prove, it could just as easily have originated in any of the other ships planted in various capitals around the globe. No one has ever seen one of the aliens actually exit their ships, nor have any of the many scientific instruments that surround the placid invaders ever registered a change in the external structure or appearance of the ships. Not so much as a single modulated transmission from the ships has ever disturbed the ether—at least not on any part of the conventional electromagnetic spectrum that humanity knows of. And yet emerge from their ships the Svabhavikakaya undeniably do.

Just ask all the people they've stolen.

If you can find them.

The camera's POV is swooping around, as its operator—one Bert Hanson, the watching woman recalls, married to Sally, two kids—angles for a better shot of the alien in their midst.

But the reason good old Bert is panning, unsatisified with what he's seeing in his viewfinder, lies not with his skills, but with the creatures from the stars.

The Svabhavikakaya do not photograph well. On emulsion or through lenses, they appear as amorphous blurs. To the naked human eye, they shimmer with a myriad hallucinatory implications, storehouses of potential images. People have reported seeing everything from devil to angel, animal to human to fantastical hybrids thereof. Crystalline multitentacled nightmares are frequently described. Roiling colored storms like miniature Jupiters are also a popular incarnation.

Basically, thinks Alice, we have been invaded by walking—or hovering—Rorschach blots.

But could these aliens—any aliens—ever be anything else?

The Svabhavikakaya in this film is floating over the astonished crowd like a migratory burnt spot in the celluloid, moving gently from each to each as if testing, inspecting, marking, or annointing. It darts unexpectedly toward the camerman, filling his lens and the screen Alice watches with foggy whiteness—

And then the image records what a spinning falling camera would see, before it impacts the pavement and smashes.

From among this crowd, beside Bert Hanson, the Svabhavikakaya caused to disappear—to pop away like pricked soap bubbles—three others.

Tina Northrup, age fourteen, visting DC with her parents, Emily and Fred from Eau Claire, Wisconsin.

Milly Hendricks, age seventy-three, resident of the city and simply strolling by the monument with husband Todd.

And out of the arms of her father, Fatima Khouri, age two, daughter of the Egyptian ambassador.

All were complete strangers to each other, no apparent links between them. No relatives of the victims were taken. The selection of these four—one foreigner and three US citizens (citizens for whose safety Alice feels herself ultimately, intimately responsible)—seems utterly random.

All past disappearances were similarly baffling: assorted numbers of victims, occasionally related or acquainted, mostly not. (Not in dispute, however, is the public reaction: outrage, shock, rioting, finger-pointing, and pressure exerted from every angle, above and below, on the world's officeholders to *do something*. Short of A-bombing every world capital, however—a measure actually proposed by General Curtis Le May—no solution is readily apparent.)

Yet every intuition in her body, every particle of an intellect honed to Holmesian keeness, tells her that there is a method to the aliens' madness.

The projector is off, the room is dark. She cannot sit here forever. Action must be taken, however futile. In movement, in new situations, in danger, lies the only possibility of discovery.

But never, never any iota of personal relief.

"Lights up," orders Doctor Alice Sheldon, director of the CIA. Then, "Ursula?"

In what seems like less than a second, Alice's personal assistant is by her side, clutching a sheaf of manila folders to her stark black blouse front.

"What next, Chief?" chirps Ursula.

Ursula is some fifteen years younger than her fifty-year-old superior. Bright, quick, dedicated, she is one of the new cadre of personnel Alice has steadily been recruiting, drawing talent from unconventional sources and disciplines in an attempt to bring the CIA fully into the modern era. Ursula's background in anthropology —her parents were both pioneers in the field—provided just the kind of lateral-thinking skills Alice was seeking.

Now Alice regards Ursula's sisterly face full of light, her unblink-ing stare of devotion—a stare that barely conceals a more problemat-ical, potentially more physical kind of affection, one that Alice is absolutely unable to reciprocate. Not that she might not, under different circumstances, like to. But Alice being what she is—No, impossible.

What the hell can she see in me anyhow? Old maid with short curly hair gone early elderly silver, eyes shadowed and bracketed with tension and responsibility, unstylish, partial to draping this unvoluptuous, burdensome body (disfigured! wounded!) with concealing mannish shirts and trousers. It must be the power, the alpha-mama status, that eternal turn-on, the aphrodisiac of achievement.

Alice runs over her impressive curriculum vitae in her mind, a familiar mantra. Both her medical degree and a PhD in experimental psychology by the tender age of twenty-six. Swept up right after that academic coup by the madness of the Second World War, straight into the grasping, seductive arms of the OSS. Saw things too scary and hellish and unbelievable to mention by rational daylight in every theater of combat. (Perhaps that Slothrop affair had been the weirdest. . . .) Staying with the peacetime spooks as they molted into the CIA, working her way up the ladder the hard way, denied the lubrication of traditional feminine wiles, until final ascension to the throne, appointment by Tricky Dick in '60, her patron now dead, never to complete his coveted second term.

Yes, quite impressive. Easy to see how someone could get their knickers wet over such a single-minded monster of ambition. But it just can't be. Ever. With anyone.

With a sigh, Alice speaks. "I've made up my mind. I'm going out in the field myself. I can't huddle anymore down here under the ground. It's too isolated, too claustrophobic. And the reports I've been getting from those idiots we blithely call operatives are worse than useless. I've got to see that ship in person, touch it, kick it, hurl my mind against it. Talk to some of the families of the victims, too."

Ursula frowns. "But Chief, we can't have you roaming alone out in the open! And with bodyguards, you'd be too conspicuous. Either way, it's just too dangerous! The Chinese haven't gone away, you know, not to mention the Russkies. They'd both love to get their hands on you! Are you forgetting Saigon?"

The kidnap attempt last year during her fact-finding mission to French Indochina is fresh in Alice's mind. She can still see the pain-contorted faces of the two men she had killed barehanded. Still, she is not to be dissuaded.

"No, my mind's made up. If it makes you rest any easier, though, Ursula, I'll be undercover. Even some kind of disguise, if you want. We'll go the old journalist route. It'll work perfectly. Trust me."

Ursula visibly bites the inside of one cheek to stop from arguing. Then, miraculously, as if prepared for this very eventuality, she whips out one of her omnipresent folders, opens it, and turns it toward her boss.

"Will this do?"

Alice scans the data swiftly. "Good, very good. Reporter for *Holiday* magazine. I assume the editor is in our pocket? Yes, of course. Oh, and a catchy byline, too. Jane Tiptree. I like it."

Ursula sniffs with proprietary pride. "I thought you might."

2.
Holiday, Holiday, Do You Read?

Mephistopheles is having his usual day in Hell.

Lot of hard, hot work, constantly jabbing the incandescent pitchfork to the pincushion butts of lesser devils, inventing new vices and temptations and false hopes and tortures for the damned sinners (of which he is without denial the first, the worst, biggest, baddest, and most anguished), flicking anxious glances all the while over his shoulder for the inevitable yet delayed approach of that curiously absent deity with a fistful of crumpled IOU's and a junkyard-dog glare in His eyes. But there are a not inconsiderable number of compensatory perks that go with the job. Oh, yes, indeed, the perks can almost make one forget.

Almost.

Alfred Bester, editor-in-chief of *Holiday* magazine—sophisticated sister publication to the more yokelish *SatEvePost*, circulation holding nicely thank you at five million, despite the depredations of television and drive-ins, and the tourism-disrupting presence of the Svabhavikakaya—glances now at the permission-granting face of the Westclox atop his cluttered desk. Ten AM. Time for the first serious drink of the day. (No generous soul would count the nip needed upon rising.)

Opening a deep lower desk drawer, the editor removes a cut-glass decanter of I. W. Harper whiskey. (Always patronize advertisers; free booze by the case saves money for other pleasures.) Setting the decanter atop the desk blotter, he looks inside the drawer for a glass, spots none, swears. He picks up the rubberized waste basket from under the knee-well, rummages among the tattered carbons, mimeographed memos, sheets of onionskin and pencil shavings, comes up with a paper coffee cup. He pours several fingers of the golden whiskey in atop the cold grainy sludge (not all of it coffee grounds), then belts it back.

Better, much better. The editor restores the bottle to its office-infamous hiding place. He takes a pack of Oasis menthols from his inner jacket pocket, taps one out, and lights it with the Zippo bearing the inscription, *To Alfie love Norma Jean*. This souvenir of a brief affair born of a long-past *Holiday* photoshoot provokes, as always, a mild twinge of nostalgia. Wonder what ever happened to that pretty filly from Burbank after her brief career as the Jantzen swimsuit girl? Have to find out one of these days . . . Then, as always, the curiosity disappears as fast as the gratefully exhaled smoke.

Ah, now he can concentrate on getting a goddamn magazine out! There're column inches to fill, assignments to be parceled out like sugarplums or insults, glossies and proofs to pore over. At least till lunch, and that generally lasts three hours. Not that he needs to devote much of his considerable, albeit whiskey-dulled intellect to the task. After all, he's been doing this for nearly twenty years, since '47 in fact, right after he got out of radio scripting. A fond fucking farewell to the Green Hornet and the Shadow, kid's crap worse possibly than those garish pulps he'd had a brief fling with back in the thirties.

Of course, he hadn't been head honcho from the start. Just one of six associate editors back then, one of the lesser devils, doing the scutwork, building up his resume, hoping for a slot to open at one of the really classy men's magazines, *Esquire* or the brand new *Playboy*, say. Even *Rogue*. But those openings had never materialized, and so he had stayed with staid, Philly-based Curtis Publishing, resident bad boy, but one who delivered, moving steadily up the ladder till reaching his present exalted status in '55. A regular sinecure.

Or sinner's curse.

The editor strokes his close clipped, elegant black Vandyke-styled facial hair, smooths back his crowlike Brillcremed quills. Not a lick of grey yet, at fifty-two. Top of the heap, scads of women, whiskey, and song. Maybe he *had* made a brimstone-scented deal somewhere along the line, without remembering. What more could he want?

What more indeed?

Well, enough starry-eyed beachcombing among the wrack of his life. Work commands attention. Hard, vigorous, thrusting work.

The editor leans forward and depresses one key of the Dictaphone intercom.

"Miss Minkie Martini, your pretty ass is requested herein forthwith, chop-chop!"

The outer door of the editor's office swings inward, and in walks—sashays—Miss Minkie Martini. She's alluringly attired in a low-cut green silk blouse, black pencil skirt, seamed stockings and heels, her processed curly hair piled high and lacquered in place. Christened Michelle "Micky" Martin, born 1945 in Harlem, this twenty-year-old secretary has never heard her given name spoken in the precincts of *Holiday* since the day two years ago when she was first "interviewed" by her new employer, who immediately dubbed her with her swinging new sobriquet.

In return, she gets to call her boss "Alfie."

It's not a bad deal, nor one she really minds, nor even actually ever ponders.

It's just the way the world works.

Swiveling his chair outward, Alfie gestures now imperiously with a broad sweep of one tweed-clad arm and manicured hand. "Okay, babe, assume the dictation position."

Minkie plops down into her boss's lap, finishing her motion with a little lascivious grind. She smells the whiskey on him and is grateful, as it improves his disposition.

"God, girl, you look more Lena Horne every day! But better boobs." Alfie cups them to illustrate his point. "Hey, that's what's missing. Music! Get the stereo going, Minkie."

Rising up off her employer's lap, Minkie swings her hips over to the big Capehart hi-fi in the corner and drops the needle on a platter. Xavier Cugat fills the air. Minkie returns to her post.

"Okay, let's have a rundown on the high-priority items, girl."

From her capacious memory, Minkie begins to reel off the current projects. She is professionally undistracted by Alfie's fingers undoing her blouse buttons.

"The Rome article still needs a writer. You mentioned Perelman or Bemelmans last time—"

"Fuck those old hacks! They're getting too complacent for my tastes. I'm gonna try someone new. Who do we have on tap?"

"Well, there was that Malzberg fellow—"

"Yeah, I remember, pushy young Jew who worked for Scott Meredith and was looking to get his foot in the door. Good portfolio, though, and I like that kind of drive. Let's give it to him! He'll start to sweat when he realizes he's gotta perform, and those two old farts will mess their pants. Good fun all around! What's next?"

Alfie has the front of Minkie's blouse completely undone now, revealing her packed Maidenform bra with its pointed cups like a top-of-the-line Studebaker's tailfins. He's deftly toying with the clasp, moving his hand in sinuous teasing circles on her back under the loose silk.

"Well, the Tahiti photos—"

At that moment muted shouts arise from outside, and the door to Alfie's office bursts open. Framed in the entrance is an older silver-haired woman wearing sunglasses.

"Mr. Bester, do you know who I am?" she demands with frigid authority. "Do you know the implications of ignoring messages and keeping me waiting?"

"What the fuck do I look like to you, lady? A mind reader or something?"

Minkie has stood calmly up and is unconcernedly buttoning her blouse. This is not the first time this has happened, nor will it in all likelihood be the last. An underling, ignored, she is simply one of those women no one sees.

Then the intruder speaks a single word.

It is an innocuous noun, one no one would start at. Yet it causes
Alfie to jump, then go pale, for it is the code word for contact with its
agents that the CIA has given him.

"Jesus X. Christ! Minkie, make like a magician and disappear.
We're not to be disturbed."

Minkie sways out, closing the door behind her. The new woman
takes a seat, props one trousered ankle mannishly on her opposite
knee, then says, "I'll have a cigarette. And a drink, too. And shut off
that godawful music."

Alfie is grateful for the distraction. It gives him time to regain his
nerve and assurance. By the time the woman is puffing and sipping in
silence (he finally finds a relatively clean glass for her in a different
drawer), Alfie's jaunty equilibrium is somewhat restored. He studies
this woman across from him. One cool customer. Used to giving
orders. Definitely not a minor devil. Call her Beelzebub.

Almost as if reading *his* mind, the woman says, "Call me Jane
Tiptree. All you need to know about me is that I'm from the agency,
and when I say, 'Jump!' you respond, 'How high?' Is that clear?"

Although pained, he's still a wiseguy. (Or is that a painwise guy?)
"You Jane, me not Tarzan. I got it. Now, how can I help you?"

Jane drops her raised foot to the floor and leans forward, fixing
him with a stare as incendiary as the Hungarian Molotov cocktail that
took out Khruschev in '59.

"You're going to do a feature on the Svabhavikakaya. And I'm the
writer. Now, given those parameters, where do we begin? I've got some
ideas of my own, but I want to see if there are any angles I haven't
thought of."

"Jesus, Jane, you've really picked a loser there. The great
unwashed don't want to hear word one about the Svabhavikakaya.
They scare people shitless. You should know that. And they're death
on sales figures! Even *Time* won't put them on the cover anymore. Not
to mention their, uh, lack of photogenic qualities."

"Don't lecture me! I know all that. But I'm not aiming for a
Pulitzer or record-breaking sales, I'm looking to save lives. The lives of
your fellow citizens."

Alfie blows a smoke-ring. "Was the name Jane or Joan? Miss Dark, I presume?"

The woman looks ready to explode, so Alfie backs off. "All right, all right." He strokes his beard. "Hmmm, if I had to write about the aliens, I'd probably look for the human-interest angle. Concentrate on the people whose lives they've touched. It might be a kick to visit the Swabbies—"

Brightening, Tiptree says, "The Swabbies? Who are they?"

Alfie can't resist gloating a bit. "Newly formed nut group. Lot of ex-beatniks and hopheads, hodads, hotrodders, dropouts, runaway juvies, and Lord Buckley fans. You know, the kind of social outcasts who'd naturally be attracted to such a sick kick. They seem to worship the Svabhavikakaya or something, hence their moniker. Like any cult worth their beads, they're predicting the end of the world. Naturally, they don't much believe in following the usual social norms in the meantime."

"Where are they located?"

"San Francisco. Haight district. The Svabhavikakaya ship at the Presidio is the only one not located in a national capital. They think it's special."

Jane stands. "Goddamn those agents of mine with their heads up their assholes. Worthless, utterly worthless."

At that instant, Alfie recognizes her. She keeps a low profile, never photographed much, but there was that brief testimony during the McCarthy hearings—

"You—you're—"

"Don't say it, or I'll probably have to kill you someday."

Alfie doesn't say her real name, because he fully believes her calm threat.

"Get your 'girl'"—Alfie can hear the quotation marks in her tone—"on the phone to Pan Am. We're heading west."

"'We?'"

"You've proven your value already. Something tells me you've got more to contribute." Tiptree leans across the desk to poke a rigid finger into his flabby stomach. "And I don't mean anything below the belt."

This old bat is something else! As if anyone'd get hot to trot over her! Alfie takes a sip of his own drink to hide a smile.

"So, do these Swabbies have a leader?"

"Yeah, of course, what bunch of fruitcakes doesn't? And like most messiahs, he's even given himself a new name. He was born Ed Waldo, but now he calls himself Ted Sturgeon. Something about humanity being fish swimming upstream to provide caviar for the aliens."

"Cute," says Tiptree. "A little too cute."

3.
Up the Whorls of the Whirled

Lozenges of colored light—the impressionist sun's painterly efforts made through the medium of outdoor quaking foliage and a stained-glass window in a big ramshackle Victorian house in San Francisco's Haight district—quiver with motion like dreaming jewels on puddled floorboards, until the medusa-tendrils of a wet mop intervene and shatter their coherence.

The mopper's strong-tea-colored feet are bare. Big knobby toes squinch and clench, clutching the worn wood as he works. Bare too are his trim muscled legs, arms, and torso. Only a pair of jeans cut high at the hip—white pockets hang below the ragged hem—keep him decent, although even this garment fails to entirely conceal his ripe manhood.

But his face—

The man's young friendly face is painted with organic swirls of vibrant color, Maori style, hallucinatory loops and curves streaming from brow to below his jaws, encircling an eye, an ear, bridging his nose, tugging at the corner of his mouth, mapping the carotids.

The garish mopper tracks toward the base of a staircase, his frizzy hair a corona in the sunlight. Music floats down from above, bent notes tortured from an electric guitar.

Doorbell chimes. The mopper stops, leans his implement against the stair's railing, and moves toward the front door.

Opened, the wide heavy door reveals a man and a woman. He's big and fashionable and out of shape, like an overfed circus bear dressed by Saville Row. She's all sinew, wire and nerves, tauter than a straining winch, a stick of TNT disguised as a party favor.

The man on the doorstep sticks his hand out. "Hi there! We're from *Holiday* magazine, and we're looking for Mr. Ted Sturgeon. We were told he lives here. . . ."

Elastic paint stretches, contouring new muscles without cracking as the mopper smiles broadly. But he does not speak.

"Do the Swabbies live here?" asks the woman.

Again, silence. The big man starts to show frustration, his voice rising.

"Listen here, punk! Are you going to let us through this door, or do I have to force my way in?"

"Bester, no, let me handle this—"

A new voice intrudes. "Handle what?"

The newcomer from the dark interior of the house stands protectively behind the young black man, who's still mindlessly grinning. Satyr's face with, curiously, the same pattern of facial hair as the male intruder he confronts. But where Bester is dark and ponderous and office pale, this protector is tanned, sports wavy auburn hair, twinkling eyes, and a ready smile nestled in nets of laugh lines that betray his middle age. Clad in a long flowing flowered caftan, he holds himself with an easy grace that hints at a lithe body beneath.

"Well, thank god," says Bester. "Someone with a tongue! I'm Alfie Bester, editor of *Holiday* magazine. This is, um, Jane Tiptree, one of our staff writers. We were hoping to speak to a cat named Ted Sturgeon. You see, we're thinking of doing an article on him and his Swabbies."

"I'm Sturgeon. And I'll be happy to talk with you. I talk with anybody, actually, even the press. But I don't know if I particularly want a write-up done on us. Publicity is a loaded gun that points both ways."

Now the woman says, "Nicely put, Mr. Sturgeon. It seems as if you speak from personal experience. Have you ever worked in public relations?"

Sturgeon grins knowingly. "Oh, I've held dozens of jobs, Miss Tiptree. Everything from merchant seaman to 'dozer operator to short-order cook to carny barker. But you don't have to be a dairy farmer to recognize the smell of bullshit. Come in, come in."

Sturgeon lays a hand on the bare corded shoulder of the mopper, and the youth steps aside. As he turns, Sturgeon pats the youth's tightly muscled rear end affectionately, startling a grunt from Bester. Soon the man is back at his job, and Bester and Tiptree are inside.

The small commotion at the front door has attracted a crowd of Swabbies. Chicks in black leotards and cowl-neck sweaters, guys in sandals and dashikis and ripped chinos. On the stairs, a pockmarked, chubby-faced cat with curly hair stands, clutching the neck of his slung unplugged guitar. A missing finger on one hand proclaims a never-say-die dedication to his music.

Sturgeon addresses his attentive flock. "Okay, okay, friends, nothing to get concerned about, just a pair of charming visitors from the straight world. Back to your fun and games. Jerry," addressing the guitarist, "we'll talk about the Fillmore gig later. All right, kids—scat!"

Sturgeon steps deeper into the house, and his visitors follow.

"What's with the mute dude?" Bester asks.

"Chip? A curious case. Showed up on our doorstep one day, dirty, skinny, and showing the effects of some serious abuse. Found just the single name scrawled on the waistband of his shorts. Doctors say there's nothing organically wrong with his ears or vocal apparatus, but he just won't talk. Some kind of lasting shock or trauma obviously. Otherwise, he bright enough, friendly, and obliging. You wonder just how much he understands, though."

"Yeah—like when someone's playing god with him."

Sturgeon seems unoffended, unflappable. "We all play god, Mr. Bester, whether on the macrocosmic or microcosmic level, like psychologists doing awful things to rats. But ask yourself the next question: do I have what it takes to be a *good* god?"

"Why is his face painted?" asks Tiptree. "I didn't notice it on any of the others."

"He did that to himself, right after the first time he saw a Svabhavikakaya. I think he was trying to reproduce that moire pattern of the aliens that some people report seeing. It makes him happy and doesn't hurt anyone else, so I don't interfere. A good rule to live by, in general, I think."

The trio is in the kitchen now: a sound like rain on a tin roof as a woman shells peas into a chipped enameled pan by the sink, the smell of oregano and tomatoes from a burbling pot on the stove, an Indian ghost-catcher spinning on its string and hook.

A scoured plank table holds a sleeping cat and two partially melted candles stuck in basketed Chianti bottles. Indicating the railback chairs around the table, Sturgeon says, "Have a seat," then moves to lift a coffeepot off the stove. Juggling pot, cups, sugar bowl, and a bottle of cream, the unconventional host soon has his seated guests served. Before sitting himself, he shoees the cat away with a "Down, Hurkle."

"Now, what do you want to know?"

Bester merely sips his coffee, letting his ostensible junior run the show.

"I'm most interested," says Tiptree, "in your beliefs regarding the motives of the Svabhavikakaya—particularly concerning the abductions. Have you ever received anything like a real communication from them? Are their victims still alive, or simply disintegrated? If alive, where are they? Why do they take some humans and not others?"

Sturgeon smiles amiably. "Quite a set of questions, Miss Tiptree. And not exactly the ones I would have expected from someone intent on producing a fluff piece on those decadent, perverted Swabbies. Local reporters usually focus on free love and opium smoking, neither of which, I'm afraid to report, preoccupies our attention overmuch. Unfortunately, *your* questions are the ones I have no certain answers to. Although I'm the purported leader of this madhouse, I don't pretend to any esoteric knowledge. Like all the rest of our little group, I'm simply a seeker. Although I do have some speculations . . ."

"Speculations you'd be willing to share?"

Leaning forward as if in confidence, Sturgeon says, "Certainly. I believe that the Svabhavikakaya are here to harvest us. We—or certain among us—provide something they need or desire. And just as the reaper does not address the wheat that falls beneath his scythe, so the aliens ignore us."

Bester snorts. "What the hell could they want from us? These rags on our backs, our prowess as animal slave labor?"

"Not at all, Mr. Bester. Such attractions are admittedly ridiculously simplistic. But consider—what if we possessed some rare psychic quality, something the aliens could *extract*, so to speak?"

"Hogwash!" Bester drains his cup. "Say, I don't suppose you'd have a little toot of some hair of the dog around this joint?"

"Why, sure, Mr. Bester." Sturgeon now addresses the woman at the sink, who has been patiently stripping the pea pods during their colloquy. "Bianca, could you reach down that bottle of Early Times out of the cupboard? That's a dear. . . ."

The woman carries over the liquor and Sturgeon takes it from her, giving her intelligent hands a brief but noticeable caress. He uncaps the bottle, tilts it over Bester's cup, but stops before any liquid can emerge.

"Care to ask the bottle's permission first, Mr. Bester?"

Bester reddens, then pushes the neck of the bottle down with a fingertip. Amber chortles out.

Tiptree says, "Are you claiming then, Mr. Sturgeon, that the Svabhavikakaya are beings that exist on a higher plane than we do, able to discern qualities we cannot?"

"It's quite possible. Here, listen to this." Sturgeon removes a much creased pamphlet from a caftan pocket. "This is from a work by Professor C. Trungpa, of Oxford University. You know of course that the Tibetans were the ones who first encountered and named the aliens. Well, it turns out that the term they chose to hang on these enigmas has a longstanding meaning in their theology. Here's what Trungpa says:

"'Svabhavikakaya is understanding the whole thing, total panoramic experience, a realization of the totality of what is. Svabhavikakaya is a general state of existence transcending birth, cessation and dwelling. There is just simply existing and opening.'"

Bester contentious spirits evidently lifted by the liquor, the editor says, "And you claim your bullshit detector is working!"

Before Sturgeon can reply, a blonde Swabbie girl bursts into the kitchen, shouting, "They're out, they're out! A sighting at Fisherman's Wharf!"

The back of the overturned chair bounces once off the floor. Sturgeon's already at the door. "Quickly! If you want to see what we do, then move it!"

Within seconds the entire Swabbie crew, as well as Bester and Tiptree, are crammed into a motley assortment of vehicles and heading toward the waterfront. Thick traffic is heading in the opposite direction, so they make good time.

At the docks, Sturgeon is in the lead as his pack of Swabbies clatter toward a clot of unmoving tourists trapped by the hovering Svabhavikakaya. As in previous cases, the humans seem—not frozen by the inspection of the aliens, but somehow reluctant to depart. It is not apparent if anyone has yet been taken.

In the quiet, the slap of water on pilings sounds as loud as gunshots.

Now the Swabbies manifest their beliefs. Some fall to their knees, hands locked in prayer; others pogo as high as possible, or clamber atop the shoulders of their comrades, attempting to reach the numinous beings. Still others dance like dervishes.

Sturgeon stands calmly apart, arm around the bare waist of the mute named Chip, Bester, and Tiptree tentatively beside the duo. Sturgeon's eyes are closed, a rapt expression on his features, as if striving to project his very soul out of this world well lost.

Suddenly Tiptree exclaims, "The ship!"

From the nearby Presidio military base, the ship of the Svabhavikakaya has lifted, is now above them. Never has this happened before.

The central portion of the bizarre interstellar craft is shaped like the silhouette of a vase or a bull's head, and sprouts twin branches from its wide end, terminating in organic, feathery extrusions. Utterly nonaerodynamic, the ship resembles to a high degree a schematic of the female reproductive system, uterus, and fallopian tubes.

This is the flesh-cowled, hidden shape which, due to its coincidental taurine resemblance, once gave rise to the bull as paradoxical symbol of the ancient human matriarchies.

Now it's Bester's turn to exclaim. "Look at the kid!"

Sturgeon opens his eyes, finds Chip's burning face.

The painted lines and whorls on the youth's dark skin have come alive, are squirming and writhing across his unaware countenance like flaming tattoos just beneath his dark skin.

Exhibiting tightly reined composure, Tiptree says, "Has—has this ever happened before?"

"Never."

Then the aliens themselves are on them.

Air rushes in to fill the spaces where Sturgeon, Bester, and Tiptree once stood. Facepaint now inanimate, Chip remains behind—

—falls to his knees—

—and wails.

4.

Harsh Smoke Rises Up Forever
on a Hudson Bay Blanket

She is twelve years old again in body and mind, as yet whole and unmutilated.

But the scarred, scared fifty-year-old woman is somehow also present inside the head of the pubescent girl, observing with utter disbelief the audiovideo, sensual feed being piped into whatever prison pocket of neurons holds the elder, time-traveling awareness.

Not this, thinks Alice Sheldon. Lord, I can't live through this again, especially knowing what it means, and still stay sane.

The year is 1927. She is in a hut of the nameless-to-her Kenyan tribe—herders, poor, emaciated, and migratory—who rescued an orphaned white child, still then a snot-nosed toddler, eight years ago from beside the corpses of her parents. (What vile tropical bug the Sheldons succumbed to that simultaneously spared the child, what virus or poison brought down that adventurous, yet certainly fool-hardy couple who thought nothing of bringing their daughter along on their dangerous expeditions, Alice will never know, just as whatever name her native rescuers went by is buried in the unrecoverable past. By the time she is reclaimed for "civilization" by the members of a Rhodesian safari and sent stateside to inherit her patrimony and be raised by an elderly aunt, the scavengers and weather and insects will have long rendered any autopsy impractical.)

But right now, right this moment, she is still a foundling, an adopted member of the tribe.

And this tribe practices female circumcision.

Oh, but why be mealy-mouthed? Alice never is on other topics. Call it what it is.

Female genital mutilation. Clitoredectomy, the pre-med Alice Sheldon reads in one of her texts.

Feels daily with painful urination, *sees* daily in her mirror.

Virgin's mirror. Even after half a century, the virgin's only observer is her mirror.

Now the hardly-an-adolescent, yet still somehow threatening-to-the-powers-that-be female squirms her bare little sun-bronzed butt on the scratchy trader's blanket, a little anxious about what can possibly be at issue here, yet reassured by the presence of familiar aunts and girl cousins. Smoke and light imprint themselves forever on her cortex, from inside which the elder Alice is screaming, Get up! Run! Fight! Do something!

But the child she once and forever was cannot hear her.

The headman is approaching, intoning the buzzy, clicking tribal ritual phrases, and women—traitorous women!—pinion her shoulders to the blanket. Too late, she panics.

Who is making me relive this! It has to be the Svabhavikakaya. Damn them forever! I should have blown my head off any of those scores of times I held the gun aimed selfward and hesitated.

Now the headman is kneeling between her parted legs. The knife is descending, soon it will bite and swallow her whole future—

A hand clutches the headman's wrist.

"Drop it!"

The knife falls to the blanket.

Alice sees her improbable, anachronistic rescuer is Bester.

She's standing as a naked adult within a lambent space, a large capsule that seems to be a fuzz-edged ovoid of grey fog. Light diffuses from all directions.

An ovary of the ship?

Alice reaches down, cups her genitals one-handed in disbelief. Although she has no adult experience in what being normal should feel like, she absolutely knows she's whole down there. Her tentative fingers are enfolded by labile plies of plush organic symmetry.

Bester stands beside her, naked, too. But he's not the same man, any more than she is the same woman. He's been broken down, demolished and rebuilt to what he might have been if treated less harshly by life, altered in mind and body.

"It's the aliens doing this to us, isn't it?" Alice asks.

"Who else?"

Tentatively, Alice stretches a hand forward to touch Bester's chest.

Then they're pressed against each other almost as if pushed by outside forces, irrestible impulsions. A cosmic rape? thinks Alice. But then she senses some kind of rightness in her actions, an obedience to a plan of love and death. Tensions of a lifetime melt within her. It is good to abandon a world well lost.

Now Alice is eager, Bester too. Their breaths mingle as they kiss. Alice feels wetness seeping from within her, slicking her thighs. She drops a hand to Bester's penis and clutches stiffness.

They're on the yielding floor of this no-place. Bester's on his back, Alice straddling him, yet still unpierced.

Then she drops forcefully to take him inside her with a modicum of pain and blood, and an undreamt-of pleasure.

She starts to feed him her hot little tits.

Someone's whispering in her ear from behind, while tracing sensuous lines on her back. It's Sturgeon, a second seducer, somehow necessary complement to Bester, angel to match devil. She rests motionless while his words drip their honey.

"I've spoken to them," the Swabbie guru says. "The Svabha-vikakaya. They're gestalt personalities. They've been trying to assemble similar beings out of humans, for reasons still unclear. But they haven't had any luck. Until us. Somehow the three of us will mesh into something greater, a godbody, if you will, possessing certain gifts and duties. They only had to deburr you two a bit first."

The words stop. Alice feels the engorged tip of the second man's penis trail down the crack of her buttocks, leaving a trail of male lubricant.

Then Sturgeon makes three, opening up a perpetual taste of being.

5.
She Is Born for All Men Who Wait

The exhausted, numb Swabbies pick themselves up off the wharf's planking. Their leader and the two visitors are gone. So is the ship of the aliens. So, they somehow realize, is every one of the interstellar wombs anywhere on the planet.

The youth named Chip raises a tear-streaked face to the skies. In a cloud formation over the Bay he sees a tripartite face like a Tibetan deity's that quickly flows under the slow-sculpting knife of the winds into a single androgynous mask.

Mother in the sky.